I WAS THE HUNTRESS

... and suddenly, unwillingly, I knew who I must ultimately destroy.

Not the pilgrims. They would eventually destroy themselves.

Not the heretics. They were so few they hardly mattered.

Not my parents. My earthen Mother, my fiery Father.

Instead ...

"Trebb, wait!" I cried desperately. I ran after him, knowing that if I were alone in the meadow, the terror that had been revealed to me would destroy me also.

SUNWAIFS

SYDNEY J. VAN SCYOC

BERKLEY BOOKS, NEW YORK

SUNWAIFS

A Berkley Book / published by arrangement with
the author

PRINTING HISTORY
Berkley edition / October 1981

ISBN: 0-425-04645-1

A BERKLEY BOOK® TM 757,375

PRINTED IN THE UNITED STATES OF AMERICA

FOR SCOTT

SUNWAIFS

PROLOGUE

NADD

I sit at my desk gazing at my rough-hewn wall and I wonder how many of the younger generation remember conditions as they once were on Destiny. Sometimes I feel our younger people are strangers: strangers to the reality that once ruled our villages so harshly, strangers to our hardships, our legends, even to the ceremonies and prayers of my own youth.

And so I begin my account thus: stranger, you stand upon the soil of Destiny. Aptly named, Destiny lies directly in the path our great-grandparents' ship took from Earth-Then. And despite Destiny's benevolent appearance now, it was not always a hospitable world. Even in my youth, not so many years ago, the web-rooted grasses of the meadow yielded access to the black soil reluctantly at planting time and grew back quickly, strangling newly planted crops. Periodically the entire plain was swept by flooding rains. Then mosses and fungi appeared and blossomed overnight, releasing spores that drove our livestock to furies of self-destruction. The bull butted its skull against the trunk of the fingerpalm until it shattered the bone and drove sharp splinters deep into its own brain. Screaming porkers contorted their lardy bodies to gnaw their own entrails.

No, Destiny was not entirely hospitable. But when the pilgrims found their fuel dwindling, when they found their tempers growing as short as their vanishing food stocks, when every other planet they had probed on the long journey was either scalding desert or jungle hell—then Destiny became destiny. The little ship set down and the pilgrims straggled from its holds. The dark beards of the youngfathers curled bleakly as the men surveyed the small world at their feet. The women and children peered around with eyes that dared not hope. But then every pulse speeded with dawning joy.

Because at first glance Destiny appeared well met. Broad meadows spread from the heavy-booted feet of the pilgrims, the grasses emerald green and lush. Here and there trees erupted from the densely carpeted soil, fingerpalms reaching their giant five-fingered hands for the gold and lavender morning sky, bluewillows spreading drooping limbs in broad canopies, creating shadowy havens at their gnarled roots. Smaller vegetation grew in glossy-leaved clumps, brittle foiliage catching sunlight and shattering it like tiny mirrors, throwing it in brilliant shards across the grass.

Such was Destiny at first glance. The elders fell to their knees. Nodding, the youngfathers bade the women and children to prostrate themselves. Then they too knelt. *"O Secret Power, who sees these few children who are your own, who feeds and clothes these few children, who has guided them first through the poisoned Eden of Earth-Now, then through the yawning void of the galaxial arm, who has whispered to them constantly of hope, of worlds where their young may grow straight and tall and joyous . . ."*

But set to paper the litany of landfall lacks the resonance of two thousand pilgrim throats. It becomes words, empty words.

And some of you may not even know the story of the First Warning. Two days after landfall, shelters had begun to rise on the meadow. They were rude constructions, but they were the best our elders had been able to wrest from the hostile economy of Earth-Then. The ship was already partially dismantled; every component was to be used in the establishment of the colony. A joyful chorus rang from the morning air as men, women and youths worked to glorify the Secret Power. The younger children played in the meadow, shrieking at the clouds of sweet-voiced crybirds which had appeared from the trees. Feathered bundles of color, lavender, scarlet, emerald and gold, the birds blessed the morning air like a mobile rainbow, sweeping playfully at the children, crying at them with piercing sweetness.

But then, as if some indwelling demon were angered by the pilgrims' joy, the sky-face of Destiny changed. The lavender sky grew first violet, then indigo, and thunder rumbled ominously from clouds that had not been visible a quarter hour before. In the distance lightning gashed the dark sky and the subsequent thunder was followed by an unnatural stillness, as if some sky-fury had sucked its breath and held it. Crying in alarm, the crybirds gathered into a flock and swooped away. They did not flee to the tall fingerpalms or to the densely cavernous bluewillows but plunged to earth in a flock, disappearing into the deep grass of the meadow.

Alarmed, the children ran back from the meadow. "The birds flew away! The birds flew away!"

By then the workers had dropped their chores and stared up at the ominous sky. "The birds see danger coming," Youngfather Doss proclaimed. "We must shelter from wrath."

Headfather Grumann concurred and raised up his mighty voice. "Shelter yourselves immediately, my people. A storm comes to challenge our right here."

But where were the pilgrims to shelter? The ship was partially dismantled and neither the half-completed cottages nor the main dome were roofed. One small group of pilgrims immediately rushed toward the nearest bluewillow, but Headfather Grumann summoned it back. "You must avoid prominences. Electrical fingers are attracted to trees and outcroppings," he reminded them. He scanned the frightened knot of people. "Youngfathers, people, we have packing crates and tarpaulins. Hide yourselves in them and under them. No one must expose himself to the storm. We will not carelessly feed ourselves to the hungry elements."

And so the pilgrims huddled near their half-finished structures, some packed into shipping containers, others crouched beneath heavy tarpaulins, and watched cloudy indignation sweep across Destiny's sky-brow. The storm stalked the distance on flickering white legs, grumbling. Then it moved swiftly from horizon to foreground and hissing electrical tongues tasted the grounds around the colony. They spat at the trees. One glimmering tongue split the nearest bluewillow—the very one from which Headfather Grumann had summoned the fleeing pilgrims—and the tree's heartpulp burst into blue flame.

Then the lightning moved into the colony grounds and snapped angrily at the main dome, the colony's one substantial structure. With a single stroke, it melted not only the plastic panes that had been fitted into place but those still stacked on the ground. Next the storm moved to sample the ship itself, bellowing with stormy rage at its presence on the plain.

The pilgrims huddled for what seemed hours while the storm expressed its displeasure. Finally, when every eye was glazed with fear too long sustained, a greedy wind swept across the meadow and shepherded the vicious black clouds away.

"Stay," Headfather Grumann commanded. "There may be more to come."

The pilgrims stayed as the wind teased them, groping beneath the tarpaulins after them, sweeping at their hair and slapping their sweat-soaked garments. Then it whirled away after the thunder, to be superseded by a heavy rain. Wet grey clouds spilled water in icy fury. As the pilgrims huddled closer together, rain fell so heavily across the meadow that the soil could not absorb it. Instead rain water stood in the web-grass in shining sheets. Reluctantly the pilgrims who lay beneath tarpaulins sat and hunched together, their hair plastered to their skulls.

"The birds!" an unidentified child cried in alarm. "The birds will drown!" Immediately tens of children responded. They wriggled from shelter and splashed through the flooded grasses. None of them heard their parents call them back.

The flock floated like a rainbow flotilla beneath the tall fingerpalms. The crybirds had tucked and fanned their plumage so snugly about themselves that neither their feet nor their beaks were exposed. They bobbed on the meadow water like jewels, their glossy feathers proof against the still-falling rain.

The children furrowed through the water and began snatching up the downy rainbow. They stuffed the unresisting birds into their loosely buttoned waistlets, harvesting crybirds until their waistlets were puffed huge.

As they larked through the meadow, thunder sounded again in the distance and a nearer cloud answered its challenge, spitting lightning at the ground bare meters from the flooded colony. The children halted and stared up at the billowing sky. The distant cloud spoke again, and suddenly young Charles

Edward Dumler, eleven years old, was transfixed by light, his upraised arms caught in a web of brilliance, his head thrown back with neck-snapping force.

Alarmed parents shrieked at the children to throw themselves down. Thunder drowned their voices, and, in the meadow, Charles Edward fell limply and lay still, face down in the water. Immediately mothers and fathers burst from shelter, shouting instructions. But before they reached the meadow, lightning tasted at a second child, Heidi Helger, eight years old. When it had played its deadly game with her, it tossed her aside, a rag doll splashing convulsively in the cold flood water.

Reaching the children, the adults tumbled them into the flooded grass, holding them down while lightning hissed and snarled around them. They hardly dared raise their heads until the clouds swept away again. Then, warily, they stood.

Slowly the water soaked into the soil, leaving four bodies in the wet grass, Charles Edward, Heidi, and two younger children. The latter two had drowned, as had scores of the bright crybirds the children had stuffed into their waistlets, then submerged between their trembling bodies and the soil. Destiny had thrown her first tantrum for the human party. She had warned them with fire and rain of her displeasure at their intrusion.

But she had warned them too late. The pilgrims had neither ship nor fuel to flee this cruel Destiny. However reluctantly, they were committed to struggle upon her web-meadow, victims of her storm-fury and her cold rains of rage.

Committed, and there they struggled for two centuries. They ripped back the grasses to plant their crops, only to have the wiry roots creep back within weeks, choking their fields. When morning dew was heavy or when rain was newly fallen, they woke to a world smothered in green mosses, brown mildews and fast-forming fungi. Pillows and crusts of emerald, dun, violet and black formed upon every surface.

True, crybirds appeared almost immediately to feed upon the mosses and fungi, but well before noon of a wet day the first spores matured. They spewed through the air, an invisible tide. Then the cattle lowed ominously and tried to break down their fences to dash their heads against the tree trunks. Porkers snapped at their bellies, and the weakest among the settlers struggled to destroy themselves. Not until the crybirds had completely devoured the spewing mosses and fungi and the palemoths had strained the tide of spores from the air would the settlers be free of another suicidal storm.

Hopeless you say? Their existence an exercise in futility? Certainly the bleakness of their new lives smothered joy from their spirit. Within a single generation, the pilgrims became a grim society of harsh patriarchs, gaunt woman and frightened children. Their chants and their hymns grew stone-heavy; pleasure became a perversion, worship a duty, suffering a birthright. Only the mystic core of their faith remained untouched. In the dead of night, men, women and children lay awake listening for the whispering voice of guidance, hungry for some promise of salvation.

Ironically when salvation finally came, it was almost squandered through ignorance and the joyless rule of dogmatism. And now I see signs that a second generation of saviors is to be born, as different from the first generation as the settlers of today are different from their grim-jawed predecessors. And although these new saviors may appear as frightening creatures, barely human, you must be prepared to nurture them through their dependent years, to accept the gifts they thrust upon you, however bizarre, and to exploit their offerings for the greater good of all Destiny's people. They wait in the wings, these new saviors, fleshed by the sun, nurtured by the moon. If you do not permit them to carry you forward at the crest of their tide, you may destroy them—and them you.

And so I am asking Corrie to help me chronicle the development of the first generation of saviors. These pages will provide a poor guideline to the development of the second generation—but this is the only guideline you are likely to have. Read carefully, reflect, and prepare.

THE COTTAGE

CORRIE

DESTINY YEAR 0212

Nadd came to me today with his plan, striding down my lane like a flesh-god. But he halted when he reached the ring of drizzle that hangs over my tree-home and looked down at his soiled boots not with distaste but with something very like fear. And then instead of pulling aside the sheafs of hanging moss that drape the entrance to my home and stepping into the shadow of the cavernous branches, he stood peering up into the dense foliage overhead. For a moment, gazing out at him through the leaves, I saw the fearful child he was not so many years ago and pleasure twisted my face.

"Corrie!" His voice was deep, ringing. Yet the fear remained, haunting his powerful features.

I stepped out at his third hark, my leaf-garment rustling around my ankles. "What is it today, Nadd? You never come to me unless you want something," I said, deliberately making my voice sting. "And you never want anything from me that you can get from one of the others. So what can't you go to Trebb or Feliss or Ronna for?"

"They are—not in the village," he said, his deep-set eyes on my rustling garment, his face grey.

"They are not flesh today, you mean," I guessed. When had

9

I last seen Feliss? A month ago? Two? I had caught a fleeting glimpse of Trebb only the week before as he passed through a newly planted field, delicate seedlings yearning after his bare feet. Even then the green had been upon him and I realized he would take root within the hour. And Ronna... Smiling, I curled my right forefinger and drizzle became cold rain. Nadd took a quick step backward, then caught himself and planted his feet firmly.

"They're all—occupied elsewhere," he hedged. "And you're the logical person to share this task with me anyway."

"And the task?" I demanded. "Come inside and tell me about it. There are seedcakes, and I have bark tea steeping."

His tongue flicked at his lips. Rain darkened his hair and beard, but he would never step into the musty haven of my home voluntarily. "I don't have time today," he lied.

Even my delight in teasing Nadd knows limits. With a surge of displeasure, I rapped lightning across the meadow and shook my head with a thunderous clap. "Then tell me your task," I said imperiously, "before I am called away."

He glanced uneasily at the sky, which darkened ominously. Then, stumbling over the words, he told me of signs he saw, of the births he anticipated. And he confided his fear that unless the settlers were prepared, they would behave as badly as they had when we were born. This led him to the manuscript he wanted us to prepare in collaboration, to bring the people of the villages to some understanding of the evolution the six of us had undergone in our early development.

And so to save you from drowning in Nadd's sentimental prose, and partly because I find the task appealing, I agreed to contribute certain chapters to the proposed narrative. "Of course we begin the story with our birth," I speculated as he peered uneasily at the clouded sky. "Or do we? Doesn't life begin with conception instead, with the conception of one's father and mother, with the conception of one's grandparents? Or does the story begin with the journey from Earth-Then? With—"

"I have already dealt with that material," he said stiffly. "Your portion of the story begins with our birth."

"And you are afraid to stay and talk with me for a moment longer," I jibed, whipping tendrils of wind at him, tugging his wet beard. "You are the only one of us permanently body-bound and you are still a frightened child."

"I am a man grown," he said huffily, steadying his god's body against the rising gale of my scorn.

"You are a man afraid." I could read the fear in him now as surely as I had read it once in the gnomish child. When I flicked lightning across the meadow again, then played it upon the upper branches of my living home, he retreated, his legs carrying him down the lane at a fearful half-stumble. Delighted, I threw back my head and let my laughter lash after him. I would write the material he wanted, but I had extracted my price for it.

And he was off the mark as usual in wanting me to begin with our birth. Our tale necessarily begins with conception. In fact I will not even carry you to our births. Surely you have already heard that part of the tale: the birthing couch, draped in heavy curtains, the groaning mother, the grim attendants, watching bleakly for the emergence of—what? Whom?

The answer may depend upon the sun. I am told it is large in comparison with Earth-Sol. Each morning it looms like a consuming orb in the east, painting the dawn sky with color: scarlet, violet, gold, azure. Its rays break brittle upon the mirror-leaves of the brightbushes and are scattered by their glossy foliage. Some say the sun is no more than a globe of gas, indifferent to our activities. But when I look up I see a face, and I know the sun is more than a distant gaseous conjugation.

At the time my story begins, Destiny children were conceived to be born during the winter recess, when their mothers were not needed in the fields. The first recorded sunstorms occurred in the month of our conception. For no conceivable reason, arms of brilliance flared angrily from the sun. They reached out into the lavender and golden sky and hung there, glowing, before they were slowly drawn back. Loops and whorls appeared, cosmic tatting decorating the sun's gassy body.

The eruptions marked a year already badly launched. Late winter storms had flooded Dorsonville and Henches' Plowbourne. Lightning had ignited homes and granaries in every community and livestock had been driven into frenzied panic. After the storms, every surface was padded with swift-growing mosses and fungi. They released their maddening spores and by Destiny-February, the designated month of conception, the settlers' strength was drained. There were the mad to be protected, injured stock to be butchered and smoked, and soon it would be time to rip web-grass from the fields again for spring planting. In the midst of this turmoil, the sunstorms were noted briefly in Headfather Dressler's log and then scarcely noticed by the distracted settlers.

As spring progressed however, other aberrations appeared. Palemoth husks hung from every fingerpalm, like so many paper lanterns. But at hatching time, the parchment-winged insects appeared in sparse numbers. Whole husk clusters failed to produce a single living moth. And for the first time moths flirted through the spring air not upon pale yellow, pale green or pale orange wings but with garish violet and scarlet ones. Some appeared with barbed feelers, while others hatched with their tissue-paper wings permanently folded. The elders puzzled. Certainly the moths' scarcity was not due to lack of spores to feed upon; the air was full of madness this spring. Thanks to the inexplicable scarcity of palemoths, it remained full.

Still later in the spring, the crybird hatchings were small too. Normally no one was permitted near the heavy-limbed bluewillows at hatching time. This year young Jode Dunn was dispatched to see if unhatched eggs remained in the nesting baskets. Jode found the grassy baskets completely empty. But the ground beneath the trees, he reported, was littered with tiny skeletons, strange skeletons, hardly the skeletons of crybird nestlings. But what else could they be?

Disease? Had some virus, some bacteria unaccountably attacked both palemoths and birds? Did they share some common vulnerability not evident until now?

The elders and youngfathers watched the encroaching web-grasses anxiously. If the slugworms were affected too, if they did not burrow up from their deep winter tunnels to gnaw through the roots of the strangling grass, the spring ripping would be twice as difficult as usual.

After a period of tension, the first diamond-emerald and fuchsia on grey, appeared from the soil, tooth-cones bared. Rings of bare soil began to appear in the fields, widening rapidly as the worms gnawed the web-roots to nourish their larva. Relief swept through the communities, and Headfather Dressler called the Festival of Worms. Elders and youngfathers gathered at the edges of the fields and chanted while women and children prostrated themselves upon the widening circles of black soil.

Women and children, you note. During this period of our history, devout pilgrim elders and youngfathers never soiled more than the knees of their coveralls in prayer, but women and children were required to grovel in the mud.

The first clear warning of disaster came soon after the Festival of Worms, with the late spring birth of monster porkers. They appeared in the mucking yards baroquely malformed, many scarcely recognizable as porklings. Headfather Dressler ordered them destroyed immediately, as if their very presence were a threat. His orders were carried out grimly and afterward prayer rumbled ominously through every cottage.

After the disaster of the porkers, the cattle were watched closely. Their lowing hung over the communities like a dirge. At mid-summer moribund calves were born, dozens upon dozens of them, dying with their first breath, their spindly limbs malformed, their heads grotesque. From the herds of all the communities, no more than thirty score calves survived, and half those were subsequently destroyed.

Again the tormented refrain of questions. Disease? Was there some single agent that afflicted both porkers and cattle? Did they share some common vulnerability never evident until now?

But no. Headfather Dressler studied every text the original pilgrims had carried to Destiny. Soon he recognized the nature of the disaster. During the critical months of February and March, the storming sun had thrown out unusual concentrations of radiation. It had penetrated husks and nests, mucking yards and barns alike to warp unhatched moths and birds, unborn porkers and cattle. Only the slugworms, sheltered by intervening layers of rock and soil, had escaped its deadly effect.

But the human contingent did not shelter in caves, and now the women of the communities were committed to advanced pregnancies.

Ironically, this year of all years the Secret Power had conferred almost universal fertility. Even the maids and the mauds, pubescent girls too young for marriage and older women mateless through widowhood or failure to marry, had been almost universally impregnated by dutiful youngfathers.

Fortunately many of these miscarried in the mid-stages of pregnancy. But by late summer the Council knew that monster births were imminent and declared Council guardianship of every infant to be born that winter. No parent must wrestle alone with the onerous decision whether to preserve or destroy. Certainly no able hand could be spared from the spring labor force to attempt the solitary preservation of some frail, misconceived infant. And so the women were secluded and the colony waited in agony for us to be born.

Us? Do I validly categorize *us* with *them*? Or should I deal separately with the fifty odd who were ultimately consigned to cages and the three hundred others who had the good grace to die soon after birth? Let me term them us and us them for a few paragraphs more. One of the stillborns was my own twin, a circumstance Nadd insists has contributed to certain rifts in my character.

One by one we appeared, three hundred sixty-two of us, and were whisked to a special nursery built beyond Drae's Crossroads. We lay in trestled baskets in a dirt-floored storage house, wailing thinly. Imagine a malformation: it appeared in at least one infant, usually in more than one. And worse than the grotesque were the pitiful.

Only six of the entire crop appeared normal, or relatively so: Ronna, Trebb, Nadd, Feliss, Herrol, myself. We were set aside in a special row and attended with special concern while the dozen nurses treated the others with a species of silent neglect. Feedings were forgotten. Tiny bodies were left unprotected against the night chill. Remediable defects were not treated. Within weeks, three hundred sixty-two had become two hundred forty, one hundred twenty-five, then one hundred. The count lingered there stubbornly for several months.

Five weeks after the last birth, the six of us were taken to a smaller nursery specially prepared for us. There we practiced our newly focused eyesight upon painted walls and sanded wooden floors, amenities few Destiny infants knew. Soft blankets and fuzzy garments were lavished upon us. The cooing faces of our nurses hung over us.

Cooing faces, beaming faces, radiant faces—why could I never forget that other face, grimacing at me through a cloud of amniotic fluid, dead eyes accusing?

Faces. Who says I can't remember Headfather Dressler's expression when he came to examine me soon after we were moved to the new nursery? He hung sternly over my crib, his brow etched with some private pain, as a tense young nurse drew back my gown and cottie, exposing me. Headfather Dressler peered down at me, stroking his full white beard, frowning.

"Both?" he demanded finally, distaste tugging his shaggy white brows. "Why wasn't this aberration reported to me sooner? Why has this infant been termed normal and brought here? Of necessity a normal infant must be either male or female."

"But you can see—" the nurse began, then bit her lip. "You can see that except for this—"

"I can see that this infant has been brought to the wrong nursery. It clearly belongs in the other nursery with the irremediables."

At that point Healer Caine appeared clasping his lame left hand, his white robes billowing like wings. "No, no, Headfather, this condition is fully remediable," he declared, projecting hearty certainty. "We have only to decide which we want, male or female, and dress the child accordingly. In a few years it will be whatever we term it, male or female."

"It will be neither," Headfather Dressler crackled.

"Both," the nurse corrected tensely.

"Both *is* neither," Headfather Dressler corrected her. "And clothes do not make the youngfather, Healer Caine."

"We will give it female clothes then," Healer Caine proposed, still forcing heartiness into his tone. He massaged his withered left hand nervously. "Who cares, after all, what lies beneath a woman's skirts or coveralls? Who sees?"

Headfather Dressler snorted, his larval brows crawling. Briefly his eyes clouded with pain and he touched his abdomen, as if in entreaty. "And who would ever pair with it?" he demanded when color returned to his lips. He paced away across the nursery, his boots thumping heavily. "It would be a maud from the time it left the nursery, Healer." Slowly he trudged back until his massive face hung over my basket again. Stony eyes peered down into mine, never guessing their image would be retained. "No, either you scalpel it into a recognizable female or it returns to the other nursery." Here his granite face softened slightly. "And that would be a shame. Three males, three females—they are matched. Matched from birth." Now his eyes snared Healer Caine's reluctant gaze. "Can it be done?"

"It—of course," that good man asserted, and three days later it was done. The surgery was crude, given Healer Caine's disability, but I am a woman now, at least outwardly.

Feliss, Ronna, Herrol, Trebb, Nadd, myself: sometimes

even I can summon a certain sentimentality about our infancy.
We were waifs of the sunstorm. Our parents never knew us.
Our brothers and sisters never touched us, our aunts never
cuddled us. Instead nurses hung over us day and night. During
that first year, aside from my own offending organs, our small
idiosyncracies seemed not to matter: Ronna's lumpish jaw and
dun complexion, Herrol's earth-colored nails, the spider-thin-
ness of Trebb's limbs, the monkey-sparkle in Feliss' eyes. We
were testimony that even the worst disaster yields some good.
The Secret Power had not deserted the people. He had fought
the sun for us and we lived.

Another spring, a normal one this time, and we were briefly
the subjects of controversy. If we were perfect, why weren't
we returned to our parents? What right had the Council to retain
us without even notifying individual parents that their own were
among the survivors?

What right, Headfather Dressler countered, had six families
to joy while the majority mourned? We were diverse enough
that any family could secretly consider one of us its own. Better
to raise us as originally intended, wards of the community,
sons and daughters to all. Then no family need taste the bitter
certainty that its own offspring was dead.

A just decision. Impartial, lofty, sublimely humane.

Perhaps.

But I haven't told you yet about the events that preceded
Headfather Dressler's decision. The first winter of our life was
one of grinding hardship in the settlements. Madness had hit
heavily in the spring and summer months before our birth and,
with the scarcity of crybirds and palemoths, persisted into the
winter. Then spore density decreased, but skinspots appeared
in all but the very elderly, who spent their days near the drying
flames of the housefires. Ugly fungus patches broke out on
faces, hands, arms and necks and ran rampant, sometimes
engulfing an entire limb in a puffy red or crepey black swelling.
And finally pneurrhea, a disease peculiar to Destiny, struck.
In the course of the winter hundreds were afflicted and several
score died.

But winter went differently for our attendants. They came
to us in the first nursery bearing the ugly stigmata of skinspot.
But gradually their skin began to clear. The improvement grew
marked when the six of us were moved to the special nursery
and assigned our own two nurses. Larissa Dunn's spotted face

and splotched arms healed within the first week. Nira McCree came to us with her left eye swollen shut by a pulsating skinspot. Within ten days the skinspot had disappeared entirely. During the same period Healer Caine unaccountably regained partial use of his withered left hand, useless for years.

In a flap of excitement, Healer Caine reported these events to Headfather Dressler. Soon afterward, Headfather Dressler delegated his two youngest daughters, Daya and Miss, both wretched with skinspot, to assist in the nursery.

Soon they were silken-skinned again. And after their healing, Headfather Dressler himself began to stalk the row of cribs daily, his normally stony face bemused. As winter turned to spring, pneurrhea cases became less frequent in the communities. Skinspot yielded to spring sunlight. But no one who frequented our nursery had suffered the onset of pneurrhea or the recurrence of skinspot. And Headfather Dressler's wife was heard to marvel that certain recent complaints he suffered had been mysteriously relieved over the hard winter.

Only Ronna showed sign of weakness. She was an ugly, lumpish baby with feathery hair the color of summer dust and a strangely muddy complexion. As winter waned, she became visibly frailer. By the time spring came, she was little more than a ruffle of hair and a skeletal body.

Finally one morning Larissa found her immobile and glassy-eyed in her crib. "She's dying," she moaned, her plump hands describing panic in the air.

When Healer Caine was called, he did not contradict her. "I have examined her repeatedly and I can find nothing. No sign of infection, of bloodworm, of inherent defect. I have studied her blood and she is not anemic. Her lungs are clear. I can find no sign of heart irregularity. Yet—"

Yet she was dying. My crib stood next to hers and I recognized the falling away of flesh from bone, the corpse-baring of toothless gums. For the past months I had watched the death's head grow upon Ronna's frail shoulders with infant fascination. For me it was a return to the womb, to the days when a dead face floated dimly near my own and the rhythmic booming of my mother's heart defined the known universe.

Headfather Dressler was summoned. He stood at Ronna's cribside pensively tugging his beard. His brows drawn tight with thought, he peered down the row of cots, assessing the situation in the nursery with intent acuity. "There is something completely out of the ordinary here," he pronounced finally, examining Ronna's withered body. "Some process takes place here, a process apparently engendered—" But there he stopped, feeling the pressure of too many eyes. Slowly he paced away from the knot of caretakers: Healer Caine, Nira, Larissa, his own daughters. His eyes avoided Healer Caine's perplexed gaze. Walking the length of the room, he paused to stare into each crib in turn, as if he were seeking evidence of some hidden gift. Finally he returned to Ronna's crib. "Do what you think best for her, Healer Caine," he said, with an edge of impatience—or of something else. Inadequacy? Perplexity? Simple unwillingness?

Healer Caine sighed heavily, his white robe falling in discouraged folds. "I have considered placing her in isolation."

"It is your decision," Headfather Dressler pronounced. But his gaze sought down the row of cribs again intently. He frowned deeply. "I will continue to study the youngsters daily. This one too." Nodding, as if formulating some private resolution, he withdrew.

Those remaining stirred uneasily. "Yes, we will isolate her," Healer Caine concluded when he had examined Ronna again. "The small room down the hall, put her there. Look after her needs, Nira, but disturb her as little as possible. Perhaps her nervous system is too immature to tolerate the constant coming and going here in the big room."

An inane diagnosis. White-robed, he flapped away, unconsciously flexing his once withered hand. Tears sliding down her plump face, Larissa wheeled Ronna's crib away. Rolling to my stomach, I peered at the space where it had stood and felt a strange loneliness. I was deprived again of a presence I understood and cherished: death.

Despite his stated intentions, Headfather Dressler was prevented by the exigencies of ripping season from visiting the nursery again for several weeks. In his absence, Daya and Miss whispered bleakly about his resumed night-walkings, about the return of those sudden moments of lip-blanching pain.

After a month in isolation, Ronna was returned to the nursery, healthy again. Headfather Dressler appeared two days later, a grim presence with lines of pain etched upon his sunken features. He stood by Ronna's crib for a quarter hour, staring down at her as if he were making some irrevocable decision. "You?" I heard him murmur, the words muffled by his beard.

"Was it you? And how—how?" Then he strode away, head bowed, and never visited the nursery again. In his final delirium two months later he made his wife promise not to bring the baby Ronna to his bedside under any circumstance. The malignant force of his disease would destroy her, he pleaded, destroy her utterly. But of course by then he was irrational. Was he not?

And so with Ronna's return, the six of us met our first summer. Father Sun struck through dingy windows to finger our growing limbs and tease our unaccustomed eyes. Inarticulately we reached for him. We tried to close fists around his dust-moted sword, tried to snatch his brilliance for ourselves.

Summer. By then we had become fully aware of one another. I sat for hours watching the busy thrashing of Trebb's lanky limbs, transfixed. Feliss stared at Herrol with monkey-bright eyes, and he rewarded her with a belligerent glare. Nadd and Ronna clutched the bars of their cribs and inventoried each other solemnly.

And the web was forming, a network of tendrils which would quickly bind us into a whole. If Ronna had died that spring, perhaps the wiry filaments would never have proliferated. Perhaps the balance of six psyches and gifts was crucial to their development. Perhaps if she had never returned to the nursery, we would have eventually lost ourselves in normalcy.

Perhaps. But Ronna survived, and the web formed, binding us tightly, until we became like a stand of meadow grass, each blade bound irrevocably into the system, unable to survive alone.

And so we remain bound even today. To all outward appearances we have become independent entities. We rarely encounter each other from month to month. Yet the world beneath our feet is one, the biosphere we inhabit is one, the spiritual force that endows us is One—as are we.

NADD

DESTINY YEAR 0217

I recall the first summers of our childhood with bucolic sentimentality. A scarlet mist swirls over the meadows of memory, shading to lavender and gold on sunny days, to shimmering green and deepest indigo on days of deluge. The grasses grow high and sweet, yielding playfully to the flirting breezes. Sometimes the slugworms crawl from the ground to sun themselves, oddly elegant with their intricate emerald and fuchsia patterns. Then from nearby Drae's Crossroads comes a coven of daypilgrims, the women and children in long black robes, the elders and youngfathers stern in white muslin—all of them bound for the sanctified stream that runs beyond our cottage, where they will fast and pray the day. As they chant their way down the narrow path, crybirds and palemoths splash a rainbow across the morning sky, a pagan celebration.

Often on Destiny, summer afternoons suddenly grow deathly still. Then great cloudfaces appear on the horizon, scowling across the plain. Lavender flees before indigo and violet, and storm sweeps across the plain. When this happened, Nira and Larissa, Daya and Miss would hurry the six of us into the cottage. There we crouched together at the end of the dark hall, trembling with anticipation as the sky bellowed and rain swept noisily against the roof and windows.

Invariably Trebb and Feliss managed to squirm free and escape into the rain. Then Nira and Daya leapt up and scurried after them. Breaking free of Larissa and Miss, the rest of us ran to the windows to watch the chase.

Trebb liked to gallop through the whipping sheets of rain, his head thrown back, his mouth open to catch the cold moisture. Dodging and twisting, he raced across the play yard and into the meadow. As he ran, his feet dashed sheets of water into the air and the grasses whipped wildly, urging him on. They swirled in great green whorls when he passed, as if tugged by a ghostly wind. Quickly the emerald whorls spread outward from his path until broad swaths of grass stirred in agitation.

Feliss preferred to tease her pursuers. A compact mite with straight black hair, she ran a distance into the meadow, then balled herself against the rain like a crybird and threw herself into the grass, only to scramble up again when Nira or Daya approached. Then she darted away to toss herself into the grass again, arms clasped around her legs, her head tucked tight against her chest.

Larissa and Miss moaned in suspense as fingers of lightning punctuated the chase. Ronna reached blindly for a hand to clasp, her heavy-jawed face dappling with apprehension. Herrol stamped his feet and Corrie peered hungrily into the rain, her dark eyes glittering, anticipating some unsavory deathfeast. I was the only one, with my still-infant gift, not yet even recognized as such, who sensed the shape of the occasion, who sensed that it was only a pantomine of crisis. Accordingly I was the only one who did not sigh with relief—or regret—when the offenders were carried kicking back to the nursery and locked into the linen closet.

Not that Feliss and Trebb were intimidated by the shadows of the closet. Briefly the heavy wooden door bulged with their protests. Then silence fell, and finally Miss and Daya pressed their ears to the door, eavesdropping on the resumed antics of the captives. "This is no punishment," Nira complained, pacing up and down the hall. "They're learning nothing from this, and I'm not pleased that they're together in the dark."

"They're only little kiddies," Miss protested. "They're tumbling in play, not depravity."

"And Headfather Jones forbids corporal punishment," Larissa interjected. At this Nira usually retreated in displeasure, her wet clothing clinging to her rigid body, and Miss and Daya returned to the door, giggling. Had it been left to Larissa, Daya and Miss, we would have grown into savages. But Nira was determined otherwise and fortunately she was our senior attendant.

But I proceed as if you know us, as if you can clearly picture each of us. Stop for a moment, close your eyes, and let me paint images for you. First Feliss: she is tiny, her eyes are bright and mischievous, her approach to life flirtatious. Her hair is black and fine and scatters about her head when she moves. She always moves within a halo of crybirds, and sometimes, when the sun strikes her bare arms, they seem to be plumed in a rainbow brilliance that matches the plumage of the birds.

Trebb is long and lanky. His hair is sandy; his eyes are green; his face is long and thin and the features are in constant motion, reacting to the rapidly changing scene. He seldom stays in one spot long enough to bring his scattered attention to focus. In some ways he is like a rapidly growing vine, constantly sending out tendrils, spreading restlessly in every direction, yet without ever achieving any real depth or penetration.

Herrol is our bull, with thick neck, massive shoulders, hefty arms and legs. His eyes are dark and perennially belligerent. He lows instead of speaking, and his gaze is a threat. At first glance you note the hair that grows low on his forehead, the broad nose, the densely muscled jawline. Upon closer examination you find that his nails are the color of mud and that dark hair grows down the backs of his hands to his fingertips.

Ronna is as unprepossessing as Herrol. Her dust-brown hair falls in feathery streamers, like plumes that have been dragged in the dirt. Her skin is muddy brown and dapples white when she is chilled or apprehensive. Her eyes are dull and brown. Normally they have two moods: apprehension and apathy. She is dull, brown, inward.

Corrie is a paradox of gender, her face sometimes hard with emotion more suitable to a fledgling youngfather, at other times unbearably tender. But the object of her tenderness is not likely to be a nestling crybird finding its wings or the lavender shadow cast by a distant golden cloud. Instead it will be a groundweasel gorging himself on writhing slugworms or a palemoth desperately flapping torn wings against the afternoon breeze. And

Corrie's perverse tenderness can turn to chilly rage in an instant.

Myself? I'll let Corrie describe me, unflatteringly I'm sure.

By now you have probably already paired us: Feliss and Trebb, the one mischievous, the other never still; Ronna and Herrol, both dull and inarticulate; and Corrie and myself, her intensity balancing my timidity. By the time we could totter across our nursery floor, our nurses had made the same three pairings. If Herrol crouched in a corner hammering his wooly-bear against the wall, Larissa or Daya would quickly snatch Ronna from the window and deposit her beside him. If Trebb racketed through the playroom, Feliss was urged to pursue him, shrieking. And if I studied a picture book, soon Corrie was plopped down beside me with a rebuking, "Here, Nadd. You must not leave your girlie alone." Trapped, I would peer up into Corrie's turbulent eyes and squirm, reading things there that made me whimper.

Or Corrie would be intent upon the slow destruction of some plaything, only to have it whisked away and myself offered as a more fit diversion. Then her black eyes would flare and her nostrils would dilate with desire to pick me apart tissue by tissue. But if I backed away, our keepers scurried me forward again. "See," they tittered. "He knows he'll never escape his little girlie." They giggled when Corrie snatched my arm and bit it. "He must learn to defend himself," Larissa observed primly, while Miss and Daya laughed. "After all, when they grow up..."

Defend myself? Against a black-eyed fury who had spent her final months *in utero* with her twin floating lifelessly at her face? Apparently I was the only one who wondered how he/she had died. Grimly I imagined wiry fetal hands groping through the bath of amniotic fluid, seeking prey, and I recoiled from Corrie's fierce black eyes.

"See him squirm? He'll never get away from her." More gales of laughter.

Fools.

Or was I the fool, to think I could escape? To think any of us could throw off the invisible filaments that already bound us? We learned to walk, to talk, to manipulate toys and nurses, but the most important lesson of early childhood was recognition of the fact that we constituted a unity, that the tensions and attractions that bound us were more vital than any tenderness offered by nurse or any punishment imposed by aide. We learned that despite Corrie's destructiveness, despite Feliss' mischief and Trebb's restlessness, despite Ronna's dull ugliness and Herrol's bullish rages, despite my prickly righteousness, we could expell no one from our group. And no one could withdraw.

Until we were six our routine seemed pleasant enough. We took first lessons together in the classroom which had been added to the cottage. Nira was headmistress and Daya paced around the room slapping hands and stifling whispers. Late each Sabbath, Headfather Jones appeared to lead us in an abbreviated chant. Day-pilgrims frequently murmured down the lane which led from Drae's Crossroads to the streamside, the children stumbling along in caped black robes, their faces blanched as they peered wide-eyed at us.

But soon after our sixth birthday, I realized that while children from the Crossroads joined in chapel worship and participated in pilgrimages, the six of us never did so. And it wasn't long before I recognized other differences, disturbing differences, both in myself and in the others. When we played in the meadow, web-grass curled lovingly around Trebb's ankles and crybirds followed Feliss wherever she ran. Certainly no pilgrim child commanded such tribute. Yet the highest power of all ignored us.

Hesitantly I began to question Nira. She brushed off my queries with an evasive frown. Finally, one day as she shook out the linens, I demanded furiously, "Is the Secret Power punishing us for some offense? I've called to Him every night this week and He's never even whispered an answer. And when I asked the others, they said He doesn't whisper to them either. Trebb said—"

Nira rounded on me, her eyes widening with offense. "Never say that again," she rapped. "He whispers to everyone, even the offender and the outcast. You simply haven't listened, Nadd. You haven't attuned yourself properly, none of you have."

"But how will any of us learn to hear Him if we're never permitted to make a pilgrimage?" I persisted, trying to plumb both our lack of grace and Nira's chronic irritability. "There aren't enough voices here for a true Sabbath chant. Headfather Jones, six children, four women—with those few voices, how does the Mighty Power even know we're praising Him?" And did our differences make us alien to Him? There lay my central doubt. Yet how could I put it into words when Nira was already angry with the direction of my questions?

"He knows everything, Nadd. He is all around us, protecting us, setting our feet right. He knows your heart and He knows mine. He whispers to you every night, offering guidance, unless you're too young or too heedless to listen."

"Then why—"

But her lips bunched in a tight knot and I knew she was going to evade me again. "I have no time to discuss this now, Nadd. If you don't hear, it's because you haven't consecrated yourself to hear. You're only a child, after all. And as to the pilgrimages, look to yourself for the reason you've never been called to join one. Look to your brothers and sisters." And she hurried away, her lips drawn into a thin white line.

Crushed, I was forced to look. I tried to imagine Feliss stumbling meekly down the path in a black robe with peaked cowl. Instead I saw her bounding away through the grass, wrapping herself up tightly in the consecrated garment and throwing herself into the shadows of a bluewillow, choking with laughter. I pictured Trebb's long limbs entangled in black as he capered away from the coven to run after Feliss. I imagined Corrie glowering at the elders and refusing to prostrate herself with the other children.

"Ronna, Herrol and I could go with the pilgrims," I insisted when I located Nira again in the kitchen. "Ronna never misbehaves."

Nira's lips compressed. "Many years ago Headfather Dressler forbade Ronna to join any outside group. Never until she is much older and much stronger is it to be permitted."

My eyes narrowed. While I had not anticipated her answer, it was more a confirmation of my growing suspicion concerning our status than a surprise. "Why is that?" I probed.

"Reasons," she said tersely.

Which meant she didn't know. "But Headfather Dressler is five years dead," I pointed out.

"He recorded his will in the matter in a special log," she informed me. "Headfather Jones has sworn to respect it."

"Herrol then," I pressed, chewing my lips thoughtfully. "There's no reason Herrol couldn't—"

"You saw what happened last week when I instructed Miss to shave his hands for Sabbath. Miss could have been permanently scarred—and Herrol's fingers are still covered with bristles."

That much was true. Miss had led Herrol bellowing to the

washroom, where he had snatched the razor and slashed out at her. Blood from her wounds had sprayed the washroom walls. Fortunately the wounds had closed in a day's time without any sign of scarring. But that did not render Herrol's hands presentable. Nor did it make him any more like the children of the Crossroads in other respects. "There remains me," I argued in a hollow voice, trying to forget the gnomish tot I met each morning in the mirror, his head poised precariously upon his thin shoulders, visions sometimes disturbing in their clarity, sometimes equally disturbing in their lack of clarity flashing across his mind's eye.

"You cannot go alone," Nira declared stubbornly, edging away from me. "I will not permit one to enjoy special privileges. Don't ask again, Nadd." And she slipped past me and hurried away, her shoulders rigid.

And so very soon after my awakening, I faced the fact that during our first few years we had been gradually consigned to isolation: social, spiritual, educational. Our special nursery had become an orphange so slowly even our attendants had hardly noticed the change. Seasons had passed and normal infants had been born to the families who had briefly grieved us. The outer communities had largely forgotten us, and the people of Drae's Crossroads, I realized heavily, sensed our alienness and regarded us with something closer to fear than curiosity or warmth. Left alone with us, our nurses had failed to socialize us properly, despite Nira's best efforts. It was vaguely anticipated that one day we would become youngfathers and mothers, but how were we to develop the required characteristics when our day to day existence was so far removed from the lives of pilgrim children? How was I to learn the proper manner of command when I so seldom saw it exercised? How were Feliss and Corrie to learn meekness and humility from a pack of giggling nurses? And how deep-rooted were our differences from the children of the Crossroads, I wondered? Couldn't the pilgrim leaders see that our isolation only emphasized whatever inborn eccentricities existed?

One day I reached a conclusion. If I could train my siblings, if I could demonstrate that we could learn the sacred rituals and perform them in an orderly manner, perhaps we would be accepted. And so that spring, as the crybirds hatched in the bluewillows and as new flights of palemoths papered the sky pastel, I organized a game of pilgrims. I suited Herrol, Trebb and myself in white sheeting and Feliss and Ronna in black storm curtains. When I refused to permit Corrie to wear white, she withdrew to the bunkroom window to watch with hateful eyes.

I marched my pilgrims back and forth across the play yard, leading them in a melancholy chant. At first they were orderly, but by the time Nira appeared at the schoolroom window, Trebb had begun to caper and Herrol to glower. I scowled at them, holding myself very erect as an example. But when I launched the final chant, mischief glittered in Feliss' eyes and she began flapping the wings of her makeshift black robe. "I hear! I hear!" she shrilled. "The Secret Power whispers to me." And abruptly she spilled forth a scalding stream of obscenities, her face knotted with fierce joy. "I hear! I hear! I hear!" she screamed, and threw herself down convulsing like a soul possessed.

Nira ran from the schoolroom, her thin face white with fury. "Halt this sacrilege!" she cried. "Stop it immediately!" But instead of snatching at Feliss, she ripped away my white robe and smacked me fiercely across either cheek. "If you ever, ever commit this blasphemy again, Nadd, I will call in Headfather Jones himself. You are to return these sheets to the linen closet immediately and stay there yourself. Don't come out until I call you."

"I didn't do anything wrong!" I tried to plead, but my words emerged a babble. Already Feliss and Trebb were capering away across the meadow, dragging their robes after them. Ronna's lips quivered and Herrol ripped off his white robe and trampled it, glaring at me.

"Go to the closet," Nira pronounced, her lips pale. "Call yourself fortunate I choose not to switch you. Even Headfather Jones couldn't object in this instance."

They were hopeless, all of them: Feliss, Trebb, Corrie, even Ronna and Herrol. Mortified, I crept away. I was exiled until the next morning when I followed Nira down the hall to the classroom with bowed head. I peered around the room, seeking sympathy. The others refused to meet my eyes. Even Larissa denied me her smile.

And the others had not even been punished. Feliss beamed up at Nira with clear-eyed innocence. When Nira turned to the chalkboard, Corrie leaned across the study table, her eyes sparkling maliciously. "If you have the gift of sight, why didn't you see the shape your pilgrimage would take, Nadd?" she taunted.

Why? I brooded over my slate. Over the past year I had

become convinced that my fleeting visions represented a dim glimpse of the future. Too many times when the others were apprehensive, I was possessed by a great calm. At other times I woke in the night whimpering with some tormenting foresight while the others slept peacefully. But if I saw the future, why did I see it so spottily? And why were my glimpses of it so often contradictory? Was my gift nothing more than a boast, a lonely child's attempt to make himself important? Certainly the visions were not infallible; all too often they were incomprehensible.

That summer brought increasingly frequent parties of day-pilgrims past our yard. It also brought decreased vigilance on the part of our nurses. The winter before, the Council had determined that Nira, Larissa, Daya and Miss could no longer be excused from productivity. And so at the proper time, each of them had disappeared to the maiding house for rendezvous with a masked youngfather. With summer, Nira grew increasingly tense, her face aging into a grim mask. Larissa and Daya dwindled to pale gauntness, as if they fed their growing pregnancies at the cost of their once sleek limbs. Only Miss blossomed with pregnancy. She was gripped by an unnatural euphoria and danced around the cottage singing inanely.

"Miss, still yourself! The children," Nira snapped angrily.

"But I'm full of life!" Miss caroled and continued to dance.

Accordingly our keepers were not alert when a large party of pilgrims passed the play yard one morning, filling the summer air with their litany. I gazed after them, suffering my exclusion keenly. I felt the potential of a headfather developing within me, struggling for recognition. Yet all the pilgrims saw was a tiny sunwaif, his head too large, his eyes too piercing, an object of pity and superstitious fear. If I stepped into the path and begged to accompany them, the children would shrink from me, the women would edge away nervously and the eldest pilgrim would reject my plea with a stern flip of his hand. None of them would recognize my common humanity. My chin trembling, I turned and crept away from the fence.

Minutes later I heard Feliss shrill from the meadow. Whirling, I saw Trebb, Corrie and Feliss race through the high grass that skirted the path, a cloud of crybirds swooping after them, the grasses themselves celebrating their passage, whirling into crazy-lace patterns either side of their running feet. I stood paralyzed on the classroom steps, staring after them, unexpectedly gripped by a vision of terrible clarity: the chanting pilgrims, the rioting forms, the celebrating birds and the dancing grasses—and completing the pattern, disaster, like an imperfectly defined storm cloud hanging over the scene.

I hesitated on the steps. If I ran after the others, if I called them back to the play yard, if I prevented the dark cloud from towering toward its storming climax... But did I trust my vision? I debated for only a moment, then yielded to the compelling fear that gripped me. Desperately I clattered down the steps and hurtled across the play yard. As I ran across the meadow, I called hoarsely.

A white-robed youngfather turned and stared blankly at me, his senses anesthetized by the chant. I threw myself into the grass and hid until the pilgrims' litany faded in the distance. Then I stood and cautiously surveyed the meadow. Far ahead, I picked out three bobbing heads. With a cry, I stumbled toward them.

Daya and Miss had often remarked that near our cottage the web-grasses grew more perversely than elsewhere, forming a deep tripping-mat that entirely covered the soil. Certainly it was treacherous that morning. It snared my boots repeatedly, bringing me to the ground. Finally, bruised, my coverall stained, I heard Feliss' voice ahead. I cried. "Wait!" "Wait for me!"

I reached them a few minutes later, guided by the strange agitation of the grasses and by the flock of birds that surged around them, a mobile rainbow. As I approached, Feliss rolled herself into a ball and threw herself into the grass, her head tucked under one arm. Immediately the crybirds swept into the grass and settled in brilliant balls all around her, lavender, scarlet, emerald, gold. They wrapped their wings tight and hid their heads.

Confused, I peered at the sky. But no storm gathered. Abruptly Corrie laughed and snatched up a single golden ball of feathers. Her fingers closed tight, crushing the bird's fragile bones. "We're making a pilgrimage to the stream, Nadd," she challenged, her eyes as old as the ages, as old as death.

"No," I breathed, staring at the dead creature in her hand. "No. No one invited you. And I see—"

"Don't tell us what you see," Corrie commanded impatiently. "We have eyes of our own, and we're going to the water, where the pilgrims are. There's no reason we can't."

"The water, the water," Trebb chanted, flinging out his arms. Grass rippled in confusion, dancing away from him in agitated whorls. "Feliss! Race you!"

With an incontinent shriek, Feliss leapt to her feet and danced away after him. Corrie seared me with a defiant gaze, then ran after them both, her long black hair flowing. I stared down at the dead crybird she had tossed aside, then peered after the three of them. Sunlight broke on a nearby clump of brightbushes and scattered across the grass in shimmering prisms. Three children ran under a lavender sky, the meadow grasses surging wildly to mark their passage, a brilliant cloud of birds swooping after them. But I did not see beauty; I saw disaster, its dimensions still undefined, yet its presence clear, immediate and real. Calling hollowly, I ran after them, stumbling through the thrashing grass.

Gradually the grass became less luxuriant, less wild. Ahead loomed the trees which lined the stream, fingerpalms splayed like solemn hands against the lavender sky, bluewillows spreading to form a series of dark caverns. Feliss, Corrie and Trebb sprawled in the grass just short of the trees.

Corrie cast me a deprecating glance as I threw myself down beside them, panting. "All the streamside is sanctified," I warned them hoarsely. "Everything that falls under the shadow of the trees is sacred to the Mighty Power. Only pilgrims are allowed under the trees. If we trespass—"

"But we *are* pilgrims, Nadd," Corrie said acidly. "When the coven passed the play yard, the voice of the Secret Power called us to the trees too. We knew Nira would be angry, but He commanded us. And who can fault us for obedience?"

"He—He called?" Briefly I stared at the three of them, confused. If it were true, if the Secret Power had called them, when He had never even whispered to me—

Abruptly Feliss giggled. "I hear Him now!" she shrieked, bobbing up from the grass. Running a distance, she threw herself down in a whirl of birds, her compact body convulsing rhythmically. "I hear Him, Nadd! He whispers to me!" she shrilled, and proceeded to foul the air with the same obscenities she had used a few weeks before.

My face suffused. "Stop that!" I kicked my way through the pile of birds that surrounded her to seize her coverall and shake her. "Stop that, Feliss. The Secret Power hears everything you say."

"I hear everything the Secret Power says!" Feliss shrieked jubilantly. Her eyes popping, she leapt up. "Run, He tells me! Run and scream and yell!" And in a flurry of limbs, she dashed toward the streamside trees.

With a yelp, Trebb dashed away after her. Corrie leapt up, but I snatched at her arm. "Don't let them do it. I see—I seee—"But Corrie didn't care what I saw. She pulled free and, with a last malevolent glance, ran after the other two. Grasses rippled and brilliant clouds of crybirds disappeared into the trees.

Alone, I caught a painful breath and held it. Should I run after them? Plead with them? But dread gripped me, wrenching my will. Whatever sacrilege they committed beneath the trees, I did not want to be involved. Inevitably, when it was reported to Nira, she would remember the practice pilgrimage and blame me.

But if I did not follow them, did not plead with them . . . Bleakly I stared at the point where they had disappeared. I heard faint voices, muffled by dense foliage. I took a single step forward, then bit my lips, turned and ran back toward the cottage, my breath hissing sharply between my teeth.

Soon the cottage's long, low shape rose reassuringly from the meadow. But when I ran into the play yard, the nagging sense of impending doom did not abate. I peered around desperately and realized by Larissa's distracted gaze from the steps where she sat that I had not even been missed.

Heavy with doom, torn by it, I ran inside, threw myself into bed and huddled under the prickly covers, whispering fiercely to the Secret Power to guide me. Should I go to Nira and be ostracized by the others for telling? Or say nothing and hope Nira would never connect me with whatever happened? Abruptly my prayers turned fierce. If I could not see clearly, I didn't want to see at all. I didn't want to be tormented by dimly apprehended shapes sweeping dimly toward me. Instead I begged the Secret Power Himself to color my perceptions, to shape my vision, to lift the terrible burden of this anomalous gift from my shoulders. Then perhaps I would be able to hear His voice when I called to Him every night in the dark; perhaps I would be blessed with the same whispered guidance Nira assured me the good children of the Crossroads received.

I pleaded and I prayed. For answer I received silence and a continuing sense of doom.

CORRIE

SPRING 0217

Running after Feliss and Trebb, I picked my way through a bramble of brightbushes and crawled into a dense thicket of drooping bluewillow branches. Penetrating it, I found myself on hands and knees in a musty cavern of foliage. My hands sank into the mouldering residue of fallen leaves. Making a face, I scrambled free and ran toward the water. The stream flowed sluggishly, a broad strip of brown water. Massive trees loomed out over the water, hoary sheets of unfamiliar hanging moss depending from every limb. The sloping stream bank was slick with mud. I was momentarily intimidated. But the mute force that had sent me running after the pilgrims, that had propelled me here, still commanded me. I peered up and around. Grey moss grew everywhere, curtaining out sunlight, creating a musty pall in the air. Even the broad leaves of the occasional fingerpalms were coated with unfamiliar mossy growth.

I sucked a deep breath and analyzed the mingled scents of the streamside: mud, decay and an unfamiliar spicy aroma. Then from somewhere nearby I heard a murmur. With a tingling sense of unreality, I pawed my way through the sheafs of moss that hung from every branch. It tore easily in my hands, showering my coveralls with grey dust. "Trebb?" I called, choking on the fine dust. "Feliss?" My voice was muffled.

Nearby brush rustled and Feliss popped into view, her black eyes round with fright. Simultaneously Trebb appeared from behind a tree, his eyes as huge as Feliss'.

"Where are the pilgrims?" I asked.

Feliss shook her head, her fine black hair falling across her shallow forehead. "I don't know," she said querulously. "I don't like it here, Corrie. I don't understand why you wanted to come here."

"You could have stayed at the cottage," I hissed. "You didn't have to come just because of me."

"But you said—"

Trebb summed up the situation succinctly, cutting her protest short. "It stinks here."

"You smell the dead leaves rotting. And the moss—" Frowning, I ripped down a clinging grey beard and shook it, creating a cloud of dust. I inhaled experimentally, my fingertips tingling with the onset of numbness. The aroma was cloyingly spicy. And suddenly, as if the grey dust were affecting my senses, my voice seemed to come from very far away. "The moss smells like spice and mold. The moss—" I lifted my hand and peered at it, expecting to see it float away across the muddy water. "Shake the moss, Trebb," I said distantly. "Shake it before I float too far away." Was this why I had come to the trees? This floating sense of timelessness?

His face loomed preternaturally large in the dim air. His eyes huge and solemn, he pulled down a beard of moss and swished it through the air. Instinctively he retreated from the resulting cloud of grey dust.

"Smell it," I urged him as I inhaled again, my voice faint. Past, present and future telescoped dizzily into a single time frame, now and forever melding and blending. And when was I? Who?

"It—" Bracing himself, he sniffed sharply at the grey dust. Then, smiling inanely, he sniffed again. "It smells—"

"It smells bad," Feliss whimpered.

"It doesn't smell bad, 'Liss." His grin widened oafishly. "It smells like spice cake. It smells like Miss just baked spice cakes."

My own voice said dreamily, "It smells good, 'Liss. Try it."

"Try it, 'Liss, try it," Trebb urged, a half-drunken chant. "It feels good when you try it, 'Liss." His thin lips twisting into an inane grin, he broke free a fat sheaf of moss and shook it at her.

Feliss retreated from him, squealing with fright. "I don't want to smell it, Trebb. It smells rotten. It smells terrible. And I don't like it here. Everything feels funny here."

With a yelp of laughter, Trebb lurched after her, pawing aside curtains of moss. As they dodged along the streambank, Trebb staggering and bellowing incoherently, dust puffed from disturbed beards of moss and enveloped them both. I plunged discordantly after them, sucking the cloying dust into my lungs. With every step, I lifted my feet a meter into the air and set them down with a hilarious slap. My head bobbed drunkenly far above, connected to my body by a thin stalk. I was barely aware of drunken laughter burbling from my lips. "Try it, 'Liss," I raved. "Doncha wanna fly away with me?" Fly away through now to then, to when. Fly through centuries as if they were days, through days as if they were centuries. Fly, wingless and blind, yet all-seeing, all-knowing.

The drunken chase resolved into slow motion, an airy thrashing of attenuated limbs, a series of incoherent squeals. Abruptly Feliss succumbed to the effects of the dusty spore-cloud we had stirred up under the trees and threw herself to the ground in a tightly curled ball.

"Birdie!" Trebb shrilled as she rolled away under a brightbush. Quickly he wrapped his own limbs around his body and rolled away after her.

I slowed and stopped and it suddenly seemed very still under the trees. I closed my eyes, listening intently. Despite the giggling in the bushes, I heard a voice speaking to me from the very depths of time, a compelling voice, the voice of the stream that ran beneath the trees—that had always run there, eternal, fluid, yet never-changing. Heeding its call, I turned, slowly, slowly, magnetized. The brown waters ran serenely in their broad channel, beckoning me with an ageless murmur. Mesmerized, I stumbled to the streambed and stretched out on my stomach, reaching for the water, for time. All my perceptions altered, I studied the water like some mysterious fluid I had never seen before. It slipped through my fingers like a lifestream that nourished but could never be possessed, like the soil's own sweet blood, flowing thick and brown and cool from the earth's subterranean heart-spring.

When I had dandled both arms in the mysteriously changed water, I slid forward in the mud and flicked my hair into the stream. The water tugged at it, bathing my scalp, cooling it. *I baptize myself in your blood-water, Mother Destiny*, some lisping voice within me declared, wakened by my changed perception of the water, of the world. For only when time telescoped could I see that inert soil and mindless-flowing water were indeed animate, sentient—powerful. And I, who ran on rapid feet, whose perceptions came and went within the space of a second, was no more than a mote of life floating helplessly in a shaft of eternal sunlight. *See how I crawl to you, see how I give myself to you. Bleed through my hands, bleed into my hair, pour out your sustenance for your loving daughter*, I pleaded, eager to taste the eternity of the waters, to make it mine. *Bleed for me, my Mother.*

And my Mother-waters bled for me as I lay on the stream-bank, my arms thrown out, my eyes half-closed in ecstasy, my hair swept by the water. She bled for me and in an orgy of thirst, I wallowed in the mud of the streambank and splashed blood-water brown and cool across my face and down my coverall. Then I knelt in the stream and plunged my arms to the elbows into my Mother Destiny's throbbing vessel. Cupping my hands, I cradled the silty waters, straining them through my teeth as I drank my fill. *Feed me, feed me, feed me!*

And she did. As I sprawled in spore-fostered incoherence in the water, she fed me placidly, she fed me well, she fed me as a mother feeds her daughter, sweetly. She fed me time; she fed me eternity; she fed me the very stuff of forever.

At last I was sated. I crawled away from the water and threw myself into a pile of rotting leaves, staring up at the faint pattern of light created as the sun tried to finger through the dense bower of trees to touch me. Blandly I watched its futile efforts to lay rods of light across my face. Then I dozed.

As I slept under the trees, caked with mud, the sun pawed restlessly at the trees, then slithered from its zenith and reached obliquely for me. But my Mother Destiny provided moss and foliage to shelter me and I was safe from its burning rays. Finally Feliss squirmed near me and said softly, "I'm a birdie person. Did you know that, Corrie?"

With effort I lifted my head. Focusing my eyes, I studied her as she sat there, rainbow crybirds perched upon her shoulders and her head. They blinked solemnly down at me, their gold and emerald wings drawn snugly around their downy bodies.

"Did you know I'm a birdie person?" Feliss demanded again, peering at me as solemnly as the birds. "I command all the birdies. When I call them they come, and when I tell them to fly away they go. The birds do whatever I want, Corrie."

"I know it," I murmured, and wondered how I had known it.

"And Trebb is a grassy person and a tree person. Everything green grows for him, all the meadows, all the forests."

"Mmm-hmmm."

"Then what is Corrie?" Trebb demanded in a muffled voice. He leaned against the moss-cushioned trunk of a fingerpalm, his limbs for once still, his face slack.

"What are you, Corrie?" Feliss wondered, his echo.

"I—" I blinked around the mossy cavern that enclosed us. "I'm opposition," I said, not certain the reply made sense. It came of its own volition. "I'm the opposition of forces. I'm my Mother's child and my Father's child. My Mother feeds me and my Father warns me. I—"

"Your youngfather?" Feliss giggled.

"My Father Sun," I said with thick-tongued impatience. "My Father warms the land and my Mother cools the air. My Father pulls the clouds up into the sky and my Mother draws them down again in rain. Then my Father booms and my Mother crackles. She scratches her hide with lightning and my Father scolds her with thunder. My Mother—"

"It's not seemly to scratch," Feliss informed me. "But if my skin was mud and grass—"

"I'm the grass person," Trebb interjected.

"If my skin was mud and grass and it itched—"

"Her skin is mud and grass and rock. Her muscles are mountains and valleys and meadowlands. When she combs her hair, it grows out into tall trees. Somewhere there is a spring, and that is her heart. It pumps her blood through all the streams that are her veins. It pumps her blood to me and I drink it. I wash my face in it, I wash my hair in it. I splash her blood on my clothes. A long time ago I drowned my brother and sister in it. My brother, my Father's frowning son, and my sister, my Mother's smiling daughter—they were one person and I'm one person. I'm one person and two, even if Headfather Dressler did try to murder my Father's son." On and on my voice meandered, an accompaniment to Feliss' dreamy babble and Trebb's wonderstruck murmuring and the contented cheeping of the crybirds that clustered upon Feliss' shoulders and head.

Time passed and I told them the tale of creation. Time passed and Feliss told us why the crybirds fly and why they sing. Time passed and Trebb murmured tales of the meadow grasses and their eternal union. I swept wind over the land, Feliss beckoned up clouds of crybirds to ride the wind and Trebb bade the grasses to bow and dance before it. And during that isolated moment all these powers were real, actualized by the grey dust that sifted from the gently stirring moss.

Then, through some intricate internal evolution, the time for dreaming passed and we stood. Sensing our purpose, Feliss' birds fluttered back to the trees. Then the four of us—four because I am my Father's son as well as my Mother's daughter—moved silently upstream, solemnly pacing off the length of my Mother's heart-vessel. We moved slowly, we moved carefully, cautious not to disturb the heavy sheafs of hanging moss and shake down fresh clouds of grey dream-dust. We did not want to lie down again, to return to burbling helplessness. We were sated with ecstatic insights. And the slight concentration of fine dust that hung in the air, stirred by the faint turbulence of our passage, served to maintain the floating grace of enchantment.

We moved upstream. Beside us, the water spun a soothing refrain, beckoning us on toward some deep heart-spring that lay far in the mountains. We moved upstream until we found ourselves at the mouth of a ghostly clearing. Brush had been uprooted from beneath the trees and the lower limbs of the bluewillows had been amputated to form a deep moss-hung cavern. Sunlight propelled a few weak rays against the musty air. The perimeter of the clearing was marked by a coven of abandoned robes, black and white, hung upon brush and limbs. Hoods and limbs splayed, they were so many muslin skins abandoned in the wilderness.

Silently I gestured for Feliss and Trebb to halt. Alone, I crept forward into the silent clearing. Mud-coated forms lay naked upon broad couches of rotting leaves. Male and female, elders, youngfathers, mothers and children sprawled together under the trees, their intertwined limbs weaving them into a common humanity. They lay with eyes open and glassy, peering up into the moss-hung trees. A faint breeze stirred their ghostly robes and circulated motes of grey dream-dust through the air. My breath caught, I stared at their slowly writhing lips and realized they were joined in an inaudible chant.

My gaze shifted to the muddy streambank. Pilgrims lay there too, their fingers trailing in the water, blissful abstraction rendering their disparate faces identical. With rising gorge, I stared at their pallid bodies, coated with my Mother's slippery brown blood. I glowered at their lank hair, wet with the same sacred blood. Rapidly the pleasant sense of satiation I had experienced as we walked my Mother's heart-vessel curdled into disbelief, anger and finally jealous rage.

They stole my Mother. They sucked at her breast, drawing off the cream of her blood before it could flow downstream to my eager lips. Like greedy bloodworms, they diverted my nourishment and flourished upon it. And they despoiled this spot sacred to my Mother with their own false deity's name and praises. As I peered at them from the shadows of the bush, my eyes darkened with rage. My fists clenched and muscles cramped all through my body.

Slowly Feliss and Trebb crept forward and stared round-eyed at the pilgrims.

"They're stealing her blood," I uttered. "And they're using her trees as a cathedral to their god." I expected to find my own rage mirrored in Feliss' eyes, in Trebb's. Instead they peered at me quizzically, their usually bright gazes still dulled by the spicy dream-dust that hung in the air. "They're drinking up her blood. They're taking it from me," I repeated, but neither of my companions tensed in jealous anger.

Finally Feliss blinked and tittered uneasily. "They look funny without their robes. Is that what Larissa calls sinfulnaked?"

Trebb ventured a grin, eyeing me. "We could take off our coveralls. There's no one here to scold us."

"We could run around with mud on our tummies," Feliss agreed, sparkle slowly returning to her eyes. "I could rub mud in my hair."

"Like Corrie."

"Then I could call my crybirds and tell each one to pluck me out a feather. Then I'd glue the feathers to my skin with mud and flutter my wings and cry like a birdie and fly away."

"But I'd grow tall enough to pick you out of the sky," Trebb cried, feeding on her fantasy. "I'd reach my hand up after you—"

"And it would be a blade of grass instead."

"And I'd twine it around you so you couldn't fly. It would be like a big green ribbon tying your wings against your body. They you'd fall down and break your bones and Nira would have to bury you. She'd have to bury you in the field and chant over you."

"You'd all chant over me," Feliss declared ecstatically, groping at the placket of her coverall. "You would say, 'Here lies Feliss, she died in bliss; here Feliss lies, she died in the skies.'" Quickly she peeled off her clothes and tossed them in a heap, presenting herself in the flesh: tender and white. Then, raising her arms, calling out in a sweet bird-voice, she covered herself all in crybirds. She beckoned to them and they came from every tree. They clung precariously to her flesh with tiny claws, making her a rainbow. Those that could find no perch fluttered around her, a feathered guard, entirely hiding her.

Trebb tongued his lips, peering intently from Feliss to me. We were like the two sides of a coin, joy and fury. Feliss covered herself in celebration while I raged, my eyes demonic. Which of our two ecstasies would he choose?

"The pilgrims are drinking the blood that should flow to the meadow grasses," I urged in a hypnotic undertone. "They're sucking it into their sinful-naked bodies, Trebb, sopping it up to feed their own weedy growth. When the stream comes out of the trees, it will be no more than a trickle and all the grasses will have nothing to drink but the rain. And when it rains the pilgrims will set our their rain barrels and steal every drop for themselves. Then the grasses will wither and dry. The grasses will brown and burn. The grasses—"

Trebb's eyes had grown huge and glazed. "And the trees?" he demanded. "The trees?"

"Are you a tree person too?" came Feliss' sweet voice from the chittering cloud of crybirds.

I had woven a successful spell. Trebb did not hear her. He peered intently at me, falling deeper into the black lakes of my eyes, and asked again, his voice rough with emotion, "The trees?"

"See for yourself," I said. "The pilgrims are lapping up the water that belongs to the trees too. The trees were stationed here by my Mother Destiny to guard the stream. They were put here centuries before the pilgrims ever thought of leaving Earth-Then. They hunch over the stream, rattling their limbs to protect it from sunlight. They hold it in their arms, protecting it—saving it for the grasses and for themselves. If the pilgrims suck up all the water, the trees will shrivel and die. Without the water, all the trees will soon be gone, the bluewillows, the fingerpalms—"

"The brightbushes?" Feliss interjected, shaking crybirds off her face so her bright black eyes shone through.

"The bushes will die too. There will be no berries to feed the nestling crybirds. There will be no bluewillows to hold their hatching baskets, no fingerpalms for them to gather in at sunset. There will be no grasses where they can hide from the storm. There will be—"

"There'll be nothing good left!" Trebb cried. "If we let the pilgrims drink all the water, there'll be nothing good left for the plants and the birds." Wildly he peered around the clearing. His inflamed gaze clawed high into the trees, inventorying every brutally amputated limb, and he began to flex his arms and legs rhythmically. An absence came into his eyes, as if he had fled his strangely thrashing body and invested himself elsewhere.

At the angry rattling sound overhead, I stared up and, fascinated, saw the rhythm of Trebb's limbs repeated in the limbs of the trees. Angrily, violently, they swayed and dipped, their mossy grey beards shaking with ancient rage. Great clouds of spicy must shook free and swirled in the dim air. At the edges of the clearing, brightbushes rattled their mirror-leaves in anger and vines snarled and tangled, rapidly, reaching out for human flesh.

Feliss shrieked in blood-joy and shook clouds of crybirds into the air. "I can do it too, Trebb! I can do it with my birds!" As she crowed and called, inciting them, the birds darted at the entranced pilgrims and began pecking at their naked bodies. Their little beaks were fat and shallow, fashioned for hulling meadow grass seeds, but the birds buried them to the nostrils in human flesh, creating scores of wide, shallow bleeding punctures.

Pain-prodded from the depths of reverie, the pilgrims were driven groaning to their hands and knees, to their feet. Instinctively they clasped at their private parts, trying to protect them from the vicious rainbow that swirled through the clearing. Fear-eyed, they peered up into the agitated trees, peered down at the thick vines that snaked from the shadows to snarl at their feet. Their eyes were hollow with incomprehension. Inhuman sounds crawled from their throat. Finally, despite the intensifying cloud of dream-dust that filled the clearing, they summoned enough presence of mind to flee.

"Eat them!" Feliss shrilled to her crybirds as naked pilgrims staggered and stumbled into the bushes. "Drink them!"

"Nothing else left!" Trebb raved as trees, bushes and vines grew increasingly violent in their efforts to destroy the intruders.

Groaning with terror, the stragglers fled into the narrow band of vegetation that separated them from the meadow. We ran after them, three young furies. Feliss screamed and Trebb cried, and the limbs of the trees reached down to slash naked flesh. Vines appeared and dragged the unwary to the ground, where brightbushes scored bare skin with hard little mirror leaves. The crybirds harried the fleeing pilgrims with grating cries. And everywhere beards of moss puffed clouds of cloying grey dust into the air, intensifying the hysteria.

Finally, bleeding, the pilgrims reached the meadow. They choked and sobbed with fear and pain, their eyes clouded with whatever mystic fantasy had gripped them at the streamside. As they fought to gain the footpath, the meadow grasses tangled wildly around their ankles, felling them. Fresh flocks of birds brightened the sky, summoned to the melee by Feliss' shrieks. They fell upon the struggling pilgrims, rapping gleefully at their bare skin, pocking them with blood.

I emerged from the shadow of the trees and viewed the massacre with a heady sense of creation. The pilgrims had stolen time and revelation from me, splashing their naked bodies with it. Now their bodies were wet with blood instead. And ecstatically I sensed an intensified celebration of power rising upon the horizon. The grey dust had activated abilities rooted so deeply within my unconscious that I had never guessed they existed. I paused at the edge of the meadow, the grass thrashing at my feet, and arched my body erect, rising to my toes, tossing my head back. I raised my arms and clouds of vapor were whipped from the soil and sucked up into the late afternoon sky. I flicked my wrists and the moisture condensed into an ominous line of black cloudlets. I splayed my fingers and the dense little clouds diffused into towering grey thunderheads. They blew swiftly from the horizon to blanket the meadow, turning the sky midnight dark. I shrieked with joy. Then, as I ran, whooping with exhilaration, I heard the first crackle of thunder, saw the first shimmering finger of lightning, felt the first drop of rain on my mud-clustered cheek.

I had summoned the storm. Together my Mother and my Father had built it upon the horizon for me, and now they dispatched it to the meadow where I required it. "Run!" I shrieked to Trebb and Feliss. "My Mother will scratch out their eyes with electric fingers. My Father will deafen them with thunder. Run before the birds drown in the storm, Feliss! *Run!*"

The pilgrims turned fear-haggard faces to the driving rain as they struggled against the writhing grasses that clutched at their feet. I shrieked and swiftly lightning reached down and tasted ground around them. Thunder rolled, the voice of an angry Headfather admonishing his errant young. With whimpers and groans the pilgrims threw themselves flat upon the ground. They scrabbled at Mother Destiny's pelt with clawing nails, cowering before the anger of the skies, crying to their Secret Power to deliver them.

With a cry, Feliss called her crybirds back into a dense, bright cloud. Quickly she dispersed them to the safety of the grass. Trebb called out incoherently and behind us the angry trees ceased to thrash. The grasses calmed, to offer the birds shelter. Only my own rage continued to express itself, storming down from the skies, swirling heavy sheets of rain across the meadow.

"Run! The storm won't hurt us," I called. With a cry of exhilaration, I led way through the grass toward the footpath, leaping over the prostrate bodies of pilgrims, pausing only to snatch up a scarlet crybird from the grass. It was warm and soft in my hand, vulnerable, totally vulnerable. Trebb and Feliss darted after me. Shrieking with wild joy, the three of us—the *four* of us, Father Sun—plunged through the storm, invulnerable to the tongues of death that tasted earth behind us.

Reaching the path, we ran until our breath was a hard pain in our chests. Then we slowed to a trot and finally to a walk. Behind us, the worst fury of the storm gradually dissipated, raining away into the trees. Slowly bleak forms rose from the meadow. They stared after us with dead eyes, their punctures and lacerations dripping scarlet.

Slowly my head settled firmly back onto my shoulders; my limbs ceased to float. And the grasses had grown taller and lusher. Our cottage lay ahead. I caught my breath and a finger of anxiety touched some deep nerve in me. The storm had passed and I was young again, vulnerable again. "Nira," I said involuntarily. Of all our attendants, she was the one to reckon with.

"She'll thrash us tonight, no matter what Headfather Jones says," Feliss moaned, peering at me from beneath strands of wet black hair.

"She'll shut us in the closet for a week."

"Nothing to eat."

"No blankets to sleep with."

"No taste of water or broth."

Resolutely I knotted my hand. The crunch and crackle of the bones of the little bird I still carried was reassuring. "No one will ever believe what the pilgrims tell on us," I said strongly. "Because now we know what everyone else knows: there's madness under the streamside trees. The pilgrims go there to breathe dream-dust and draw mystical revelations. When we're accused, we'll say we were only walking through the meadow from the picnic grove and ran home when we saw rain coming. If the pilgrims saw us walking, if they attach some fantasy of persecution to our presence—"

"But don't use those words, Corrie," Feliss urged, hope bringing the sparkle back to her eyes.

"I'll say it in child words," I promised, making my jaw hard. "I'll lisp if I have to, and you'll giggle, Feliss, and Trebb will hoot and run around."

"And no one will ever know their stories are all true," Trebb concluded triumphantly.

"No one," I agreed. We would dash into the play yard wet and flushed with youthful innocence. We would shed our wet clothes on the stoop of the cottage—hoping Larissa did not notice when she gathered them up that Feliss' were missing— and run to towel ourselves and put on dry clothes. By the time the pilgrims straggled back to Drae's Crossroads with their tale of trees gone mad, of crybirds attacking in waves, of children calling down storm from the sky, we would be innocently at our supper. After the first wave of hysteria passed, the pilgrims' wounds would be explained away as a manifestation of spore-madness, as would their incoherent tale. No one could ever know that everything they said was true. No one could ever guess.

NADD

SPRING 0217

At the supper table, I hunched over my porridge mug, too miserable with intimations of doom to plumb the nervous excitation I sensed at the table. Corrie, Feliss and Trebb had returned just as Daya was warming the pot. Nira had not quarantined them to the linen closet, despite their wet hair and mud-spattered faces, but had permitted them to put on fresh coveralls and come to the table. Through my own misery, I stared the length of the table at Nira. She peered into the fireplace, one hand resting on the slight mound of her pregnancy, her face drawn with some concern unrelated to us.

A hiss at our end of the table, and Ronna's muddy complexion dappled. Her eyes suddenly became sharply attentive to something in Corrie's hand, which rested in her lap under the table. Ronna reached down. Corrie jerked and uttered a sharp expletive, but before she could prevent it, an involuntary exchange took place under the table. Then Ronna slid from her chair and fled to the bunkroom, cradling something small and bright against her cheek. Corrie half-rose, her face darkening ominously.

"Corrie!" Nira snapped, her attention returning to the table.

"Have you finished your meal and whispered your devotions to the Secret Power?"

Rebellion played across the surfaces of Corrie's dark eyes, a stormy presence. Unaccountably she whisked it from sight and sank back to her chair. "No, Nira," she said meekly.

"Then do so before you leave the table," Nira instructed, her gaze sliding away into reverie again. "And offer a special stanza tonight, all of you. Tomorrow, thanks to the rain the Secret Power has seen fit to send, the mosses will bloom."

"Yes, Nira." Composing her features into a fair semblance of piety, Corrie bent over her mug and spooned up the thick porridge. With each bite, she murmured a devotion, her black eyes playing up and down the table, covertly testing for reaction to her supplicant pose. Feliss giggled and Corrie elbowed her, her eyes momentarily blazing with annoyance.

I had pushed my own mug back and mouthed my ritual gratitude when Miss, who had flittered away from the table earlier to dance restlessly through the rooms of the cottage, suddenly appeared in the doorway. "Nira, Daya, Lariss—come see the pilgrims!" Her voice was high, flirting with hysteria. "Come see how the Secret Power has clothed them for the storm." With a wispy burst of laughter, she danced away.

Nira's features tightened into tense annoyance. "More nonsense," she declared, pushing back her chair. "Continue your devotions, kiddies." With a thrashing of long skirts, she hurried after Miss. Daya and Larissa glanced at each other, then slid from their chairs to follow her.

Glancing down the table, I caught a spark of dark delight in Corrie's eyes. Feliss sucked a long breath, obviously fighting an attack of giggles, and Trebb jumped up from the table and flung his limbs out in strange calisthenics. Only Herrol showed no reaction. A stab of apprehension blanched the blood from my face. Quickly I slid from my chair and ran after Nira.

The door into the play yard stood open. Framing myself in it, I stared unbelievingly at the cortege that wound up the path from the stream. Pilgrims staggered toward Drae's Crossroads in twos and threes, every one of them mother-naked. Mud was smeared across bare buttocks and abdomens. Their hair was lank and wet, and they bled from scores of oddly shaped punctures and lacerations. Haunted, they peered into the play yard as they passed. They did not chant; they did not even mutter. Instead they staggered silently from the dusk, gazed balefully

into the vacant windows of our cottage, and then stumbled
ahead into swiftly falling darkness.

At the sound of choked laughter, I turned to see Corrie pinch
Trebb savagely. With a high-pitched giggle, Feliss slipped past
them both and ran into the play yard. At her appearance, a
haunted moan rose from the passing pilgrims. They fled the
path, stumbling into the grass of the meadow as if pursued.

Nira turned, her lips tightening. "Children, this is no sight
for your eyes." In the dusk her complexion was so pale that
it took a greenish cast. When we did not budge, she slapped
her skirts around her ankles and strode toward us, her face
grim. "Into the linen closet—all of you!" She snatched Feliss'
arm and twisted her around, pushing her roughly toward the
door. "Go! And send up a song of contrition, that your eyes
have seen of this madness."

"But Nira—" I pleaded, retreating before her anger.

"No argument, Nadd. You were told to stay at the table and
you did not. Now, into the closet, all of you."

Corrie snatched Feliss' arm and drew her ahead of me as
we were shepherded into the closet. The heavy door closed,
then opened again as first Herrol, then Ronna was pushed in
after us. Finally the key turned in the lock and footsteps hurried
away. Blindly I stared into the darkness as the others shifted
around me. Was this the disaster I had foreseen? This unaccountable column of traumatized stragglers? "Corrie—"

"Hush!" she grated, from somewhere in the shadows.

"Did you see all those bare titties?" Trebb demanded of the
darkness. "Did you see—"

"I don't see why we can't tell—" Feliss began.

There was a swift movement and Feliss' protest ended in
a shriek of pain. "We aren't going to talk about it," Corrie
hissed. "Not one word."

But I could not contain the cloud of foreboding that had
been building inside me all afternoon. "Corrie, you told Nira
and Larissa that you went to play in the meadow today. You
told them you went no farther than the picnic grove. You—"
I whimpered with pain as nails suddenly reached from the
darkness and closed around my forearm, slicing into the flesh
mercilessly. "You—" I bubbled, tears coming to my eyes.

"We went for a walk in the meadow," Corrie grated vengefully into my ear. "We played peggins in the picnic grove and
then hide-seek. Then we saw the rain coming, so we ran. But

it was already storming by the time we got home, so our clothes got soaked. And I fell down and got mine muddy too. And that's all." She clawed my other arm for good measure and then slid away. "Ronna—" I heard her hiss. The sound was followed by a tussle in the dark.

"It's already flown away," Ronna said clearly from the back of the closet, her voice trembling. "I turned it loose from the schoolroom window while everyone was in the play yard."

"That's a lie," Corrie grated. "You have it and you'd better give it back."

"It flew away," Ronna said again. "Herrol saw it. *Herrol*!"

Herrol's voice rumbled sullenly from the front of the closet. "If you want your broken crybird back, it's too late, Corrie. Ronna turned it loose when she healed up its bones."

"If you're lying to me—"

"It flew away," Herrol muttered obdurately.

Corrie's breath hissed angrily and Ronna moaned as Corrie inflicted punishment. Then Corrie slid away to the back of the closet and refused to speak to anyone. Soon even Feliss and Trebb fell silent, oppressed by the closeness of dank air.

We hunched together in the closet for what seemed hours. Outside, first from the play yard, then from the classroom, I heard a deep rumble of voices and an occasional hysterical outburst, immediately muffled. Burdened with my own private misery, I crept to the closet door and laid my ear against the heavy wooden panel. Indistinctly I heard Nira's voice rising persuasively. It was immediately smothered in a babble of protest. Then deep voices again, stern and troubled by turns. The discussion went on for an hour or more, but I could not distinguish the words.

Nor could I read Nira's eyes when she finally released us much later. When she swung back the door and stood silhouetted in the opening, her spine stiff, her shoulders rigid, I crouched against a shelf, expecting some denunciation. But although her features were grim and white, she said only, "Go to bed," and glided away down the hall without a backward glance.

We slipped warily to the bunkroom. Daya huddled in a chair near the door, her heavy nightrobe hugged close to protect her from cold—or from something more pervasive, something more chilling. As we entered the room, her eyes were round and glazed. "Put on your nightclothes and say your devotions," she instructed, but numbly, as if she were too shocked to do more than mouth words.

Awed into compliance, we donned our nightgowns and knelt meekly beside our beds. Only Corrie glanced around with sardonic black eyes as we begged our Secret Power to whisper to us in the night.

Then for the second time that day I hid under my covers, sick with a sense of disaster. Bleeding pilgrims marched through my dreams, a series of ominous phantasms. Over and over the rumble and murmur of voices rose from the classroom. But if whatever had happened under the trees was the disaster I had seen earlier in the day, why did this sense of foreboding still oppress me? Why did it still loom if the damage had already been done? Tears of misery welling from my eyes, I tucked the covers around my ears. Later when I peeked out, I saw Daya at her station by the door, peering at me with fearful eyes.

Daya was gone when I woke next morning and menacing shadows darkened the ceiling. Biting my lip, I got up and padded across the room. Sheets of brown mildew grew on the windows, straining the grey light of early morning into grotesque shapes. Peering through a clear spot on the pane, I found our play yard covered with green, violet and dun moss. It grew in pads upon the play equipment and clung in puffy clusters to the fence posts. The exterior wall was a downy patchwork. Sunrise probed the wall with pale violet fingers. Squinting, I could distinguish the first tiny yellow blossoms opening their throats.

Blindly I staggered from the window. Feliss slept around her pillow. I shook her, anxious for companionship. "Feliss, the moss is everywhere. *Feliss*!"

Her eyes popped open, momentarily startled. "What? Did Headfather—"

"There's moss growing on everything. The swings, the climber, the classroom walls. We'll have to stay inside all day unless the crybirds clean it up."

Rubbing her eyes, she got up and followed me to the window. Her shallow forehead creased as she peered out at a muffled world. "I don't like the mosses," she said petulantly. "The spores make me cough. And I don't like to stay indoors all day." Then apprehension came into her eyes. She peered around the dim room. "Our nurses—"

"They let us sleep past first devotions," I realized, startled. Normally we were on our knees beside our beds at sunrise. "Feliss, the people who came while we were in punishment last night—"

"I heard Headfather Jones," she said slowly. Her gaze flickered to Corrie's bed, where Corrie was lost in a tangle of covers. "And there were women too. Not just Nira and Miss— women from the Crossroads. They were here a long time'."

I clasped her forearm. "Feliss, I know something happened at the stream yesterday. I know—"

"You don't know anything!" she declared, shaking free. "And I'm not going to talk about it." Darting across the room, she flung open the play yard door. She slipped into the play yard, her nightgown dragging in the dirt. "I don't like the mosses!" she cried to the sky, her voice shrill. "I hate the mosses! *Hate them, hate them, hate them!*"

Like a mad apparition, Larissa appeared from the hallway. She scurried out the door, snatched Feliss, and pulled her back into the bunkroom. Larissa's dark hair stood out from her head, snarled and knotted, as if she had spent the night twisting and tearing at it. "We've all told you, Feliss—never, *never* open the doors when the madness is coming. Do you want all your nurses to go mad and burn you up in the fireplace?" She stooped to peer directly into Feliss' eyes with her own fierce, red-rimmed ones. "Do you want us to pluck out your eyeballs and pull off your limbs to feed the raging death-wish?"

I stared at her, at the fright-wig she had made of her hair. Over a surge of nausea, I protested, "Larissa, none of our nurses—"

Abruptly she released Feliss and dug harsh nails into my arm. "None of your nurses ever suffers the death-wish?" she demanded in a grating voice. "None of your nurses ever run wild when the spores float in the air? But none of your nurses have ever been with child before, little master. And none of your nurses have been frightened for their lives before, shut up here with the six little sunwaifs."

My lips turned numb. "Frightened—"

She snatched at Felissa again and pulled us together, her deranged gaze flaying us. "Or haven't you told little master Nadd the tricks you played on the pilgrims yesterday, little birdie girl? Haven't you told him how you drove the pilgrims out of the sacred trees and threw thunderbolts at them, leaving four dead in the meadow? Haven't you told him how clouds of birds attacked elders and little children alike? Haven't you told him how Headfather Jones' oldest daughter was maimed and blinded by slashing tree branches? Haven't you—"

Quickly Nira swept into the room, her thin face taut with anger. "Larissa, you were told this nonsense was not to be repeated to the children."

"Nonsense?" Larissa demanded on a rising note. She flung Feliss and me away and whirled to address Nira directly. "You heard with your own ears the same story I heard. You—"

"I heard madness speaking, the same kind of madness the rain-spores bring. Certainly you've made pilgrimage yourself, Larissa, and remember the unearthly feelings that are stirred under the streamside trees."

"You know very well I've been there," Larissa responded acidly. "I remember the Secret Power speaking to me there when I was only a child—*to me*—and instructing me to employ wisdom and charity in all my doings."

"Then employ them now!"

"And I saw his face in the trees," Larissa continued relentlessly. "It was stern, with deep eyes and thin lips and a flowing beard. I'll never forget it. I watched his lips as they formed words for me to live by. And if you're saying that the appearance of the Secret Power can be compared to a spore-delusion or to a hysteria of malign powers set loose by these demons we have nursed at our bosoms—"

"I'm saying, as Headfather Jones himself finally allowed, that the dust of the streamside mosses contains some agent capable of inducing a trance-like state. And when a pilgrim is in such a condition of suggestibility, he can very well be deluded into seeing and hearing things which are nonexistent."

"Blasphemy!" Larissa spat.

"If it is blasphemy, why did Headfather Jones himself agree with me? Why did all the three Council elders who came here last night finally support me?"

"Because they weren't among those driven from communion by the furies!" Larissa countered. Her pinpoint pupils blazed at Feliss and me, at the others, who had crept from their beds and hovered at the perimeter of her hysteria. "My own sister saw Corrie call the storm down from the skies. And her infant was one of the dead! My own nephew, my little Helmer—"

"You're hysterical," Nira said sharply. "Go to bed and stay there until you can compose yourself."

"I'm testifying to the truth! Oh yes, I remember when Feliss and Trebb were precious babies. I remember how we petted them and spoiled them. But you know yourself what perverse creatures they've all become. Corrie with her poisonous eyes; Herrol who is more an animal than a child; Nadd with his swollen head. They should all—"

"We won't speak of it!" Nira said fiercely. She seized Larissa's arm and propelled her from the room. Their argument continued in the hall, in strangled whispers.

Stunned, we clustered together at the center of the room. Feliss trembled, tears spilling from her round black eyes. Herrol lowed dangerously, stamping his feet. Trebb dropped to the floor and wrapped his arms around his head. Slowly Ronna sank down beside him, her muddy complexion mottled with white.

Corrie glared at us all. "I told you they wouldn't believe what the pilgrims told on us."

"Larissa believed it," Feliss wailed. "I love Larissa. She gives me extra sweets almost every night."

"Well, she'll give all her sweets to her own baby after this."

I tongued my lips. "You—you—"

"We went to the picnic grove and played peggins," Corrie said firmly. "Now I'm going to get dressed so I can have breakfast."

"If Daya will cook us some," Feliss said forlornly.

"If she won't, we'll cook it ourselves," Corrie retorted, and hurried to her trunk for fresh coveralls.

The porridge pot stood in the center of the table, cold. Our mugs were ranged around it, still sticky from the night before. Silently we served ourselves. No one initiated devotions. We were listening too intently to the insistent murmur from the nurses' quarters.

When we had eaten, we slipped from the table one by one and went to the classroom. The rise and fall of voices was more distinct now, but no one ventured to eavesdrop. Sitting at the study table, I pinched my eyes shut, willing the day to return to normal. Let Nira appear and command us to take out our slates. Let Larissa come and wink conspiratorially as Nira drew figures on the big slate. Let Trebb jump up with a hoot and race around the room. Let Feliss—

Instead, when I opened my eyes, Feliss and Trebb, Corrie, Ronna and Herrol peered stiffly toward the windows. Following their gaze, I caught the bright flutter of wings as birdies pecked lightly at the mildew, creating minute clear spots on the pane.

But the others were not staring at the bright wings or the mildew. They were peering beyond into a sea of faces. With a whimper, I was drawn to the window. I flattened my face against the pane. Silently a crowd had gathered in the meadow beyond our fenced yard. Men, women and children, they were dressed in mourning garb, dark brown gowns slashed to hang in long ribbons, revealing their black undergarments. In their faces was a quality I had never seen before: an other-worldly bleakness, as if all individuality had been erased, as if man and woman, elder and youngfather had merged into one. On their gaunt cheeks were charcoaled black mourning circles. They pressed against the fence, staring up at our windows. In their hands they carried every imaginable implement: shovels, picks, hatchets, hoes. Black mourning banners fluttered in the morning breeze, lending the final touch of madness to the gathering.

I cringed from the window, a fresh wave of foreboding crushing the breath from me. "Nira—" I cried involuntarily.

Corrie appeared beside me, baring her teeth in a smile of strange tenderness. Her eyes glittered darkly. "Sit down, Nadd, if you're frightened. They can't see us through the mildew."

"Nira—" It was all I could utter over the rising tide of panic as I clutched at the windowsill, bracing myself against the roiling blackness. *Disaster*.

"I hate the mosses and the spores." Feliss' voice reached me faintly from across the room. "Nira hasn't even hung the storm curtains today."

Trebb sprang from his chair, limbs flying. "I'll get the sprinkler can and the curtains. We can hang them ourselves."

"Then we won't have to look at their faces," Feliss echoed in relief. "Then Larissa won't go mad today. And Miss and Daya."

"Larissa is already mad," Corrie hissed, her lips still drawn in that chillingly tender smile. "So is everyone else, Feliss. My Mother and my Father like the taste of madness. Today the people will cry and bleed in the meadow so my Father can suck their blood into the sky to create a special storm. Because my Mother is thirsty for the taste of blood and tears raining down on her grassy pelt. My Mother—"

With a whimper I fled her encompassing smile. In the hall-way I barreled into Nira as she hurried from the nurses' quarters. She caught me by the shoulders, a distracted frown drawing her thin brows together. "Go back to your bed, Nadd," she instructed, hardly looking at me.

"Nira, the people from the Crossroads—"

"I've seen the people. Headfather Jones sent a runner half an hour ago to warn me they were coming. He'll be here soon himself to talk them back to reason. But until he's done so, you must all go to your beds and remain very still. Ugly things are happening in the world today. And the people of the Cross-roads—"

"The people believe Corrie and Feliss made them happen," I blurted.

"And Trebb," she added distractedly, sweeping me down the hall before her. "But the danger is to all of you. If you won't go quietly to your beds, I must lock you in the closet again until the madness is past."

But as we stepped into the classroom to fetch the others, a dirge-like chant rose from the meadow beyond our fence. Beginning softly, it quickly swelled, shuddering through the chinked timbers to thunder in the classroom. Nira halted, her features blanching. Seizing at her skirts, she ran to the window.

I followed, pressing my face to the glass again. In the meadow women and children had thrown themselves face down in the grass, their arms extended, palms upward in supplication. Elders and youngfathers joined arms over their groveling bodies and swayed with the rhythm of the chant, implements and mourning banners bristling above them.

"The litany of the damned," Nira said in a low voice. She turned to stare down at me.

I tongued my cracking lips, backing from the window. "I've never heard it before."

"Nor have I," she whispered. Her eyes had grown round and glazed. "I've never heard it, yet I recognize it. Just as no one in the Crossroads has ever uttered it before, yet it comes spontaneously from their throats."

"But is it—is it for *us*? Are they damning us?"

Slowly she shook her head. "It's their own damnation they are celebrating, the damnation of a people routed from their sacred place and driven in disgrace under the mocking sky.

They are acknowledging their ultimate unworthiness. And when they have completed the final stanza—"

I caught my breath, waiting for her to continue. Instead she suddenly seemed to come to life again. She whirled from the window. Corrie stood at the center of the room, her arms spread wide, as if she were receiving unholy tribute. The others were hunched at their study tables, paralyzed by fear. Even Trebb was still, his long arms wrapped around his chest, his eyes frozen, large.

"Come, children," Nira said briskly, catching my hand and Feliss'. At a half run, she hurried us to the bunkroom and to our beds and tucked the covers around us. As she bent over me, the sonorous chant of damnation rattled the panes of the windows and shuddered the walls.

"Stuff your fingers into your ears, Nadd."

"They—will they—"

She shook her head, looking at me with pity. "They won't harm you. The danger now—"

"The danger?" I whispered, my body shuddering with a new onslaught of foreboding. "The danger?"

But she did not reply. She shook her head and hurried away.

Danger. But I knew some force darker than danger moved in the meadow today. Danger implied hope of escape, of deliverance. And there *was* no hope.

I curled into a ball of misery, my fingers in my ears. But the litany was more than sound. Uttered by two hundred throats, by three hundred, it took physical substance. Insistently it thrust through the walls of the cottage and forced itself into my chest cavity, into the space behind my eyes, into the interstices of my brain cells. I choked and coughed. Unable to dislodge it, I struggled free of my covers and tried to focus my bulging eyes. In agony, I peered across the room and met Corrie's black eyes pouring hungrily over me, feeding.

Inarticulately I mouthed a protest. But the volume of the chant, the mass of it, increased relentlessly, pressing at me, suffocating me. Barely aware that I had moved, I found myself curled in a ball on the floor, my mouth open in a shrill scream.

Nira and Daya appeared an eternity later and waded through the sea of sound to me. Nira plucked me off the floor. She mouthed something at Daya, something at me. Daya nodded, ghost-like with her long fair hair hanging to her waist, her face round, white and frightened. She took me from Nira and carried me to the linen closet. When the door closed behind us both, I began to sob convulsively.

Doom and damnation. Terror unfathomable; pain unendurable. Eternal death. I was gripped by a searingly clear vision of disaster, an ecstasy of horror. I clung to Daya until finally the intensity of my vision became too great. Then my body arched and, convulsing, I lost consciousness.

It was night when I swam reluctantly back to awareness. My bed had been pulled into the classroom. A fire crackled in the fireplace, casting ominous shadows up the wall. Nira sat beside me in a straight-backed chair, her hair disarranged. But a strange serenity marked her face. I blinked my eyes and tested my limbs. Like a fever, the terrible sense of impending doom had broken and passed, leaving me weak. "The people—" I said stiffly, thick-tongued.

The same uncanny serenity that marked Nira's features distinguished her voice. "Today will always be remembered," she said, the words soft and almost sweet. "Two madnesses met in the meadow, one lingering from the streamside yesterday, the other swirling from the mosses that grew everywhere this dawn. Many, many were lost who had survived previous sieges of spore-fever."

"They—they killed each other," I said. "When they finished chanting—"

She nodded. "Yes, when they completed the final stanza of the litany of the damned, they turned on each other and hacked and beat each other to death. I watched it all from the windows. Men and women tore off their mourning gowns, copulated, and then battered each other to death. Left unguarded, the cattle broke from their enclosures and joined the melee. They trampled and gored all those who could not flee—or would not. Children and elders slaughtered each other and bled in the grass."

Dimly visions of carnage moved in the still room, deep-eyed, bloody. "If they had just stayed home," I moaned. "If they had just hung their storm curtains and wet them down to catch flying spores—"

"But they did not. They could not. Headfather Jones pleaded with them, as did all the Elder Council who were not mad themselves. It was useless. The remnants of yesterday's madness drove them out into the meadow. And there today's madness caught them, full strength, and destroyed them."

"But they didn't attack the cottage," I quavered, trying to grasp the convoluted dimensions this new madness had taken. "They gathered outside our fence with axes and hoes but they—"

"At first they intended to massacre Sunwaif Cottage. Head-father Jones sent a runner to warn me of the danger. Perhaps if it hadn't been for the spores stimulated by yesterday's rain, we'd all be dead. But the rain-spores incite not murderous fury but suicidal rage. Every child knows that. And gathered as they were, all in a body, joined by the lingering madness of the previous day, they must have felt they had indeed become one person. And so to strangle your neighbor, to hack at your mate was little different from assaulting yourself." Her forehead was faintly scored with a frown. "Does it disturb you to discuss all this, Nadd?"

"I—*no*." No, I realized. I'd carried the burden of disaster alone too long. Speaking of it diluted its corrosive force.

She nodded and settled back in her chair, her gaze retrospective. "Yet even if the fever hadn't turned suicidal, we were granted some protection. When the litany of damnation began, flocks of crybirds began to appear from the sky. They settled upon the roof and timbers in layers five and six deep. More birds than anyone has ever seen at one time swarmed to protect us. They uttered a sweet cry that countered the screams of the people as they died. They remained until sunset, when they all took wing. And did you know that tonight there is no speck of mildew or moss remaining anywhere on our exterior walls?"

"'*I hate the mosses*,'" I whispered, Feliss' shrill protest echoing in my memory.

"What?"

"Nothing," I murmured. I was hardly even surprised to learn that the crybirds had appeared to protect us. "Is everyone, are all the people—"

"Dead?" For the first time she sighed. "Fortunately not all the people of Drae's Crossroads joined the mob. However Headfather Jones fell shortly after noon, trying to restore sanity. He's laid out in the pantry. And there are many dead in the meadow, oh so many. But there were survivors too. And when the first blood-fury passed, they took up torches and marched to the streamside. Later we saw the trees burning, burning for kilometers up and down the stream. I watched until dark, hoping to see the survivors return to Drae's Crossroads, but I saw no one. They may have died in the flames."

What could I say? I licked my lips, trying to soften them. "Larissa—"

"No one's seen Larissa since this morning."

Weak tears welled in my eyes. Larissa: soft, dark and sweetly mischievous. My voice grew hard. "They murdered her. Corrie, Feliss and Trebb."

That roused Nira from her reverie. Her voice snapped like a whip. "Say no such thing, Nadd. If the pilgrims in their moss-drugged state imagined Corrie, Feliss and Trebb powerful and malevolent, it was nothing more than an illusion. And now all who subscribed to the illusion are dead. It dies with them."

"They were at streamside. They—"

"They're children, Nadd. Particularly Feliss and Trebb. Impulsive children, certainly not above mischief. They have never, after all, been permitted to mingle with other children and so they haven't learned normal decorum. Much as I argued with Headfather Jones, he refused to permit children from Drae's Crossroads to attend classes here. And when I proposed that all of you take your morning lessons in Drae's Crossroads, he cited certain entries Headfather Dressler recorded in his special log years ago and again refused me."

I stared at her in surprise. "I thought—I thought you were the one who didn't want us to mingle. I thought you were ashamed—of Trebb's pranks, of Herrol's hairy hands."

She bowed her head, the frown biting deeply into her features. "Ashamed? Yes, now and again. But more I have been bitter and unhappy because I was never given the opportunity to mold you into normal children. There was such uneasiness about your birth, then later about petty details of your appearance. There was even some suggestion that you were little more normal than the others, the ones who are never spoken of. And there were Headfather Dressler's instructions in his special log. His dead hand was always upon you, holding you back. I fought Headfather Jones for you and lost. He refused to permit you to mingle with the children of the Crossroads, even casually."

A long sigh escaped me. I had interpreted her sternness, her chronic tenseness as evidence that she rejected us. Instead she had advocated for us and in her lack of success lay the cause of her bitterness. Inevitably I said, "But Headfather Jones is dead now."

"Yes," she said with a distant smile. "Yes, he's gone, Nadd. He's laid out in the pantry, awaiting burial. And Headfather Dressler's special log, which Headfather Jones carried in his breast pocket, has disappeared." Covertly she glanced toward the fireplace, where a crackling fire burned. "No one will find it now, Nadd. And all the people who were afraid of the sunwaifs are dead in the meadow. When help comes from the other communities, I'll point out that memories of the terrible slaughter will always cling to this place. Your tender minds can only be salvaged if you're removed to a normal existence."

Normal. The word echoed hollowly in my mind. Move the six of us into a longcottage with a dozen pious pilgrims? Delegate Corrie, Feliss and Ronna to the kitchen? Send Herrol and Trebb to the fields each afternoon with hoes in hand? Once I had believed that, if permitted to live normally, we could learn to feel normally, to behave normally. Now I saw only futility in the attempt. "Nira—"

"We've been given a sign already," she said dreamily, staring beyond me at some pastel vision of normality. "When Headfather Jones' body was brought in, it was battered and torn and we didn't even have time to wash it. But Ronna slipped from her bed in the confusion and sat with it, sat with it for hours before we discovered where she had gone. And while she sat, a miracle occurred. All marks of violence were cleansed from his body."

"She—"

"He's dead, but his body is whole, Nadd. A sign to all of us from the Secret Power that healing will occur, that despite terrible wounds, despite even death, our wholeness will be restored. A sign too that the wholeness of the community must be restored by returning the sunwaifs to community life." With a floating smile, she rose from the chair and moved toward the classroom door. Her feet hardly appeared to move. "So you see, the day is not entirely evil, Nadd. We've been given clear sign of that." And she disappeared into the hall, her shoes making no sound on the floor.

I stared after her, nausea twisting my mouth. A sign? If only I could believe the miraculous restoration of Headfather Jones' body was the work of the Secret Power. If only I could believe it had been performed by the same benevolence that had guided the first pilgrims to Destiny, that remained with them, a fostering presence grounded in the human spirit.

But Ronna's strange power, I knew with a sinking heart, was grounded in the same base as Corrie's fierce destructiveness, as Feliss' impish mischief, as my own tormenting gift of vision. And the basis for none of these could be human. We were other, deeply, inexplicably, inalienably other.

And now Nira proposed that we live among the pilgrims, that we work and study with them, that we worship with them. Once that had been my own dream. Now I lay in the classroom staring at the dim ceiling, listening not to the crackle of the fire which had consumed Headfather Dressler's special log, but to the peck-peck of lingering crybirds at the roof, seeking some last morsel of moss. And tears slid down my cheek.

CORRIE

DESTINY YEAR 0217-0222

Often, after the Day of Damnation, I woke before dawn and walked through the Meadow of Tears, reanimating it. Here the shade of a grim youngfather swung his axe. There a phantom bull and bellowing child galloped toward fatal intersection. Elsewhere an elder groveled, bawling some wordless plea as his mate hacked at his spine with a blood-spattered hatchet. I spun through the tangled grass urgently, dew slicking my coverall to my shins, and tasted the phantom gore with my Mother's hungry tongue. Then inevitably my Father appeared on the horizon, his scarlet face distended with sleep. Yawning, he reached out brilliant fingers for me, drowsily determined to possess me, and with a defiant snort I skipped away through the grass to Sunwaif Cottage.

The day after Damnation passed with a strange weightlessness, an eerie timelessness, as if it lay outside the stream of time. Distractedly, Nira hung black storm curtains in every room, hiding the carnage in the meadow. Then she glided through the long hours with a floating serenity which gradually deteriorated into nervous agitation, while Daya and Miss secluded themselves, shrinking to brittle remnants of themselves. Ronna and Nadd, Herrol, Feliss and Trebb slipped up and down the halls with death fixed in huge, staring eyes. I was the only whose memories held relish.

It was late afternoon when the first death patrol appeared from Drae's Crossroads. Nira gathered up her skirts and hurried to escort them to the pantry where Headfather Jones lay. But when she ran down the lane, the death patrol shrank from her. Sketching the sign of the broken cross in the air with their forefingers, they fled across the meadow like men and women pursued by a nightmare. Ignoring her increasingly vehement pleas, they doggedly gathered the remains of the damned into black body bags and dragged away the first group.

Desperately Nira hurried back to the cottage and persuaded Miss and Daya to help her carry Headfather Jones' bier out into the play yard. Then she mounted watch at the window, waiting for the patrol to reappear. When it did so at dusk, she rushed out to entreat them again. In vain. Despite her efforts, Headfather Jones lay in the play yard for two days, and the death patrol refused to approach.

Finally, on the third day, we woke to find that his body had been dragged away and the sign of the broken cross had been splashed on our play yard fence. Nira paced the play yard path in growing agitation, chewing her lower lip, peering anxiously at the witch sign. "I must know if they examined the body," she said finally. "If they didn't, if they don't understand— Miss, Daya, keep the children inside again today. I'm going to the Crossroads. I'll be back before supper." And she disappeared down the lane, her shoulders rigid.

Although the last dead had been removed from the meadow the evening before, black curtains still masked the windows and memory of madness hung heavy in the cottage. By midmorning Miss was running through the cottage in shrill hysteria and Daya had locked herself into the nurses' room. While the others clustered in the classroom, I swept aside the black curtains and peered across the meadow. The grasses were shaggy and wild. Crybirds and palemoths hung thick in the air, so many suspended rainbow particles. At the streamside, I knew, precious seedlings were already pushing up from the ashen waste of the fire. Soon trees would loom over the brown water again and moss would hang down in dense grey beards. Peering across the meadow, I could already smell the spicy must in the air; I could feel it striking visions in my mind, delivering special power to my fingertips.

"I'm glad the villagers burned the trees," Feliss murmured. "I hated the way it smelled by the stream."

"Now the pilgrims will never go back and drink up the water," Trebb said. "They'll be afraid. No one but us will go."

"*I'll* never go there again," Feliss countered, hugging herself.

"We'll all go back to the stream," I whispered. I turned, a slow smile pulling my lips wide, and read the slowly dawning consternation in their faces. Smiling, I saw the truth of my prophecy in Nadd's suddenly haunted gaze. "One day we'll all go back to the stream," I repeated, and Nadd pressed his hands to his mouth and lurched to the wash room, retching.

Feliss, Ronna and Nadd watched all afternoon for Nira. At dusk she finally appeared at the play yard gate, an apparition. Her grey gown hung in shreds and her hair had been pulled roughly from its knot. Her face was bruised, gouged and grotesquely swollen. Tottering forward, she steadied herself upon the gate post. "Children," she gasped, her voice wispy with pain.

Nadd reached her first, dusk laying down shadows of fear in his eyes. "Nira! The pilgrims—"

"They took Headfather Jones' body and burned it. They burned it like carrion, without even examining it, because he stood with me against the damned." With a sob, she staggered into the play yard. One eyelid had been torn half-loose and dangled across her eye grotesquely. Weakly she raised a hand to her forehead. "Children, fetch Miss and Daya. I cannot— I—"

"Miss isn't here," Feliss piped up. "She ran away at noon and Daya won't tell us where she went. She—"

"Because she went nowhere," I interspersed sarcastically, "except mad."

"She cried all morning and Daya cried too," Feliss babbled, tears swimming to her own round black eyes. "They both said bad things about us. They said—"

Weakly Nira stumbled past her and up the path and mounted the steps. She clutched her abdomen spasmodically and her face blanched. "Please," she cried, her eyes brimming with pain. She peered back at the darkening sky, as if seeking some merciful presence. *"Please."*

Only then did I notice the trail of blood that had followed her into the yard. It grew from a series of scarlet droplets near the gate to a widening swath at the foot of the steps. Gradually a puddle was growing beneath her grey skirt. Fascinated, I stared at its frothy richness, at the pallor of Nira's tortured face. Realization brought a smile of ineffable sweetness to my lips. "Your baby—your baby's dying, Nira," I said clearly. When I closed my eyes, I could already see its dead face, contorted with the agony the survivors of Drae's Crossroads had inflicted upon Nira.

Her lips moved numbly. "My baby—" Abruptly her teeth closed on her lip and her face tightened again with pain. Blindly she turned and stumbled into the classroom, dragging a trail of blood after her.

I hurried after her eagerly, but Ronna brushed me aside and took Nira's arm. My gorge rose. Vengefully I snatched at Ronna's hair. She whirled, an uncanny strength welling in her muddy brown eyes. Momentarily I felt my will neutralized as we mentally contested custodianship of Nira's unborn child. Ronna's brown eyes seemed to dilate into deep brown vortices, which drew me irresistibly. The taste of death turned sickly sweet in my mouth, like the curdled juice of the tannis vine. I grimaced, trying to expell the saccharine taste. But it poisoned my saliva, turning it to sticky strings in my throat, choking me. Involuntarily I released Ronna's arm, breaking contact with her compelling gaze.

She turned back to Nira, tightening her grip on Nira's arm. "I'll sit with you, Nira," she said huskily.

Feliss ran after them as they left the classroom, still intent upon the day's injustices. "Daya won't get out of bed, Nira. She never did fix our supper and there isn't any porridge left in the pot."

Nira paused and peered down at her, reeling weakly. "Then you must make your own supper tonight, Feliss. I cannot help you until—until my baby—"

Until your baby is dead, I hissed silently. But as she disappeared down the hall with Ronna and Nadd supporting her, my throat filled with the gall of defeat. When I reached the nurses' room, the door was shut. Nadd barred my way, his gnome's eyes huge and deep and for once not frightened.

"Let me past," I demanded. "Let me past, Nadd, or I'll bring down a storm that will shatter every window in this cottage. Let me past or I'll whip the rain in and tomorrow moss will grow everywhere, in the classroom, in the kitchen, in the pantry—"

Somberly he wagged his head. "No."

"I'll flood the fireplace and burn the roof," I threatened, but his flat stare rendered my threat a bluster. From beyond the door, I heard Nira moan. Ronna murmured. My jaw set. "You can't see what I'll do, Nadd, if you don't open the door. You don't know."

"I see enough to know you won't do anything," he countered, without quavering.

"You can't see anything!" I insisted shrilly. "You tell lies to make the others think you have a gift, but I know you're nothing but a spindly necked weakling. You can barely hold up your own head. You—"

"You won't make a storm tonight, Corrie," he hissed. Then he slipped through the door and slammed and barred it.

My teeth ground as I leapt against the door and rained a storm of blows upon it. The only reply was a weak cry of pain, then silence. Enraged, I threw myself down the hall. Outside first darkness lay upon the meadow and a slight breeze stirred the grasses. With a wordless cry, I arched my body erect, rising to my toes and tossing my head back. I raised my arms, flicked my wrists and splayed my fingers.

No heady sense of power rushed alive. Nor did the evening breeze whip vapor from the soil and suck it into the evening sky. Instead the first stars of evening winked benignly and a single pastel moon smiled blandly from the horizon. A raw cry surging from my throat, I fled the play yard and ran into the meadow. But there was no excited lashing at my ankles, no grassy caress as I passed. *Mother, I fed you blood laced with pilgrim tears,* I accused. *Now give them back to me in thunder and rain. Give them back, rain them down, give them back!*

If my Mother heard me, she gave no sign. She was like a huge, dead animal as I pounded through the meadow. My boots sank into her rotting hide. I kicked at her rock and soil but received no answering ripple of muscle, no rising of neck-hair. *Give them back!* I shrieked, but my words were lost in empty air.

My feet carried me to the picnic grove and past. They carried me to where the stream flowed brown and silent by moonlight. Its guardians lay beside it in ashen mounds. Occasionally a black stump loomed from the debris of the fire, but nowhere did grey moss hang in long beards. Angrily I plowed through the grey ash, digging in it like an animal. My breath came in harsh grunts. Somewhere spores survived. If I dug deep enough, if I kicked ash high enough, I would unearth the spicy mustiness of vision dust and power would flow again to my fingertips. I would rise to my toes and bring storm from the sky.

But if there were spores, I didn't find them. I choked and coughed, but the brown waters remained water. I snuffled and gulped, but my Mother did not stir alive under my angry feet. Desperately I threw myself down on the streambank and wallowed in thick brown mud. I sucked at running water.

I remained powerless. Despite my arrogance, I was dependent upon the vision-dust of the grey moss to draw lightning from the sky. And the demented pilgrims had torched every beard, had burned every mossy streamside elder. I ran along the stream for kilometers, encountering nothing but ash and charred stumps. I vented my rage in angry tears, raining them into mud that was nothing more than mud. At last, hours later, still strangling with frustration, I stumbled back across the meadow. The sky echoed above me, a cosmic emptiness lined with mocking pinpoints of cold light. Moons trailed across it in rainbow succession, drawing dawn over the horizon. The earth beneath my feet was nothing more than particles of ground rock, inert, unresponding.

When I stepped through the gate at dawn, my final defeat was announced by the infant's cry that wafted from the cottage. Nira's child had been born living. Its lusty protests lacerated me. Numbly I stumbled up the steps. Feliss and Trebb came barreling to the door to greet me, almost hysterical with joy. "It's a girl!" Feliss shrilled.

"It was just born. Ronna's carrying it to the kitchen now to wash it," Trebb amplified. "Come see it, Corrie. It has the funniest red face and its hands are all wrinkled up."

"That's because it's been floating in water," Feliss enthused. "Ronna—"

"It will never live," I asserted harshly. "It wasn't supposed to be born until after harvest. It will die before noon."

"But it's big," Trebb crowed. "Ronna sat with Nira and held her hand all night—"

My own hands tightened to fists. I did not want to hear

more. Ronna had stroked and caressed Nira, and through the agency of her power an infant who should have been little more than a fetus howled lustily in the kitchen. But I was powerless without the grey spores of the streamside moss.

Powerless. Abandoned by my Mother and Father, cast down into common mortality. Trebb and Feliss raced back to the kitchen, where Nira's baby bawled, and I stumbled weakly to my bed, defeated.

During the next few weeks, my Father seemed to frown upon me and smile upon the others. Ronna was ill for a week after Angelicus' birth, but with isolation she recovered. Nira healed quickly and moved briskly through the halls of Sunwaif Cottage, her thin face gradually taking flesh again. Thanks to Ronna she did not even bear scars from her ordeal in Drae's Crossroads. Miss did not reappear, nor did Daya remain, but the burden of our care seemed to sit lightly upon Nira's shoulders after Angelicus' birth, although occasionally I overheard her speaking sadly to Nadd of the unheeded miracle of Head-father Jones. Feliss and Trebb scampered in the meadow and the shaggy grasses grew even denser and more luxuriant.

We soon learned that the survivors of the Day of Damnation had deserted Drae's Crossroads and scattered throughout the other settlements. Nira found a forgotten farm wagon and we carted bags of oats, barley and wheat from the abandoned granary and filled our storage shed. Soon Herrol began to wander the meadows surrounding the Crossroads each afternoon, his stocky shoulders hunched, his head lowered. Solitary cattle, grown half-wild since the Day of Damnation, followed him home, adding their lonely bellows to his. At first they were kept in a makeshift corral Nira and Trebb erected in the meadow. Nira fed them purloined grain and tried to keep the native grasses pulled back until Earth-grasses could be sown. Soon however we found the cattle not only survived but grew sleek on a diet of native grasses—grasses which had always before been poisonous to their species. Herrol spent most of his time with the growing herd, moving impassively among the big beasts, communicating with them with guttural sounds.

The next few years flash through my memory in a series of images: Herrol leading a massive bull through the meadow by the nose, the baby Angelicus laughing on its back, her yellow curls a halo; Feliss and Trebb returning from the picnic grove with buckets of purple dewberries; flocks of crybirds and palemoths converging on our cottage after each rain, filling the air with color; the placid lowing of the cattle; Miss appearing one winter evening, her arms black with skinspot; all of us gathered around the housefire on cold evenings; Miss dancing through the cottage next spring, her arms smooth and white.

Joy, you say. Peace and prosperity. Our cattle ate poisonous grasses and fattened. Herrol brought us porkers which wallowed contentedly through the worst spore storms. Our nurses bloomed. The baby Angelicus delighted everyone. And I raged?

I raged, impotently. I raged through the cottage, I raged in the meadow. I raged at the streamside, where bluewillow and fingerpalm saplings grew with maddening slowness. I raged at the morning sun, I raged at each moon and every star, I raged at grass, rock and soil.

We were eight years old, we were nine, we were ten. Gradually we realized that beyond our own meadows an ominous change had come across the land: drought. Slowly Drae's Crossroads was resettled, but not by proper youngfathers and mothers, not by staid elders and pious children. Instead the outcasts of the other settlements gravitated to the deserted cottages and barns: people displaced by dissent, by unacceptable word and deed or by the increasingly savage specters of famine and disease. Soon we saw them stalking through the sickly meadows that lay beyond our lush ones, gaunt people in ragged clothes. Their eyes followed us with an unwholesome amalgam of hunger and dread. But despite their outcast status, they selected a Headfather and one spring morning he appeared at our gate, his coarse red hair slicked to his skull, his bony face pulled tight in a rictal smile. His eyes were rust-red and watchful.

Nira framed herself in the classroom door at his approach, her body rigid, her features wary. "Good morning, Father," she greeted him noncommittally as he came up the path.

"Good morning, Maid McCree, I come to offer chant with you," replied he, in a voice pitched persuasively low. The watchfulness in his eyes did not yield to the smile with which he briefly softened his gaunt face.

Nira's features grew very still. "It has been many years since we were blessed with spiritual guidance, Father. Apparently we have been forgotten, if not by the Secret Power—who has blessed us all—then by His human agents." A subtle intonation questioned his status as agent of the Power.

Headfather Schuster bared a range of incongruously square white teeth in a placating smile. "It is unfortunate that the irrational fear which emptied the buildings and fields we now occupy also served to isolate you here. Over the past few months, we have watched your sunwaifs playing in the meadows and in the picnic grove. And we have concluded among ourselves that they are not witches but simply children, growing children."

"Undisciplined children," Nira amended briskly. "I've had no choice but to let them run wild. The settlements have refused to take them in, to train them into proper pilgrims."

"And perhaps that will ultimately work to their benefit," he interposed, stepping firmly forward so that she had little choice but to retreat and admit him to the classroom. There he peered around with alert interest, his red-brown eyes finally minutely examining the four of us who sat at our study tables. His ruddy brows arched questioningly. "There are two other children, aren't there? As well as the younger child?"

"Ronna and Herrol are tending the stock this morning." Instinctively Nira had moved to station herself at the blackboard, rod in hand. "They have little aptitude for academics."

"As well, as well," he assured her absently. Then he turned to us. Again he bared his teeth in a smile that failed to reach his watchful eyes. "Shall we offer gratitude to the Secret Power for the good estate in which I find you, children? Not only are you fatter than any child I've left behind in Drae's Crossroads, you are blessed with a snug home and conscientious care."

My teeth ground as he flicked a glance at Nira, covertly evaluating her response to his flattery. Feliss stared at him with round black eyes, her mouth open in an O of astonishment. Trebb's arms thumped to the table top and lay there. Nadd half-stood, his eyes round and dark with growing fear.

"I won't prostrate myself," I declared, jumping up from my table.

Headfather Schuster hardly appeared to notice the challenge. "Of course not. Even in spring the floor is cold. Sit at your table, young miss, bow your head, and the Secret Power will hear."

Feliss' gaze flicked from me to Nira, who gazed at Headfather Schuster with narrowing eyes. "If Corrie doesn't have to lie on the floor, I don't either," she proclaimed.

"Children—" Nira admonished, clutching her rod.

"No one has to lie on the floor," Headfather Schuster said. He turned a placating smile upon Nira, whose face had tightened into a disapproving mask. "Why insist upon the oppression of our female members when the Secret Power waits to hear all of us? The new women of Drae's Crossroads stand with their men, Maid McCree."

Nira's eyes narrowed to chill grey slits. "The new women?" she demanded, the words emerging as spears of ice. "Does the Secret Power suddenly fail to differentiate between the proper humility of women and the pride of men?"

Headfather Schuster's smile tightened. "I'm certain you've heard that in Drae's Crossroads we dissent from any doctrine that requires certain members of our community to publicly humiliate themselves. Even here you've surely heard of the schism of the Dolbrites."

"Schism? I've heard it dignified with that term," Nira said sharply. "Instead I've heard that a few misfits have been driven away from the pilgrim settlements and that they have united to form a band of malcontents and have settled in Drae's Crossroads."

"And you yourself are content? The children you're charged with have been isolated and even persecuted. You yourself were stoned when you tried to inform the pilgrims of Drae's Crossroads of a miracle. You've been ostracized for years now, made rightfully wary of approaching any settlement except under heavy veiling, to secretly visit some member of your family. Even your family, I'm told, considers you an outcast. Yet you're content with the established pilgrim order of life and worship on Destiny?"

"I'm the victim of faulty understanding," she retorted. "Had Headfather Jones' body been examined before it was bagged and burned, everyone would have marveled at the wholeness to which the Secret Power had restored it. And they would have understood the Secret Power's message to us all; that we are one, a whole, and that we must live together in peace."

Headfather Schuster's lips retracted, revealing square white teeth again. "Exactly, Maid McCree. We are one people, man and woman, elder and child. Hurt and humiliation must not be inflicted upon any of us. We're only mortals after all; we have no right to judge or to punish. And so I've come hoping to partially heal the breach that has existed these past few years.

Will you chant with me, Maid McCree? Will you permit your charges to enter into praise with me?"

Nira's features remained taut. "Headfather, how can I permit the children to partake of the heresy that has taken root in what was once a pilgrim community?"

"But you can permit them to continue to exist as outcasts?" he demanded. "You can permit them to grow up here as witches, clawing at the outer perimeters of human society? They've been fortunate in your care, but you can't provide everything forever. One day they'll require membership in a spiritual community. They'll require guidance and leadership and aid, both material and spiritual. You're just one woman, assisted by another. You're not immortal."

Reluctantly Nira nodded. "That—is true."

Headfather Schuster's rust-brown eyes widened, became vortices, and his voice was driven by passion. "Who can say the Secret Power gives more credence to form of address than to the content of the worshipper's heart and soul, Maid McCree? Who can say that the Secret Power is as petty as those Headfathers who are more eager to exert power than to demonstrate mercy?"

Nira stared into his red-brown eyes, his hands clenched, as if she were fighting a mesmerizing force. "Mercy," she echoed faintly. Perhaps she was reliving the day when she had hurried to Drae's Crossroads in pursuit of a miracle, the day when she had been stoned.

"The Secret Power is mercy," Headfather Schuster intoned, his voice dropping a register. "The Secret Power is life. The Secret Power is all things right and good and true. All life and being flow from the Secret Power and at the Secret Power's command. We come to the Power today . . ."

Involuntarily Nira's lips moved, joining him in the chant. Soon Trebb's voice took up the chorus, with Feliss wavering behind. Finally Nadd joined in, his gnome's head stiffly erect on his thin neck, his eyes stark and staring. I subsided into my chair, refusing to be drawn into the hypnotic murmur. Instead of reverence, I felt resentment, intense resentment. Our isolation was the only lasting memorial to my brief hour of ascendancy, when my Mother and my Father had answered my call and stormed across the meadow. Now this gaunt man had come to dazzle Nira with his sophistries and reestablish ties between Sunwaif Cottage and Drae's Crossroads.

He had come to destroy my fragile creation: lasting fear, continued isolation. I scowled at him as he led the chant. His face was bony and starved, a death's head. His eyelids were so thin that tiny blue veins showed through and his knobby hands were ugly with nervous pulses. Beneath his stained white robe his body was emaciated. Only his square white teeth and his coarse red hair were undiminished by hardship. And his eyes—they slid open and peered at me, coldly calculating, keenly assessing . . . hungry.

When the chant was done, Nira raised her head as if in a daze. Her eyes were heavy with tears. "Headfather Schuster, it's been so long, so so long, so very long. If we can repay you in any way, if there's any need in your parish—"

He responded almost too quickly. "I understand your milk cows are very productive this year."

Her face brightened. "Oh yes. Yes, and Herrol milked them early this morning. If you would do us the honor of sampling the take—"

His tongue darted at his lips, moistening them. He bobbed his head. "Yes, I'd like to see if the butterfat content is as high as it would appear from the condition of the herd."

"Certainly," she smiled.

In the pantry Nira dipped the creamy milk from the pail. Headfather Schuster's hand shook as he accepted the filled mug. Raising it to his pale lips, he closed his eyes tight and quaffed down the milk. When he opened his eyes again, they were unfocused, as if his attention were turned inward, to the cool wash of milk down his gullet. "Ah yes," he said softly. "Yes, yes. It's excellent."

"And your own cattle?" Nira probed, quickly dipping him a second mug.

"Our cattle?" His voice broke bitterly. Closing his eyes, he tossed down the second mug of milk and grasped at composure. "Our cattle are lean this year, Maid McCree. As I'm sure you know, the two-year shortage of rain has seriously impeded crops everywhere. All the settlements are suffering, some quite heavily. Yet I hear that the cattle in your pasture don't even require supplemental grain or Earth-grasses to fatten and bear. I hear they live entirely from native croppage."

Quickly Nira hooded her eyes. "They—they graze upon web-grass, yes."

"Yet they're the same cattle which strayed from Drae's

Crossroads just a few years ago?" he probed.

"They—yes, and their offspring," Nira agreed uncomfortably. Still evading his eyes, she lidded the milk pail and rinsed the dipper. "I haven't been trained in animal husbandry, and so I have no explanation for their ability to graze upon webgrass. I—"

"That's not your province, Maid McCree," Headfather Schuster agreed quickly, his rust-red eyes coming sharply back to focus. "An adaptation, I'm sure; perhaps even to be expected after the breed has lived so many years on Destiny." But his eyes were sharply assessing as he gazed around the pantry. "Perhaps since you are so well supplied, my people can deal with you for your surplus production. We don't have much—"

"We'll be pleased to give freely," Nira said quickly. "We have everything we require except perhaps a few bolts of roughspun and some muslin."

His gaze quickly withdrew to cover of his brows. He rendered quick mental calculations. "I'll set spinners to work today."

But did he *have* spinners, I found myself wondering. And did his spinners have fibers—and the strength to work them? Certainly he had hesitated before making the commitment. I studied his gaunt face as he and Nira concluded the interview. Starvation was etched clearly upon his skeletal features.

And gradually a smile of comprehension drew my lips. I didn't need Nadd's vision to see that Headfather Schuster had come to us not out of concern but out of hunger. We had meat and milk, while the drought-stricken people of Drae's Crossroads starved. Despite his sonorous voice, despite his smooth words, Headfather Schuster had come groveling to Sunwaif Cottage. And in his cautious approach, in his hungry alertness, lay proof that the Day of Damnation had not been forgotten. Why else approach six children and two maids with such elaborate tact? No one in Drae's Crossroads knew that until the streamside trees were swathed in moss again I was impotent. No one knew that I had no more power than any other ten-year-old. With a flick of my head, I caught Headfather Schuster's eyes and created a glittering smile for him. Involuntarily he retreated a step, a muscle twitching in his temple.

I glanced back at Nadd, victory flashing in my eyes. But Nadd scarcely noticed. His spine pressed rigidly against the pantry wall, he stared at Nira and Headfather Schuster. His face was pasty, his eyes huge, in them an amalgam of dread and anticipation. Whatever he saw for the days, weeks and months ahead, it chilled him. And whatever sent Nadd into silent spasms of dread would surely delight me. With a sharp laugh, I threw myself at Headfather Schuster. The crackling of brittle birdie bones seemed to echo in the tiny pantry as I wrapped my arms around him in an impulsive hug. Then, before he could respond, I skipped away, running down the hall to the play yard door.

Elation rampaged in my heart as I ran through the meadow. Our isolation was at an end, but suddenly I had the sense not of a precious creation shattered but of opportunity being given to create again, to create on a larger scale, to create freely and exultantly. Trebb called and ran after me, his long limbs thrashing. He caught up with me and the grasses tangled luxuriantly about our ankles as we ran through the meadow. Even my Father sun smiled down at me, his lips curling in a rictal smile reminiscent of Headfather Schuster's.

THE VILLAGE

NADD

FALL 0222

Milk and meat, milk and meat—the refrain cried through my mind like the plea of a starving man as we tramped down the road to Drae's Crossroads. Through the long drought-ridden summer, sleek cattle and pails of creamy milk had been dispatched from our pasture to the settlement. Now Drae's Crossroads proposed to honor the debt not in muslin and roughspun but in intangibles. Nira and Miss led the way toward the village, Angelicus dancing between them. Feliss and Trebb scampered at either side of the dirt track in a welter of dancing grasses and flirting crybirds. As I stumbled along beside Corrie, I tried not to betray the wrenching pain that closed talons on my heart.

"You deserve every opportunity to grow into normal children, Nadd," Nira had argued the night before, when I went to her bedroom to plead with her. "None of you have known the warmth of family life, the companionship of classmates. Of course you're frightened of the change, of how the people of the Crossroads will treat you. You—"

"It—it's not the people I'm frightened of," I insisted, groping for words. "It's—"

"But it's only natural you *should* be frightened of them,

Nadd," she assured me, smiling warmly. "After facing so much hostility at the time of Damnation, attending school in the village is certainly a frightening prospect. Even I feel apprehensive on your behalf. But Headfather Schuster assures me his people will accept all of you kindly. And if things go smoothly this winter, with spring we may take a cottage in the village. Why, within a few years, you will have forgotten you were ever an outcast. You will have forgotten all these long years of isolation." Her eyes glowed. "And if eventually you feel too uncomfortable with the heresies of Headfather Schuster's people, one day you can move on to another settlement. It's only a matter of learning to behave normally, to achieve the proper demeanor, the accepted bearing—"

"But in Drae's Crossroads—" I protested.

"Oh, certainly I realize Headfather Schuster's people are not ideal models for growing children. But they're better than nothing, Nadd. And if you're perceptive it's possible to learn almost as much from a poor model as from a good one. Now run to bed. We must be up early, all of us." And she was on her feet, escorting me to her door.

When the door closed behind me, I lingered in the hall, torn by anxiety. *If she wouldn't listen to me, if no one would listen to me, if everyone insisted upon believing we could be tailored this late into normal children*—Sucking a steadying breath, I choked back dark images, formless faces writ in black across my mind's eye, and stumbled down the hall to my bed.

And now the first cottages were visible ahead, decrepit structures weathered dark with years, their windows boarded against winter cold, their chimneys exhaling anemic streams of woodsmoke. By contrast the morning sky was clear, like a lavender jewel tinged with gold. The sun's disk was a sharply defined rim of scarlet against the glowing sky. As we neared the settlement, the grasses that had been so luxuriant in our own meadow became sickly. Despite Trebb's bounding feet, they lay dead and yellow against the soil. As Feliss ran up the road, the stream of crybirds and palemoths that followed her was like a rainbow incursion, sweeping into the grey on grey squalor of Drae's Crossroads.

As the dirt track wound between the first rank of cottages, a dark shadow seemed to fall across our little group. Nira and Miss squared their shoulders and drew Angelicus close between them. Feliss and Trebb retreated from the shoulders of the road to march directly behind Nira and Miss. I drew my head down to the protection of my hunched shoulders. For slowly, as we entered the settlement, doors opened and people appeared to stare at us: slattern women in rags, hollow-eyed children, tottering elders drooling into unwholesome beards, bold-eyed young women whose breasts thrust out in salacious challenge, youngfathers with bunching jaws and lowering black brows. They materialized at either side of the road, peering at us in heavy silence, their breath steaming against the chill autumn air.

Haunted, I peered at them. *If this was normality, if this was human society*—My eyelids fluttered, and the steaming breath of the heretics seemed to coalesce into a dense grey mist. As they continued to stare, continued to exhale cloudy vapor, the mist burgeoned into a black thunderhead, boiling ominously over the entire settlement, shadowing every face. Choking with dread, I pushed past Ronna and Herrol and snatched at Nira's sleeve.

She turned to me tensely, a mechanical smile frozen on her lips. She bent and hissed between clenched teeth, "Nadd, walk with Corrie. Hold her hand if you—"

I refused to be brushed off. I clutched her arm, desperately, my voice rising in hysteria. "Nira, the people, these people—"

Falling back from Miss and Angelicus, she caught my hands in a painful clasp. She tossed a placating smile to either side of the road, then bent to me and whispered urgently. "You must never make personal comment in public, Nadd. Even these people are capable of taking offense."

I shook my head, rejecting her admonition, and struggled to put my premonition into words. "Nira, these people, this place—" But how explain the nightmare within the thunderhead when the thunderhead itself was invisible to everyone but me? How explain the very formlessness of my fears and expect Nira to honor them?

Again she smiled tensely at our silent audience and bent back to me. Her hand tightened painfully on my arm. "Nowhere will you find people living in much better circumstance, Nadd. The drought has been long and hard. There continues to be a severe shortage of meats, grains and clothing fibers, even here, with all the surplus we are able to provide. Several communities to the north have been destroyed, all their inhabitants starved. Many others have been decimated. You can't expect a healthy, buoyant people to greet you here today."

"But there's no drought at Sunwaif Cottage,"I hissed, thrusting at her most vulnerable point.

Her eyes flittered away, a tiny frown appearing between her brows. "Indeed there isn't,"she acknowledged unwillingly. "For reasons no one can explain, rain falls upon our meadows and our water barrels remain full even when wells everywhere else have run dry. And so we must give thanks that we are able to aid these people and earn their acceptence."

Acceptance? If the silent stares that followed us was acceptance, and if it were a boon to be accepted by slatterns and brutes . . . But Nira pulled me down the road relentlessly, her teeth clenched in a placating smile. Finally Headfather Schuster appeared from a tumbledown cottage and stepped into the road to greet us. Nira's hand tightened as she dragged me forward.

"So here we have the scholars,"Headfather Schuster declared. A summer of adequate nutrition had brought a change in him fleshing out his skeletal face, making his gaze less hungry, more assessing. His red-brown eyes alert, he shook hands with Herrol, Trebb and myself and bowed to the girls. Finally his gaze lingered on Nira, detailing her clear complexion. He nodded, as if answering some silent question of his own asking, and offered her his arm.

Flushing, Nira placed her fingers around his arm. "I hope we haven't arrived too early. The children were so eager, it was difficult to keep them from running ahead."

"We've been awaiting your arrival, all of us,"he declared diplomatically, leading us up a bare path to a long, grim structure with a sagging door and discouraged roof. Along one wall was a series of boarded windows, like so many blinded eyes. He threw open the door with a flourish. "Our school house is clean, Maid McCree. That's all I can say for it now. But next spring, the necessary repairs will be undertaken. It may even be possible to whitewash it, if the Secret Power favors us this winter."

"I'm sure He will," Nira declared, and I shriveled at the swimming softness in her eyes as she gazed up at him. Compared to the hags and hot-eyed wenches who lined the road, Nira was a blushing sunset. Twice that summer when Headfather Schuster had come to lead us in chant, I had heard him whispering to Nira in the hall afterward, calling her not Maid McCree but other things, soft things. Whenever I fell under his alert gaze, I found myself keenly ambivalent. He was a man who recognized opportunities so radical or so obscure that no other saw them. At the same time, he was clearly a man who intended to wring every benefit from those same opportunities, and that made me squirm uneasily. As the others filed into the schoolhouse, I gazed up at him suspiciously. He flicked me a keen-eyed smile and urged me into the classroom.

The classroom was large, with a high ceiling and boarded windows. Lanterns burned from wall fixtures, casting unhealthy yellow light. A haggard woman in wash-worn skirt stood at the blackboard, frozen in an attitude of nervous apprehension. Along the wall housing the boarded windows stood our classmates, their bodies rigid, their gazes frozen. At the far side of the dim room, set a distance away from our new classmates' battered desks and study tables, stood six new desks, arranged in rows of three. A slate and chalk lay on each desk. For several moments we stood like hostile armies, assessing each other.

Feliss stirred restively. "I don't like—"

"Hush, Feliss," Miss hissed.

"But why is it so dark here?" Feliss insisted, raising her voice. She peered around, aggrieved. "Why are the windows all boarded over? How can I see the crybirds?"

"Your desks aren't near the windows anyway," Nira said sternly. "And you're here to study, not to stare out the window."

"But I don't like to study by lantern light," Feliss persisted. "It makes my eyes hurt. And if the birdies can't see me—"

The adults gathered around Feliss, trying to hush her. While they were thus preoccupied, Corrie slipped across the room and preempted a decrepit desk directly before the teacher's stand. She shoved aside the scribbled slate and stubby chalks that littered the battered desk top. "I'll sit here," she declared with a flick of her black hair. "Then I can see everything Teacher writes on the board."

The teacher cringed visibly at Corrie's glittering smile. Quickly Nira stepped forward to retrieve her charge. "Corrie—"

"Of course Corrie may sit up front near the teacher's stand," Headfather Schuster said smoothly, waylaying Nira. "Just let us exchange that old desk for the new one we've built for you, Corrie."

Corrie turned her glittering smile on him in all its hostile insincerity. "No, I like this desk, Headfather. I even like the slate and chalks. I'll just stay here."

The teacher gave a nervous yelp, wringing her hands. "The new desks, Headfather—You promised the parents—You promised me—"

Headfather Schuster's square white teeth appeared in a reassuring smile. "Of course I promised you, Maid Tetner." He
uncoiled his most sonorous tone. "Feliss and Trebb, these are
your desks, in the middle. Herrol and Ronna will sit behind
you, and Nadd and Corrie have been assigned the front two
desks. Nadd—"

"But I'm the smallest,"Feliss protested. "I should sit in
front. I'm even shorter than Nadd."

"But you know you want to sit with Trebb," Nira reminded
her tensely. "And Headfather Schuster has everything planned.
Tomorrow, if Nadd wants to exchange places with you—" She
caught Feliss and Trebb each by an arm and guided them to
their seats. Ronna and Herrol slid mutely into the designated
desks. "Now Nadd—"

"And I'll just exchange your new desk for that old one,
Corrie," Headfather Schuster said easily.

"No, I won't use the new desk," Corrie declared. "I don't
like the broken-limb sign you had carved on it. Look, Nira.
He had one carved on the side of every new desk."

Nira shot a glance at Headfather Schuster, who laid a pro-
prietorial hand upon Ronna's desk. I followed both their gazes.
There, carved into the wood just below the hinged lid, was a
tiny swastika. "Surely Maid McCree has explained that the
swastika is a symbol of good luck, Corrie," "Headfather Schuster said.

Corrie's dark eyes flared. "Nira's told me the swastika sig-
nifies that the Secret Power has broken the limbs of evil. She's
told me that when people want to contain some evil or neutralize
the power of a witch—"

"But no one here believes in witches, Corrie," Nira said
hurriedly. Snatching my arm, she propelled me into one of the
vacant desks. "See, now everyone else is sitting at a fine new
desk, ready to study. Surely you remember how we all pledged
to be cooperative before we left the cottage. You remember—"

"I didn't pledge myself to sit in a desk carved with the sign
of broken evil. That sign makes me think the people here *do*
believe in witches, and if they do—"

"Of course they do," Headfather Schuster intervened
briskly. "You can't expect people to be rational, Corrie, when
they meet the inexplicable every day. Who understands the
cycles of nature and the forces that cause them to follow one
upon another? Who understands why one child dies of pneur-

rhea while her sister skips through the winter in perfect health? Who understands why one family's porker brings forth nothing but stillborns while another's sow produces healthy litters? Who understands why some years the slugworms appear early and other years late? Ordinary people cannot always attribute evil as well as good to the Secret Power and still retain their faith. Their minds cannot span the dichotomy. So the inexplicable, the evil becomes the work of witches instead.

"But of course there's no reason to deny the other children the same protection conferred upon you, is there?" Slipping a hand into his pocket, he brought out a carving blade. Unfolding it, he stepped to the first row of battered desks and began cutting swastikas into every desk top. Moving briskly through the hushed room, he marked each desk. Finally he mounted the teacher's stand and incised a swastika upon her desk as well. With a snap, he folded his carving blade away. "Now take your seats, children. Whoever was using Corrie's desk may take the new one beside Nadd." When no one moved, his voice hardened. "Take your seats, children."

With an uneasy murmur, the children hurried to their desks. A tall girl with spindly limbs and lank brown hair slipped into the desk beside mine. Her entire right hand pulsated with black skinspot. She peered at me anxiously and I edged to the far side of my seat.

"Excellent," Headfather Schuster observed. "For the next few days, children, you are fortunate in having two teachers. Maid McCree will coach some of you separately while Maid Tetner lectures. If it proves a workable arrangement, it will become permanent." Alertly his red-brown eyes sought over the room, cataloguing each frozen face. "And now let us offer devotions."

As his voice slipped into the morning chant, I peered covertly around the room. My new classmates were unpreposessing, spindly and spot-ridden, with runny noses and eyes that peered slyly across the room as their lips mouthed devotions. Guiltily I closed my own eyes and surrendered to the hypnotic flow of Headfather Schuster's voice, murmuring smoothly, murmuring easily through stanzas subtly altered from those Headfather Jones had taught us.

"Secret Power, guide us in the ways of survival on this world chosen for us by our ancestors. Teach us to feed ourselves from the land, teach us to grow in the ways of self-sufficiency,

*teach us to know thy divine will and adapt ourselves to the soil
You have placed beneath our feet. Secret Power, teach us to
forgive those who term us heretics, that we may lead them to
the new light. Secret Power...*"

Disturbed, I gazed up at Headfather Schuster. Immediately,
as if by some instinct, his eyes opened and fixed alertly upon
mine. Transfixed, I stared at him, helplessly mouthing the
heresies he had set to the rhythm of the morning chant. The
force of his gaze held me until he concluded our silent con-
frontation with a nod and lidded his eyes.

"Those who term us heretics..." The same righteous people
had termed six children witches and had stoned a pregnant
woman come to plead a miracle. The pilgrims had held us at
arm's length, in fact, since late infancy. Although Headfather
Jones had come to Sunwaif Cottage weekly to chant, we had
never undertaken a pilgrimage, attended a Festival of Worms,
gone berrying with the children of the Crossroads, or been
included in any other public fest. But now Headfather Schuster's
heretics accepted us. In hunger and cold fear, perhaps, but here
we were among them, joining our voices to theirs, covertly
examining each other as the chant continued. And Nira said
that perhaps with spring...

But a new sound distracted me, forming a rising undercur-
rent to the chant. Beyond the boarded windows rose the cry
of a hundred lonely crybirds, an urgent chirping accompanied
by the scrabble of tiny claws against every exterior wall of the
schoolhouse. Feliss jumped up from her desk, her eyes shining.
"The birdies know I'm here, Headfather."

Still leading the chant, Headfather Schuster slipped across
the room to the boarded windows. Feliss darted after him.
Together they peered through a gap in the boards as he completed the stanza. When he stepped back from the window, a
spark of triumph burned in his eyes. "Children, settle to your
lessons," he instructed. "Feliss, come with me. We have work
to do." Taking her hand, he quickly led her outside.

The rest of us peered around, silently assessing each other.
Maid Tetner cleared her throat. Her voice broke on a high note.
"Well, young people, there are sums on the board. You may
have half an hour and then we will correct your work." Her
gaze flickered nervously to our side of the room. "I assume
you—you children are acquainted with your plusses and mi-
nuses."

"Those in the front four seats do well at slate work, Teacher," Nira assured her quickly. "Ronna and Herrol are not so inclined, despite my consistent effort to encourage them."

Maid Tetner's thin eyebrows rose to questioning peaks. "If you have already adjudged them incapable, Teacher—"

"I would like them to have classroom experience nevertheless," Nira said quickly. "Ronna, in fact, will be pleased to be assigned chores around the school. She's very reliable at tending little ones."

Maid Tetner eyed Ronna, who shyly evaded her penetrating gaze. She had grown into an unprepossessing youngster, her hair hanging down her shoulders in ragged streamers and her face unevenly dappled with white. Conflict etched Maid Tetner's haggard face. "Of course ordinarily there are small ones, too old for the nursery but too young to properly begin lessons. They are a distraction, but they have no other place to go when their parents tend the fields. Today we requested that only proper students attend, but tomorrow—"

"Ronna has attended my Angelicus from birth, and very capably," Nira asserted quickly. "And since we'll both be present to supervise, surely none of the parents will object."

"Perhaps not," Maid Tetner acknowledged with some reluctance. Her gaze fell over the class and hardened. "Why are there no chalks in your hands, children? Surely you can disregard the cry of a few birds."

But the sound that permeated the classroom was not the cry of a few birds. It was the insistent outcry of an entire flock, piercing in its sweetness. And no sooner had she admonished us than a woody shriek announced the ripping of the first board from the classroom window. Headfather Schuster's intent face appeared in the gap as he jimmied a second and third board from the window. Then Feliss became visible in the schoolyard, her flock darting about her, celebrating their reunion. Palemoths glided at the perimeter of the celebration, flecks of enchantment against the clear morning sky.

Drawn, the children of the Crossroads slipped from their seats and pressed their noses and foreheads against the dusty window panes. By the time Headfather Schuster ripped down the final board, the entire class peered out into a maelstrom of color. Her eyes sparkling, her fine black hair floating around her round head, Feliss danced across the dead grass, crybirds and palemoths swirling around her. Dropping the last board,

Headfather Schuster turned to watch. A spark of pleasure intruded even into his alertly analytical eyes, softening the lines of his face.

There was no sound in the classroom as Feliss concluded her floating ballet and ran back to Headfather Schuster. With a warm smile, he took her hand and led her back to the classroom door.

She skipped into the silent room with a trill of laughter, hardly noticing that her classmates gaped at her in wordless shock. "They were glad to see me! They knew I'd never come here before and they were afraid something had happened to me," she cried. With a skip, she danced across the plank floor toward our row of desks. "Come on out with me, Trebb. We can play in the yard. We—"

Quickly Nira stepped between them, her face deathly white. Her lips seemed numb as she said sternly, "Take your seat, Feliss. Teacher has put lessons on the board for a reason."

"But if Trebb and I can go play outside, the birdies—"

"You may play when everyone else takes recess, not before," Nira instructed her.

Maid Tetner moved from the window to the chalkboard like an automaton, groping for her rod. "Seats," she said woodenly to the children still clustered near the windows. *"Seats."*

But the children remained frozen at the window, staring at Feliss, staring at the rest of us with stunned eyes, until Headfather Schuster reappeared, suppressed triumph in his gaze. He ordered everyone to his seat and hovered at the classroom door for the first quarter hour of Maid Tetner's lecture, his arms crossed across his chest, his gaunt features charged with triumph.

The class sat straight and still until he withdrew. Then whenever Maid Tetner turned to write on the chalkboard, every face turned our way, eyes huge with disbelief. The lanky girl next to me peered at me covertly, her thin features slack. Twice older boys slipped across the room to brush daring fingers across Feliss' bare forearm. They darted back to their seats, staring at their fingertips, testing them.

But it was not fear that transformed every face and stilled every heart whenever Feliss or Trebb blurted out some question that first morning. It was awe. The children of Drae's Crossroads had been warned of witches and instead had been feted with a celebration of crybirds and palemoths. All through morning lessons, they peered from Feliss to the rest of us as if we were so many Winterfest gifts to be unwrapped, so many enticing mysteries to be guessed at, then savored. An hour before fear had palled the classroom. Now it emanated only from Maid Tetner—and from me. Even Nira seemed susceptible to the new mood of expectation.

Fear. At recess the six of us moved in a magic circle, ringed by silently wondering faces. Although the play period was almost over before Feliss and Trebb enticed half a dozen village children to join them in a game of gallops, we obviously had nothing to fear from the other children. And Headfather Schuster had promised Nira that the adults of Drae's Crossroads offered no threat.

Still fear encapsulated me through our first day at school, isolating me. When Headfather Schuster appeared late in the afternoon to walk us home, our departure was a triumphant withdrawal. Happily dazed by our acceptance, Nira smiled with genuine warmth at the people who appeared from the cottages. Angelicus waved from Headfather Schuster's shoulders, a princess coroneted with golden curls. Feliss and Trebb called out to classmates who slipped along the sides of the road, accompanying our march. Even Herrol managed a certain stolid dignity, barely scowling as he rubbed self-consciously at the dark stubble on the backs of his hands. But apprehension drove me down the road with the sting of a hundred little whips, tormenting me.

Fear—of what? I struggled to bring my tormenting premonition to focus, but it evaded me. Clearly it would serve no purpose to mention my dread to Nira or Miss. They would dismiss it. And the prospect of drawing probing questions from Headfather Schuster made me tremble. But if I could sharpen my dread into some single, clear image, if I could force it to take form, or at least to assume a clear outline . . .

As we left Drae's Crossroads, I lingered behind the others, peering back. This evening, silhouetted against the purpling sky, the little collection of huts and barns seemed to promise a certain sturdy security. Crybirds and palemoths floated cheerfully among the cottages and an occasional lantern-lit window promised a reawakening of prosperity. The dead grasses of the field already seemed to surge with fresh vitality.

Troubled, I turned and silently trailed the others until the grasses of our own meadows aproned the road again, tall and lush. In the meadow, cattle raised their massive heads in rumbling salute as we passed. Briefly elation gripped me as the setting sun turned the distant windows of Sunwaif Cottage to golden mirrors. But as the others ran ahead, rioting toward the play yard, dread returned to my heart, cold, amorphous, oppressive. Miserably I plodded toward the cottage, my shoulders hunched, my head bowed.

CORRIE

SPRING 0224

Despite my Father's tantalizing smile the afternoon Headfather
Schuster first appeared at Sunwaif Cottage, our arrival in Drae's
Crossroads brought the village not to its knees but to its feet.
Each morning Feliss whirled down the dirt lane in a vortex of
crybirds and palemoths, striking magic into every famine-shad-
owed eye. At recess Trebb galloped away across dead fields
and ran back through live meadows. Ronna hovered over sickly
toddlers and their pinched faces flushed with health. After
school, Herrol tramped the back lanes of the settlement and
dying cattle turned fiery-eyed and splintered their crude wooden
pens to follow him. Only my expectations and Nadd's were
frustrated.

My expectations—they were so vague. Had I expected lightning to leap from my fingertips and ignite the entire village?
Or had I simply envisioned superstitious villagers groveling at
my feet? Whichever, instead of being intimidated, our new
classmates perversely blossomed with health. Within the first
week runny noses and shadowed eyes disappeared from the
classroom. Soon skinspot became nonexistent. After a month
even Maid Tetner's gaunt face turned solid and ruddy.

Each afternoon Headfather Schuster and Nira escorted Herrol and Trebb on a ramble through the pastures surrounding Drae's Crossroads, Trebb calling dead grasses to life around his ankles, Herrol leading a herd of free cattle, his voice merging with theirs. Later, when Nira and Headfather Schuster parted at the classroom door, Nira slipped out of her cape and bonnet, her face glowing. Then Maid Tetner called us back to attention and lessons resumed.

In short we had straggled into a hellhole of starved heretics, only to see them swiftly transformed. All around us meadows greened and cattle grew sleek. Ground left fallow over the long drought sprouted with volunteer grain. Yet despite the frequent drizzle which accompanied our arrival, spore-madness never touched the village. Flocks of crybirds devoured the fresh mosses before they could bloom and spew madness. And wherever Feliss, Trebb, Ronna, Herrol and Nadd went, the villagers watched—not in fear, not in dread, but with awe.

It was an idyllic interval, and every day anger and isolation distilled fresh bitterness from my soul. Each day at recess Nadd and I sat on the schoolhouse steps, he hunched tight around his hundred fears, I glowering across the yard where Feliss and Trebb played with the village children. Finally one day I singled out four of the youngest children and coaxed them behind the schoolhouse. "I know a game too," I said, kneeling, capturing every wide eye. Of me, at least, the villagers were wary. "It's called madness. I'm the Headfather and you're the pilgrims. When I say, 'Prostrate yourselves!' you must throw yourselves on the ground and do everything I command you. Do you understand?"

They nodded uneasily and when I commanded tossed themselves down and screamed and pounded earnestly enough. But before they overcame their initial self-consciousness, Nira appeared around the corner of the schoolhouse, her face grim. "What is the meaning of this, Corrie? I saw you lead these little kiddies away from their playmates. What are you doing with them?"

My eyes flashed spitefully. "I'm teaching them to play madness. You always say true life games are the best, because they prepare us for the future."

She drew a deep breath, stung by my defiance. "I say hunt the calf and berry bucket are helpful games but I have never said the same of such a perversity as this." She frowned down at my flock. "Children, return to the classroom immediately and rest your heads on your desks until recess is over. And never let me catch you mocking tragedy again." As they slipped away, her eyes narrowed sternly. "I can forgive Nadd his obsession with disaster, Corrie. He can't control his thoughts, nor do I expect you to control yours. But each of us is responsible for his or her own actions, because actions directly affect others—too often adversely in your case."

"People gone spore-mad are not expected to control their behavior," I retorted, eager to escalate the verbal fray.

"And are you susceptible to any such madness?" she demanded. "It seems to me you're susceptible to very little, young miss. Somehow you have developed the spirit of a huntress in an environment where there is precious little legitimate prey. I've discussed you with Headfather Schuster and he agrees that you must not be permitted to be disruptive. We'll both offer whatever guidance and affection we can spare and we hope—"

"But how much affection can you spare when you spend every afternoon mooning together in the meadow?" I taunted. When her face colored, my lips curled in a malicious smile. "Or did you think you slip into a cloak of invisibility when the two of you leave the classroom with the boys?"

Her hand slipped to her cheek, half-concealing her guilty flush. "Apparently you misunderstand our motivation in tramping with the boys, Corrie. My interest lies entirely—"

"In holding hands and rubbing cheeks!" I hissed. "But if you think that's Headfather Schuster's entire interest too, if you think he insists you walk with him every day because your lips are so ruby-soft and your eyes are like clear pools—" I stopped, fascinated by her growing anger.

Her open palm cracked sharply against my cheek. Involuntarily she stepped back, startled and angry. "You've been eavesdropping, Corrie."

"Do you think I'm the only one? Ask Nadd what Headfather Schuster whispers to you each evening after we reach the cottage, when you think we've all run to the kitchen. Or ask Ronna what he coos to you late at night when he comes slipping back to the cottage."

Nira's hand flew back to her own cheek, which was scarlet. "Corrie—"

"Or do you intend to lie and say he doesn't call late at night, when we're supposed to be asleep? But we seldom are, you know. There's always someone slipping down the hall to fetch a drink of water, listening at your door..."

Slowly her hand tightened to a fist. Her words were strained. "Young miss, there are certain adult matters which you are not qualified to judge. Had I any notion my relationship with Headfather Schuster could possibly be misconstrued—"

"But I don't misconstrue it," I said quickly, my malicious smile broadening for the kill. "I understand its nature perfectly, although you don't. You think he comes for the touch of your hand, for the taste of your lips. You think it's you and you alone he's entranced with. But I know better. I know—"

"You know what, young maid?" Headfather Schuster himself demanded, emerging from the corner of the schoolhouse. A spark of derision lit his red-brown eyes. "You are how old now? Barely twelve, I believe."

"I'm as old as the ages," I snapped, stung. "I've lived forever. I know things that were born of this earth long before men and women walked here." Was it a boast? Or was the burden of agelessness as real as it sometimes felt?

"Yet there are other things you completely fail to comprehend," he said with a mocking smile. "Perhaps because you're actually as young as any other weed. I've noticed, for instance, that you haven't succeeded in making friends with your new classmates."

"I don't need friends."

"Oh? Then why do you sulk at recess while Feliss and Trebb play? Why do you try to separate them from their new playmates—without much success, I note. And why do you wander through the Crossroads every afternoon while Nira's straightening the classroom, peering in windows—peering in hungrily, I'm told, as if searching for something."

I sucked an indignant breath. "I've never—"

"No, Corrie, almost every day some citizen reports the young witch has appeared at his window, pressing her face against the pane, staring in as if she would like to feast on the occupants of the cottage."

My face darkened with rage. *The fools, the telling fools!* "And have they told you how they all scurry from any room I glance into, as if they truly expect me to gobble them up?" I demanded. When all I hungered for was some glimpse of the dark face that had haunted every household at the depth of the drought? When all I craved, as Drae's Crossroads rapidly rehabilitated itself, was some lingering hint of death's familiar presence?

Familiar? I clenched my fists, suddenly as helpless as a lost child. My lips trembled and I turned away, struggling to keep my shoulders rigid as grief gripped me. How could I consider death's face familiar when I had barely glimpsed it since the Day of Damnation? Fighting helpless tears, I tried to resurrect memory of Headfather Jones' battered body. But Ronna had spoiled even that for me, slipping from her bed to heal every wound on his body.

Alone—I was totally alone. Feliss had her crybirds and moths, Trebb his grasses. Herrol surrounded himself with beasts, Ronna with toddlers. Even Nadd had his fearful visions to cling to. But I had no one and nothing. Each morning my Father studied me with distant contempt. As I walked down the dirt lane my Mother lay like a dead animal under my feet, her rock and soil inert, unresponding. And with the passage of time I could barely remember my twin's dead face or the surge of anticipation I had felt when Nira's labor began. I was bereft.

Weak and bereft and tearful. With a sob, I abruptly turned and darted away across the schoolyard to the neglected meadow beyond, ignoring Nira's cry. Why should I respond to her when she had never responded to me? She had never petted me as she did Feliss and Ronna, never laughed with me as she did Trebb, never comforted me as she did Nadd. Nor had the others, Miss, Larissa and Daya. From the first they had hung back from me, as if there were something repellent in me.

My twin, my twin, where are you now? Have you rotted to nothing in some bleak burying yard, time-robbed even of your tiny white bones? Is that why my dreams are empty now, utterly empty—because dissolution has rendered you nothing, nothing at all? I pounded through brush and web-grass, watering them with my tears. Then a distance from the village, I saw a lone bluewillow. It was massive, its limbs burdened with foliage, its gnarled branches hunched to form a circular cavern. With a loud sob, I slipped through the arching branches into fetid darkness. I threw myself down and wailed, pounding and kicking the ground. My tears streamed down my face, too copious to be absorbed by the soil, and stood in puddles on the ground. As I tossed myself around in anguish, the shells of the spring crybird hatching crackled under me.

Finally I lay exhausted, but tears continued to drain from my eyes, as if from a flooded reservoir. I could no more control them than I could bring my Mother Destiny to life. Bitterly I let them flow. Then finally from beyond the tree came a shrilly rising twitter. It increased swiftly in volume and the limbs of the tree quivered. Frowning, I sat up. "Feliss?" My voice was hoarse with grief.

"Corrie? Are you there?" I heard the patter of feet and Feliss' face appeared between masses of foliage, her eyes round and apprehensive. Quickly her nose wrinkled and she drew back. "Corrie, it's time to go back to the cottage, and we can't leave without you."

Tears continued to stream from my eyes, an unquenchable flood. "I'm not coming."

"But you have to come. It's almost dark and everyone is waiting. If you don't come back with me, Headfather Schuster will send a search party for you."

"Go tell him not to. I'm not lost."

"But you can't stay here," she pleaded. Briefly her face materialized between the branches again, the nose wrinkled distastefully. "You can't sleep outside all night. Besides, it smells bad under here. It smells like things are rotting."

"Things *are* rotting," I said flatly. "And I'm going to sleep here."

"But—you can't!" she wailed. "Nira won't let you. Headfather Schuster—"

"You sound like a baby!" I said in disgust. "I suppose if I don't come with you, you're going to cry about it." Already her crybirds fluttered through the upper branches of the tree mewling unhappily.

"I can't help it if I'm scared of the dark."

"Then go back to the schoolhouse—and take your birds with you." Angrily I crawled around the tree to put the trunk between us.

But she did not go. Her flock continued to shift uneasily through the treetop, twittering unhappily, occasionally joining their voices in a shriek of anguish. Faintly I heard Feliss sobbing from beyond my cavern of foliage. Rising anger dried my own tears. None of them wanted me. So why couldn't they leave me in solitude? Finally, my mood hopelessly shattered, I crawled from my cavern and ran around the tree. Feliss knelt in the grass weeping, her face in her hands. "All right, I'll go back with you," I conceded angrily.

"You will?" she asked, peeping between her fingers, her voice rising eagerly.

I stiffened, recognizing her ruse. "I said so, didn't I?"

She jumped up with a laugh, her eyes sparkling through her spurious tears. "I knew you would, Corrie." She waved her arms and her crybirds swooped from the treetops in rainbow formation and darted away across the meadow. "Hurry, Corrie. Miss started back to the cottage two hours ago to cook supper. It'll be all dried out before we get there."

I sucked an angry breath, my suspicion confirmed. "You weren't even crying. You were pretending."

She beamed, her monkey-features ingenuous. "I always pretend, if I have to. You know that, Corrie. That's why you always send me to Nira when you want something. And I always get it for you too."

Yes, always, I reflected bitterly as she danced away across the field. Bright, laughing Feliss, always darting at the center of the rainbow. No one could resist her, not even me. Now she ran through the web-grass, her birds swooping after her. "Hurry, Corrie!"

Swallowing my anger, I scrubbed my cheeks with my hands and trudged after her.

When we had walked together for several minutes, she wrinkled her nose and stared distastefully at my muddy clothes. "I still smell something, something almost like—"

"Like what?"

Briefly her gaze met mine. A shadow touched her face, dampening the sparkle in her eyes. "Nothing," she said uneasily and tried to dodge away.

I caught her arm. "Like what?" I demanded again, trying to fathom her expression. But she only shook her head, then wriggled free and disappeared across the field, her birds spiraling around her.

It was not until the next morning, when I bundled my muddy clothes for the laundry, that I detected the aroma: faint, tantalizing, at once spicy and musty. Startled, I shoved my face into the muddy bundle and sucked a deep breath. Momentarily a heady sense of exaltation gripped me. My eyes swam to fresh focus, opening across a broad green meadow. The grasses writhed, as if some giant animal—my Mother—flexed its rocky

muscles and groaned to its feet. I drew another deep breath and
my arms and legs grew swiftly, dizzily, until I could stand
with my feet on my Mother's back and cup my palms under
my Father's fiery chin. His whiskers were bristles of light,
tickling my palms. I arched to my toes, making myself a con-
duit, and the power that was in them both flowed restlessly
through my elongated arms and legs. Gradually portions of it
were diverted and accumulated in a central recess deep in my
chest. There it was amplified into storm, storm that walked
across the meadow on flickering white feet.

But the scent of vision dust was so faint, so elusive, that
the storm walked no more than moments. Then my arms and
legs shriveled to their normal dimensions, and I stood alone
in the dingy laundry room, powerless.

Powerless—*for how long?* Last summer I had slipped from
the cottage and walked in fiercely contained concentration
through the feathery bluewillow saplings which had taken root
at the streamside. But they were no more than stalks, and I
had never encountered the species of moss that produced
vision dust anywhere else. It might be years before the grey beards
reappeared at streamside, before an aromatic tang hung in the
air again.

Now fresh hope gripped me. I flung down my soiled clothes
and ran to the kitchen. Miss hummed at the stove, stirring the
pot. "Tell Nira I've already left for school," I instructed and
disappeared down the hall.

Miss called after me as I clattered out the door and ran down
the lane, driven by urgency. The scent on my clothes could
only have come from beneath the massive bluewillow. Somehow, despite the drought, those dense branches had hoarded
enough moisture to prompt stray vision spores to life. Now I
visualized my solitary tree festooned and garlanded with long
grey beards. I pictured them swaying from every limb, the
morning breeze shaking free clouds of grey dust. I had only
to plunge beneath the tree and inhale that heady must, suck it
deep into my lungs, and I would become fully my Mother's
daughter again, my Father's son.

But when I ran past the schoolhouse and through the overgrown meadow, I found the tree's branches bare of everything
but foliage. I couldn't see even the wispiest beard of moss.
Disbelieving, I crawled into the fetid cavern and peered up.
Morning sunlight probed through the dense foliage, creating
a half-light—a half-light that revealed nothing, nothing at all.

There was no moss in the tree. But the spicy smell that had attached itself to my clothing must have come from here. There was no other explanation. Perplexed, angry, I crawled from under the tree and circled it, studying every branch.

Every branch was bare. Angrily I whirled and peered directly into my Father's dawning face. His gassy features regarded me impassively, betraying nothing. Rising to my toes, tossing my head back, I broadcast a silent demand to him. But there was no answer. A flock of crybirds rose from the meadow and was silhouetted against his unresponding features.

Crybirds. Blood hammered to my head. Feliss' birds had surged noisily through the tree yesterday afternoon. Had they stripped the branches of their fledgling moss? And if so, when would it reappear? In weeks? Months? Years? My hands knotted into fists. *I couldn't wait.*

I couldn't wait—yet I had no alternative. Tears began to course from my eyes again. With a moan, I retreated to shelter of the tree. Clenching my fists, grinding my teeth, I tried to stop the flow of tears. They were weak, useless.

They were also unquenchable. They flowed like some private floodtide, relentlessly washing down my cheeks, soaking into my coverall, accumulating in pools at my knees. Helplessly I let them flow.

It was mid-morning before I managed to stem the involuntary flow. By then the soil beneath the tree was muddy with my grief. Desolate, I crawled from beneath the tree and trudged across the meadow and down the lane, a muddy wraith with ravaged face and ragged hair. I slogged through the Crossroads, ignoring staring villagers. Reaching the edge of the village, I plodded down the lane toward Sunwaif Cottage.

I had just passed the last barn when Feliss' voice reached me. "Corrie! Wait, Corrie!"

I turned and stared sourly at the brilliantly feathered cloud that swept around her as she ran down the dirt road. "Trebb saw you pass the schoolhouse and Nira sent me to bring you back," she panted when she caught up with me. "You're missing arithmetic and history, and Nira says—" She halted, her nose wrinkling. "You smell bad again. You smell—"

My heart skipped a beat. "Like I smelled last night?" I said breathlessly, afraid to hope.

She nodded, putting the width of the lane between us. "Like things rotting. Like—"

Like vision-dust. With throbbing anticipation, I slapped at

my clothes, trying to raise a grey cloud. I inhaled but detected nothing. Desperately I caught Feliss' arm. "Do I smell like it did at streamside? The day we drove the pilgrims out?"

My face must have been savage. Hers contorted with fright. With an alarmed cry, her crybirds swept around us, their wings crackling against the air. "Corrie, you *smell* bad!" she cried, tears appearing in her round black eyes.

"You're pretending," I accused. "You're always pretending—and no one ever catches you at it except me."

"I'm not pretending," she pleaded. "I always tell you the truth, Corrie."

"Like you did yesterday, when you sat in the meadow crying for me to come back with you?"

"But I'm telling the truth now!" she insisted. "You smell—"

"I smell like it did under the trees that day. Don't I?"

She squealed. "*Yes*. Like things rotting. Like death, like—"

Like madness, holy madness that turned to nightmare. Like storm and death and the reign of witches. Releasing her, I turned and pounded back up the lane toward the Crossroads. Confused, her birds swooped after me, crying shrilly. "Corrie, I told Nira—"

I stopped and stared up at the swirling birds, my gorge rising. "Don't follow me, Feliss," I grated. If there were traces of moss in the tree again, if her birds consumed it. . . . "Go back and tell Nira you couldn't find me. Tell her you didn't see me anywhere."

"But *she'll* see you when you go past the schoolhouse."

"I'll cut through the fields."

"You're going back—back to the tree? Where it smells bad?" she demanded incredulously.

"It doesn't smell bad to me, Feliss," I said. Deliberately I bared my teeth in a cloying smile. "But if you follow me, if you ever bring your birds near my tree again, I'll kill them. I'll kill them all. I'll kill every crybird that ever comes near me again."

She sucked an apprehensive breath. "You—you can't kill my birdies, Corrie."

"I'll do it. If you bring them near my tree, I'll kill so many birdies Ronna can never heal them all. And the moths too—I'll shred their wings if I find them near my tree."

"But if Nira tells me to fetch you—"

"Then cry for her. She'll feel so sorry for you she'll never send you after me again." Whipping my hair over my shoulder, I turned and ran down the lane.

As I cut through the fields, barely aware of the morning chill, the earth seemed to heave beneath my running feet, like some mammoth animal preparing to take its feet. Twice I paused and peered eagerly around, waiting to see fields rear on end, the soil writhing. But despite my expectation, my Mother did not arch herself erect and bellow into the morning sky.

My tree was a lonely sentinel. Panting, I parted its branches and fell to my knees in its dim cavern, inhaling hungrily. Was it really here, that subtle musty tang? I drew a second deep breath and a third, desperate to detect some hint of the scent I had smelled on my clothing. Letting my breath seep slowly through my nostrils, I thought I detected it. It was discouragingly faint.

I jumped to my feet, peering up into the dense foliage. Tears of frustration burned in my eyes again. Had Feliss lied? Feliss with her woodsprite charm, her dancing eyes, her attending rainbow—Feliss would say anything to win her own way.

I sank to my knees and crawled around, drawing at the dank air. Without warning, a flickering image appeared in my mind: naked pilgrims kneeling at streamside, dipping their faces into my Mother's brown heart-blood. It was followed by a montage of swiftly dissolving images: trees lashing to life; vengeful flights of crybirds plunging tiny beaks into human flesh; storm clouds billowing overhead and sending down flickering white fingers.

A phantom sense of exaltation gripped me and as quickly dissolved. The vision-dust was here, but in such minute quantities that I could not breathe deeply enough, rapidly enough to build a concentration in my lungs. I moaned angrily as tears of frustration surged through my clenched eyelids and ran down my face again. I threw myself down, rolling myself into a ball to contain the floodtide. But it flowed freely without my consent, wetting my face, my coverall, the soil itself.

Much later, when my tears were almost exhausted, I heard rain. Wiping my face, I crawled from my cavern. Overhead dark clouds loomed in steep vertical banks around my tree. Rain fell in a pounding torrent to a radius of a hundred meters. But beyond that clearly defined area, the sky was cloudless, the grasses dry. Perplexed, I ran around the tree, turning my face to catch the rain. The moisture that soaked my coverall was warm.

Warm, like my Mother's lifeblood. Warm and all-enveloping, enclosing me in loving arms—and at the same time urging alive the scattered spores trapped in the foliage of the tree, saturating them with the all-vital moisture. My Mother's tears fell on my face, not tears of anger or sorrow, but a benison. In her wisdom she had led me here and coaxed my own tears from me. But the small moisture I could provide had barely stimulated whatever stray spores had lodged in the trees. And so now she shed her own tears for me. They saturated the earth and gathered in puddles at the base of the tree.

Squatting, I sucked greedily at the damp air. It tingled in my air passages. Faintly at first, then more clearly visions began to appear. Crouching beneath the protective limbs of the bluewillow, my wet coverall clinging to me, I saw Destiny as it was in the beginning, when my Father was a weak pinpoint in the perpetual night sky and my Mother lay frozen in the deeps of space, swept by cold winds. But her beauty was apparent even then, with her hide rocky and bare, her brow wreathed in ragged mountains, her blood vessels jagged gorges through which flowed not water but lava. Despite the sulphurous vapors which vented from her rocky crust, tenuously veiling her dark face, my Father reached out eager arms of gravity for her and drew her toward him. As she was tugged into his orbit, he grew bolder and brighter in her sky, until finally his scarlet face hung huge and blazing upon her horizon at sunrise. Then his loving rays touched her barren crust, reaching deep into it, exploring it tenderly.

Slowly, lovingly, he coaxed life from dead rock. Simple mosses and fungi appeared and blossomed, cloaking my Mother's rocky crust in violet, dun and green. Gratefully my Mother turned her brilliantly mottled face to my Father and smiled up at him. But as he crossed the sky on that first long day of life, his warming gaze baked the tenuous life from the tender fungi and mosses. They were too fragile, his rays too intense. By sunset, my Mother lay barren again and my Father mourned.

Through that long night, my Father pondered. Near morning he realized moisture was required to protect and preserve the delicate fabric of life. Accordingly he hung over the still oceans, staring down at them with great intensity. Concentrating his heat, he sucked the moisture from them, curled it high into the air, and swept it across the sky. He created massive clouds, towering thunderheads, which he shepherded across the sky as he again approached my Mother's rocky shores. He sucked at the thunderheads, drawing them up into unstable masses, so their precious vapors condensed and fell upon the land with dawn.

Below, my Mother caught the welcome moisture upon her back and rejoiced. And upon the third day of life she greeted my Father not only with brilliant fungi and mosses but with web-grass, which spawned just beneath her heart in dense green clumps and spread quickly across her entire hide. Soon she was entirely covered in a shimmering green coat. Prospering, the web-roots quickly wove themselves into a tight net. After that whenever rain fell, they stored the surplus beneath their dense thatch, conserving it for periods of drought.

As the web-grasses broke down the rocky crust of my Mother's outer shell, proliferation occurred rapidly. Eagerly my Mother created brightbushes to reflect my Father's glory. Other brush joined them and soon the first trees burst from the soil, uniting two realms, air and soil. The fingerpalm, with its five probing fingers, became my Father's tree. Each day at the appropriate moment, it briefly cradled him in its green palm. The bluewillow was my Mother's leaf-creature, crouching confidingly to her, sheltering her secrets beneath its drooping limbs.

But the system was not yet perfectly balanced. The web-grasses fought the intrusion of brush and trees with wiry filaments. With every rain, mosses and fungi grew in dense blankets, smothering the foliage of the trees and brush. And so together my Mother and my Father brought forth slugworms to chew through the wiry web-roots to permit the brush and trees fair foothold. Then they jointly created the crybirds, fashioned from a rainbow, to clear back the rampant mosses and fungi after each rain and the palemoths to strain surplus spores from the air.

The life history of Destiny passed before my eyes in a dazzling panorama, from inception to the present. Although life appeared to proliferate casually, without plan, in actuality my Mother and my Father had ultimately created an intricately balanced system. Everything had its place and its function: the mosses and fungi; the grasses, bushes and trees; the worms, crybirds and moths. Together they comprised a delicately balanced whole.

But a little over two centuries ago a foreign element had intruded into the ancient balance. Suddenly web-grass was chopped and ripped back, not to make room for fingerpalms and bluewillows but to permit the introduction of alien seed. After that, spring after spring, summer after summer, my Mother felt her vitality being drained by vegetable entities never designed to enhance her welfare. Oats, barley, wheat, corn, cabbages, potatoes, carrots—angrily my Mother tried to strangle them with fingers of web-grass. Persistently they recurred, unwelcome parasites sucking up precious moisture, leaching away vital minerals, pushing back native vegetation.

And the beasts—from the first day the heavy tread of the cattle and porkers was agony to my Mother. Soil that had never known a footstep heavier than that of a weightless crybird was suddenly assaulted daily, callously by tons of flesh. Angered, my Father glowered down upon the ungainly aliens. They ignored his outrage. In desperation my Mother pleaded for surplus rain, from which she created clouds of maddening spores. There seemed to lie the creatures' greatest vulnerability. Yet when the spore clouds faded, prematurely dispatched by my parents' own heedless palemoths and crybirds, the ugly beasts survived.

And the cattle and porkers were not alone. They were tended by unlikely creatures who swathed their frail bodies against rain and wind and worshipped an alien entity, a power they claimed had guided them to Destiny from beyond the stars. They built altars to him and raised their voices to him, attributing to him my Mother's every earthen mercy, my Father's every glowing virtue. Stung, my Mother and my Father sent storm to punish the intruders. But the creatures scuttled to safety and perversely praised their own Secret Power for their salvation.

For decades now the skirmishes had continued. Despite storm and drought the intruders survived, scratching a bleak life from my Mother's reluctant soil and attributing every small bounty to their own god. They praised him for my Father's warmth, for the appearance of rain in summer and the blessing of the fireside in winter. My Father and my Mother sent spore storms, and the intruders blessed their own deity when misguided crybirds and palemoths swept the air clean. Instead of trying to ingratiate themselves with my Mother and my Father, they pleaded with their own impotent god.

He was a false god, an interloper. His proper realm lay light-years away, on another world. Yet he proved as tenacious as the settlers themselves. When my Father spat long streamers of radiation at him, instead of shriveling and dying, he perverted the attack to blessing. Through a nimble chemical conjugation, he caused his people to be at once irradiated and impregnated by my Father, and nine months later was born a set of sub-deities, endowed by the circumstances of their nativity with uncanny powers.

My Mother writhed in frenzy; my Father stormed in rage. Through the devious agency of this intruding deity, they had unwittingly become parents of six creatures who commanded elements of the natural world, yet who were also the fleshly products of the intruders.

I crouched beneath the bluewillow, dark images swirling in my mind. Feliss, Trebb, Ronna, Herrol, Nadd, myself: we were at once flesh of my Mother and my Father and of the human intruders. We were a melding of the powers and weaknesses of both. And now our Destiny-parents looked upon us with as much consternation as our flesh-parents. We were their god-sons and god-daughters, at once beloved and alien, cherished and feared.

The six of us constituted a balance, just as balance had long existed between my Mother and my Father. Each of us commanded some power which contributed to our own delicately balanced system. But was it a system that would eventually restore the ancient balance of Destiny or destroy it utterly? Which set of parents would we serve? I let my head fall back. Blindly I stared up into the densely grown limbs of the tree. My Mother had sent me rain and now the heavy foliage of the tree was lightly coated with grey moss. I breathed deeply, drawing vision dust deep into my lungs. Giddily, mind and body parted and I floated away on a sea of questions.

Who would benefit from our birth and who would suffer? Whom would we serve and whom destroy? Would Herrol's cattle and porkers pierce ever-widening paths across my Mother's hide, inflicting permanent agony? Would Trebb's growing powers extend the influence of the imported vegetation, to the detriment of the web-grasses and native brush? Would Feliss countermand every spore storm by sweeping her foolish birds and moths through the madness-laden air? Would Ronna perpetually rescue sick children and frail elders? And Nadd—he was no threat now. At twelve he was a hysterical child, a pathetic figure. But one day his visions could come clear. One day the settlers might listen to his shrill warnings.

Whom *could* we serve but the intruders? It was their deity, after all, who had engineered our birth.

Unwillingly I began to cry again. Long, racking sobs gripped me as I was torn by my Mother's own quandry. We were her god-children and she looked upon us with helpless adoration, knowing that if we survived, if we fulfilled our destinies, we could ultimately destroy her.

Destroy her. I sobbed for a long time beneath the tree, helplessly, hopelessly. Then I emerged, my heart shriveled to a leathery pod, and stared bleakly across the meadow. To a distance of many meters the soil was saturated with rain. Upon the horizon, my Father's face hung in setting sadness. But before I could reach for him, before I could declare my loyalty, I saw the grasses begin to sway in a rhythmic pattern. I peered across the field. A running form approached my tree.

Trebb—his name was a cry in my heart, a cry that hurt: *Trebb, my god-brother, sovereign of the grasses, lord of the trees, ruler of all the leafy green kingdom.* Frozen, I watched him approach. He ran loosely through the dense web-grass, a heedless smile on his mobile features. The long blades tangled around his ankles, worshipping him, and my solitary tree bowed to him with a rattle foliage. Panting to a halt, he flashed me an engaging grin. "Hey, Corrie, you should see the new rice paddie we put in week before last. The sprouts are ankle high, and there hasn't even been a heavy rain yet."

"But you've gone out there every afternoon with Nira and Headfather Schuster," I said dully. He regularly visited all the settlement fields, urging alien vegetation to life, drawing it up from the soil healthy and vigorous.

"We always go out there," he acknowledged. "You know that." He glanced around, then flashed a second meaningless grin. "Hey, it's time for us to go back to the cottage. Nira says if you won't come with me—"

"I'll come," I said faintly, staring at him with sudden desperate longing. "I'll come with you, Trebb." I would go with him anywhere today, seeing him as I did with freshly opened eyes, knowing what I did: that he too was cherished son to my Mother and Father.

He laughed, not noticing the tears that slid down my face again. "Race you then!" Turning, he darted back across the grass, sweeping it alive in great green swaths. With an involuntary sob, I launched myself after him, running against the evening breeze, running against pain, running against loss.

Because deep in my heart I feared I recognized my parents' will. I was the huntress. I was the one who had been entrusted with the responsibility of destroying. That was my function within the delicate balance of our six lives. And instinctively, unwillingly, I suspected I knew whom I must ultimately destroy.

Not the pilgrims. They would eventually destroy themselves.

Not the heretics. They were so few they hardly mattered.

Not my parents, my earthen Mother, my fiery Father.

Instead . . .

"Trebb, wait!" I cried desperately. "Wait for me." I ran after him, knowing that if I were left alone in the meadow, the terrible possibility that had been revealed to me that day would desolate me, would destroy me as utterly as I feared I must ultimately destroy.

NADD

FALL 0224

Ronna threw the last bundle into the loaded cart and clambered aboard, settling herself awkwardly on a pile of bed clothing. She peered toward the bare windows of Sunwaif Cottage, her dull features concealing any flicker of excitement or regret. "We can leave now, Herrol. The others are going to walk into the village."

With an answering grunt, Herrol heaved himself onto the back of the steer harnessed to the cart and ground his booted heels into the animal's flanks. The steer waggled its horns in token protest, then lowered its head and slowly drew the cart into the lane. The morning sky was clear except for a fleece of golden clouds shining against the eastern horizon. In the meadow free cattle stood shoulder deep in web-grass, browsing lazily. As the cart wobbled toward Drae's Crossroads, Herrol's bare shoulders were outlined against the morning sky, sunlight gleaming on the pelt of glossy hair that tapered from his shoulders down his back. Uneasily I jumped down from the fence and turned back to the cottage.

Before I reached the door, Miss clattered down the steps, a sauce pan in one hand. She peered after the wagon in agitation. "Trebb, run throw this on the back of the cart," she urged, forcing a nervous hand back through her hair. She frowned irritably as Feliss scrambled down the climbing frame after Trebb. "Feliss, did you remember to bundle up Corrie's clothes and throw them on the cart?"

Feliss' face wrinkled pettishly. "I had my own things to pack, Miss. Besides, Corrie's been gone for three days now. She might never come back."

"She always comes back, Feliss," Trebb reminded her. He snatched the sauce pan from Miss, danced disjointedly across the yard and ran down the lane after the cart, stirring the webgrass into swirling agitation.

Miss peered after him tensely, then gazed unwillingly across the meadow toward the picnic grove. A dark cloud obscured the huddled bluewillows, draping them in mist. It had hung there for three days, a stormy blemish on the pastel horizon. "She's never stayed away more than five days, Feliss. And Nira told me to see that everything was brought to the Crossroads today, so you can get settled into your new home before school resumes next week." Again she forced her hand back through her hair, drawing it out in serpentine tendrils. "You'll just have to pack up Corrie's things and carry them, Feliss. Run in and gather them. I'm almost ready to leave."

Catching the distracted tone of the command, Feliss climbed back up the frame. "Ronna said she and Angelicus might come back this afternoon to play. They can pack up Corrie's things then."

Miss' face colored. "Feliss, if you think you can disregard my instructions just because Nira isn't here to keep you in order—"

"Well, she isn't," Feliss caroled rebelliously. With a taunting laugh, she threw herself backward and hung by her knees from the top rung of the frame, her fine black hair splashing against the cool air. "And if Ronna doesn't come this afternoon, then Corrie can fetch her own clothes. I don't even want to touch them. They stink." With an exaggerated grimace, she jumped down from the frame and ran out the gate. "Wait for me, Trebb!" Belatedly, a maelstrom of crybirds swept from the cottage roof and darted after her.

Miss peered around her discontentedly. "If you ask me, some people have grown up too quickly this summer," she complained. "If I'd known when I told Nira I would supervise

Sunwaif Cottage this summer while she and Headfather Schuster prepared the new cottage—"

"I'll bundle up Corrie's things," I interrupted, anxious to escape a last minute recitation of Miss' grievances. I had stayed with Miss all summer and knew the entire catalogue of her fears and complaints by heart.

"It's not natural," she persisted, "Corrie suddenly disappearing for days at a time, Herrol strutting around without a shirt on his back, Feliss turning spiteful—"

"You'll have time to catch the cart if you hurry," I urged. "I'll bundle up Corrie's things and catch up with you before the cart reaches the Crossroads."

Miss wheeled and peered uncertainly past me into the empty bunkroom. "I haven't locked the doors and windows yet. There are so many vagrants this year, wandering around searching for food. If they should break in—"

"I'll lock everything. Did you leave anything in your bedroom?"

She shook her head distractedly. "Just let me check the pantry," she decided, hurrying back up the steps. A few minutes later she emerged, an absent frown between her eyes. "You will hurry, won't you, Nadd? There have been strangers in the area. If anything should happen to you—"

"I'll catch up in just a few minutes," I promised, not eager to hear her morbid fantasies about cannibalism among the pilgrims of the outlying communities again. I slipped past her into the bunkroom. She hesitated on the steps, torn, then hurried toward the lane.

Alone, I moved through the deserted rooms pensively, locking doors and windows. The beds had been stripped of mattresses and blankets and the kitchen cupboards stood open and bare. In the linen closet, I found a stack of forgotten storm curtains. I spread one on the bunkroom floor. Corrie's clothes were piled beneath her bed in a damp heap. Reluctantly I pulled the mildewing garments out and bundled them into the storm curtain. If she did not come back this time . . .

Shivering, I glanced around the silent room, drawing ghosts from the sun-moted air. Infant, toddler and child, this was the stage upon which we had acted out our childhood dramas. But now we were twelve, less than a year from the age of first majority. Summer had already coaxed Ronna and Herrol near the boundaries of physical maturity and had launched Feliss into a perverse rebelliousness. Trebb raced through the meadow early every morning performing bizarre adolescent exercises that almost ripped the web-grass from the soil in its dancing frenzy. I was the only one who hung back at the threshhold of first maturity, afraid to cross, afraid to abandon the safety of childhood.

A chill passed down my spine. Nudged by premonition, I slung Corrie's bundle over my shoulder and hurried to the door. When I reached the play yard, an angry wind swept across the meadow. The dark cloud that hung over the picnic grove seemed to elongate, stretching tenuous streamers across the meadow toward Sunwaif Cottage. My eyes narrowed and I distinguished Corrie running through the tall grass, her hair whipping behind her, her coverall mud stained. Catching my breath, I hurried down the steps and ran toward the lane.

Before I could race after Miss and the others, a gust of wind curled around me, holding me back. The grass at either side of the lane swirled wildly, then was swept flat to the ground. I struggled briefly against invisible bonds, but they did not yield. Slowly I let my breath seep out, refusing to sob, and retreated back into the play yard.

Corrie joined me a few moments later, an accusing glitter in her eyes. "You didn't want to wait and walk to the Crossroads with me, did you, Nadd?" she demanded, tossing her head so her hair fell around her shoulders in snarled streamers.

"I—I didn't know you were coming," I lied, struggling to control my voice. "No one's seen you for three days."

"But you all knew where I was." She threw her head back and gazed greedily at the cloud that was swiftly forming over the play yard. Long streamers curled across the distance from the picnic grove and were sucked up into the growing mass, lending it altitude. "You all knew I was in the grove. But Miss didn't send anyone to fetch me. You were all hoping I'd stay there, weren't you, so you could move to the Crossroads without me?"

"No one said anything," I hedged, peering up into the cloud that had followed her. Fingers of wind ruffled my hair and cold drizzle slapped my cheek. Desperately I groped for some distraction to draw her glittering gaze from my face. Her bundle lay in the grass where I had dropped it. "Here are your things, Corrie. The cart just left. If we hurry—"

With a derisive laugh, she scooped up the black bundle and

tossed it at me. "Why don't you carry my things, Nadd?" she jibed. "Is there something wrong with them? Do they smell bad?"

My jaw quivered involuntarily as the black bundle sailed past me. "I—I didn't notice how they smelled, Corrie," I lied. Desperately I peered into the lane. Escape was so near, escape from her hungry gaze, from the gathering darkness she brought with her. "If we run, we can catch a ride on the cart." The muscles of my calves tensing, I edged toward the gate.

She stopped me with a hoarse whisper. "What if I don't want to go to the Crossroads, Nadd?"

Unexpectedly I found myself frozen on tiptoe, paralyzed by the husky malevolence of her voice. "You—"

"What if I decide I want to live under the trees instead of moving into the new cottage?"

I drew a shallow breath, testing the involuntary immobility of my limbs. *It was real.* I couldn't move. "Corrie—" I pleaded.

"What if I decide I don't want to live alone? What if I decide to take someone with me? Wouldn't you like to come live with me under the trees, Nadd? Anytime you wanted you could play in the rain. I only have to ask my Mother, you know, and the rain will pour down. I can make it rain anytime I want. I could make it rain on you right now, Nadd. I could drown you with rain if I wanted."

The muscles of my neck wrenched my gaze upward in a series of painful spasms. The cloud that had followed her from the grove towered over the play yard, its underbelly leaden. But despite its threatening aspect, the grey streamers which had been sucked into the moist air mass only minutes before were already escaping, streaming back out into the morning air and dissipating. Corrie's spell broken by a flashing insight, I sank back to the soles of my feet, my paralyzed limbs loosening. "You can't make it rain on me." As soon as I said the words, I knew they were true.

Her glittering eyes turned hateful. "I can't?" she demanded, arching her body, drawing up her arms as if to pull moisture from the disssipating cloud. "*I can't, Nadd?*"

This time her ferocity failed to affect me. I drew a steadying breath, closed my eyes and made a conscious effort to draw clear images to mind, to flesh out my fleeting insight. Only minutes before she had been able to detain me with a ghost-finger of wind. Now, despite the fierce intensity of her gaze, the cloud overhead was seeping away into the morning air. She could recapture it, I realized as indistinct images flashed through my mind, she could call down the threatened storm only if she ran back to the grove. And she could not force me to go with her.

My eyes snapped open at the sound of a mewling whimper. While I concentrated on my fleeting insight, Corrie had slumped in defeat. She stood with shoulders hunched and arms limp at her sides. When she realized I was staring at her, her head rose, and a wild, unspoken grief kindled in her eyes. It gleamed at me through a veil of unshed tears, contagious in its intensity. Disconcerted, I stepped back. But as I did, Corrie seemed to grow, becoming rapidly larger than life, the embodiment of forces I couldn't hope to comprehend. I rubbed my eyes, trying to force her back to proper proportions. Instead she continued to grow, becoming a monumental figure, her hair thrashing, her eyes burning with searing grief.

As I stared at her, spellbound, a phantom forest seemed to materialize dimly around her, blotting out Sunwaif Cottage. I sucked a startled breath, and at one and the same time Corrie stood before me in the flesh and she walked among a stand of ghostly bluewillows, their limbs arched in a series of dark caverns. As she padded stealthily among the trees, she bent and peered into each musty cavern with eyes at once hungry and stricken. In her right hand she carried a bow, in her left an arrow. A woven quiver was slung across her shoulder. Fascinated, I stared at the rank of brightly tufted arrows it held. There were four, each different, as if each were intended for some specific prey. The arrow she carried in her left hand was tufted with green feathers, its shaft tightly wound with a length of vine. As I tried to focus the vision, she wheeled and peered behind her, as if alerted by some sound. Her eyes narrowed. Recognition, then fierce grief distorted her features. She stood stiffly poised, bow and arrow in hand, paralyzed by internal conflict as the ghostly forest began to dance and sway. Then slowly, with patent unwillingness, she fitted arrow to string, drew back her arm and—

A harsh, cawing protest shattered the vision. Jarred, I realized the sound came from my own throat. Snapping my jaws shut, I drew a spasmodic breath, pinched my eyes tight, and tried to recapture the scene. But the ghost trees refused to reappear. When I opened my eyes Corrie stood before me in her normal proportions, peering at me with eyes that glittered fiercely through unshed tears. Abruptly she sprang forward and seized my arm. "What did you see?"

I stared into her swimming eyes and shook my head, instinct binding me to muteness.

She pressed her face near mine, her gaze compelling. "What did you see, Nadd?"

"I—I didn't see anything," I pleaded, trying to back away. "I—nothing. I saw nothing."

"Then why did you shout? I *know* what you saw—I know—"Her breath hissed between her teeth, a harsh north wind. "Tell me, Nadd, or I'll twist your arm."

"You—" I licked my lips and a slow quiver picked its way down my spine, wrenching me with knowledge of my own vulnerability. She couldn't call storm down upon me, but she had other means of coercion. I shuddered, knowing I must not be vulnerable now. I must not be weak, not until I understood the vision I had just experienced, not until I knew at whom she aimed her arrow and why. Stiffening, I tried to drive the whimpering child out of my heart, tried in that critical moment to become something sterner than the plaintive gnome I had been since the Day of Damnation. "You—you know you don't believe in my sight. You've always told everyone it doesn't exist."

"Well, what did you expect me to say?" She clutched my arm with both hands, all ten nails drawing blood. "*Tell me, Nadd.*"

With an angry snarl, she flung my arm back at me. I cradled the gashed flesh as she surged across the yard to retrieve her bundle. She clawed it open and tumbled out her mildewing clothes. With manic concentration, she flapped the filthy garments against the morning air. A cloud of fine dust rose. She gulped at it, holding each breath until her face was congested. The cords of her neck stood out. "If you won't tell me without a storm—"

My head wagged of its own volition, and the words spoke themselves. "You can't make a storm here, Corrie."

"Oh, can't I? There are spores on my clothes. If I can inhale enough of them—" But the volume of dust she could shake from the filthy garments had already diminished to the vanishing point. Frustrated, she threw the clothes down and hurled herself after them. "You'll tell me, Nadd."

I sucked an apprehensive breath and peered past her into the lane, recognizing my chance. Slowly, putting my feet down carefully, I crept to the gate. When I glanced back, she was pounding at the soiled clothes. Cautiously I slipped into the lane, pausing every few steps to glance back.

I was barely a dozen meters down the lane when a keening protest rose from the play yard. I froze, peering back toward the yard. The dark cloud had dissipated entirely. The keening wail rose in pitch and Corrie burst out the gate. She hesitated momentarily in the lane, peering at me with anguished eyes, then disapppeared into the web-grass.

It was several moments before I could move. Then I turned and pounded down the lane, my breath hissing sharply through my teeth. I only slowed when I realized from the swirling activity of the grasses that Trebb was nearby. I glanced back once more, then trotted until I sighted the heavily loaded cart, Ronna still atop it, Miss marching behind it, her shoulders set.

We had almost reached the Crossroads before Miss saw me plodding at the rear of the convoy. Her gaze flickered beyond me to the distant picnic grove. "You forgot to bring Corrie's things, Nadd."

Reluctantly I followed her gaze. The storm cloud hung over the grove again. Drizzle shrouded the trees like a dense grey curtain. "Corrie will bring them later."

"You saw her then?" Miss demanded sharply. "When does she intend to come to the Crossroads with the rest of us?"

I licked my lips uneasily. "I—I don't know. She might come tomorrow." My voice trailed away and again, momentarily, I saw the figure in the ghost grove, green-feathered arrow fitted to bowstring, face shadowed with anguish.

Miss peered darkly toward the grove, then sighed resentfully and ignored me.

By the time we reached the Crossroads, a retinue of refugees trailed us. The drought had deepened over the summer, scorching the pilgrim communities that lay all around Drae's Crossroads. But warm rains fell on the Crossroads. Summer crops grew lush and tall and cattle and porkers multiplied. By the end of summer a demoralized army of walking skeletons had abandoned their beleaguered settlements and tottered into the Crossroads, too weak even to beg. Headfather Schuster had provided them with tent materials and rations and assigned them a meadow north of the settlement. Now they followed our cart, their gaunt faces turned to catch whatever magic might glint from our faces. Miss cringed visibly as bony hands tapped the cart and sampled Feliss' fine black hair. When we neared the schoolhouse, Feliss disappeared between two huts with a teasing giggle. Trebb permitted himself to be fingered for a few minutes longer, then followed her. As we continued down the village lane, Herrol glared belligerently from his steer's back and I forced myself to walk rigidly erect.

Our new cottage was an elongated structure commanding a high green knoll at the eastern edge of the Crossroads, over-looking the lush patchwork of fields and paddies that sur-rounded the village. The perimeters of the drought were clearly etched in the distance. Drae's Crossroads and its surrounding fields were an island of green in a world parched brown. The boundaries of the island were irregular, a series of tender green headlands jutting into a sea of burned meadows. As I paused, a cluster of hollow-eyed refugees approached. I gazed invol-untarily into the human face of the inexplicable holocaust that moved across the face of Destiny, then shuddered and hurried after the cart.

As soon as the cart stopped, a rabble of living skeletons converged upon it to toss down our possessions. Their com-panions caught our bundles with hungry reverence. With a trembling exclamation, Miss rushed into the cottage. Briefly her face appeared at a window, haunted, and then she disap-peared.

Nira's skirts billowed as she hurried out the door to clasp my face in both hands. "Nadd, I've scarcely seen you all sum-mer. All the others came to inspect the cottage almost every day. Even Corrie came several times. But from you I heard only that you didn't want to make the long walk in the hot sunlight."

Nor had I wanted to see her new status as Headfather Schus-ter's bride blushing from her cheeks and glowing from her eyes like captive sunlight. With a jealous twinge, I forced myself to smile. "I had to help Miss at the cottage."

Nira's gaze flickered toward the exercise yard, where Feliss already swung from the rungs of the new gymnastic frame. "So I heard. With Herrol busy in the calving yards and Trebb in the fields, Miss certainly needed one man around the cot-tage." Her smile condescended to me warmly. "But now we're all together and Aldred and I will keep our wild young misses in much better order than Miss has been able to do." Her clasp descended to my hands, squeezing them warmly. "Well, we're finally a proper family, Nadd. A mother, a father, and seven young brothers and sisters, all living snugly in their own home. And I'm not the only one who's excited. The entire Crossroads has been waiting for the sunwaifs to take possession of their new cottage. There will be a festival of welcome in the tent village tonight. You've always wanted to attend a festival, Nadd. Tonight you'll be an honored guest."

My hands turned to claws in her grasp. Involuntarily I gazed at the ragged passel of refugees who clotted around our wagon. The strongest continued to unload our possessions while the weaker eyed Feliss and Trebb as they ran through the yard. All of them, I knew, had accepted heretic status in coming here, sacrificing belief to survival. But more, their hunger repelled me. Their skeletal limbs made me cold with dread. "We—do we have to go?"

Nira's brows creased. "Have to go? Certainly the sunwaifs will attend their own welcome festival."

"But we should be welcomed by the people of the Crossroads," I protested, pulling my hands free.

"Didn't they already welcome you last fall? And it was the people of the Crossroads who helped Aldred and me erect the cottage, who hammered together the cabinets and the furniture. They worked here evenings after working all day in the fields and canning kitchens. Why, when we were married, the villagers presented Aldred and me not with one quilted comforter but with eight, a large one for our own bed, a small one for Angelicus' bunk, and one for each sunwaif. Surely that's a welcome."

"That—"

"And you must remember that the refugees are people of the Crossroads now too. Some are too frail to contribute much yet, but each of them works to the best of his ability. As soon as harvest is done, their cottages will be built where their tents stand now. By next spring, when they have regained their vigor, you will hardly be able to distinguish this summer's refugees from the rest of us."

I groped for argument, peering fearfully at the wraiths who clustered at the edge of the lane, the remnants of pilgrim robes fluttering around their skeletal limbs. Suddenly Feliss tumbled through the grass, her bright eyes shot with mischief. "Nadd is afraid of the refugees, Nira," she caroled. "Just like Miss. They're both afraid the refugees will try to gobble them up."

My face burned with humiliation. "I'm not. I never—"

"You are!" she teased. "That's all Miss talked about all summer, about the pilgrims eating each other in the settlements. You'd think she'd been in some pilgrim kitchen and seen a hand sticking out of a stewpot. You'd think—"

Her voice carried to the lane. Refugees who had pressed forward at her appearance shrank back. Nira caught Feliss' arm. "Feliss, your tongue!"

"Fried—with brown gravy!" Feliss sang back defiantly. She seized my arm. "Nadd, you stayed at the cottage all summer. You missed everything we built here. Come see the nesting frames Headfather Schuster had built for my birdies. He says that by next nesting season, there'll be tens of thousands of crybirds in Drae's Crossroads, more than you can find anywhere else on Destiny."

I resisted half-heartedly as she tugged me away. Half a dozen immense bluewillows formed a grove on a shallow rise behind the cottage. Their massive under-branches had been radically thinned to permit the installation of a series of horizontal frameworks constructed of poles lashed together with rawhide cord. Set at different levels throughout the trees, the frameworks joined the half-dozen massive trees into a single immense nesting shelter canopied with dark foliage. As Feliss dodged beneath the trees, her crybirds set up a deafening greeting. Far above a single pair of scarlet birds wove a delicately constructed basket of web-grass and vine. The upper branches of the trees were spattered with the plumage of thousands of roosting birds.

Feliss scampered over the hard-packed soil, "I—can't—hear—you!" I shouted, but my voice was lost in the cheerful din. When I balked, she dragged me after her, still exclaiming happily.

Finally, irritated at my lack of response, she scampered from the grove. As we ran back toward the cottage the uproar died behind us.

"See," she boasted, throwing herself down in the deep grass behind the cottage. "See what you missed? No one in the Crossroads will have to hang storm curtains again. We'll never have to stay indoors when the air is damp either. And there's going to be a moth hatchery too. Headfather Schuster is going to put people to work on it after harvest." She leaped up again, dragging me with her. In a cleared spot east of the cottage a dozen fingerpalm saplings stood like naked poles, five vestigal leaves sprouted from the top of each sapling. "See," Feliss insisted. "As soon as the crops are in, Headfather Schuster will have the workers lash together the frames and fasten them up into the trees."

I stared at her blankly, then back at the naked saplings. "Those trees won't hold frames, Feliss, unless you're going to make them of toothpicks. If Headfather Schuster had built the cottage near a grove that was already mature—"

Feliss laughed in delight, a sound echoed by her swirling escort of crybirds. "Like the bluewillow grove where the birds are nesting?" she demanded. Leaping up, she ran through the grass and threw herself down, rolling into a tight ball. Two bright eyes peered at me, mocking. "Like that, Nadd?"

I responded warily. "Yes, if he wanted a husking shelter, he should have built the cottage between a bluewillow grove and a fingerpalm grove. He—"

Again she trilled with delight, leaping up and leading her birds in a soaring ballet across the tangled lawan. "But how long do you think the bluewillow grove has been there, Nadd? Headfather Schuster and Trebb put the seedlings into the ground the week after school was dismissed last spring. If you hadn't been moping around the cottage with Miss all summer you'd know that."

"I—" Stunned, I turned and peered back into the massive trees, their arching branches thinned to create a high, leafy vault. Something sucked at my chest, drawing out the breath. "Trees don't grow that fast, Feliss," I said weakly.

As she danced through the grass sunlight touched her bare arms, shimmering with rainbow brilliance: scarlet, emerald, lavender, gold. "They grow that fast if Trebb tells them to, Nadd." Rolling through the grass, she gave a twittering signal that brought dozens of crybirds soaring down to cover her with their own glowing plumage. "I begged Trebb to grow the trees for me, and then Headfather Schuster took him out to sleep near the saplings. He dreamed them right up against the sky for me, Nadd."

Dreamed them up against the sky. I stared past Feliss' wriggling form into the massive bluewillows, and I seemed to see a phantom grove, ominous with shadows. "Feliss—" I pleaded,

trying to shake the dark premonition. The lower limbs of the
nesting grove had been cut to permit an adult to walk upright
beneath the lowermost framework of nesting poles. Sunlight
shone through the canopy of foliage, gleaming upon brilliant
plumage. Here was no series of dark caverns, here no stalking
huntress. Yet I saw them anyway, dimly superimposed upon
the nesting grove.

"Feliss—" If only she would jump up and run away, shrieking as if we were still children, not near-adolescents with inexplicable capabilities developing willy-nilly. "Feliss, I'll—I'll
race you to the front door."

She was child enough to accept the challenge. "I'll win
you!" she shouted, leaping up and sweeping crybirds off her
shoulders and back. With a laugh, she plunged away.

I tried to follow, tried to forge my escape from the phantom
forest. But perversely ghost trees sprang up all around me,
overshadowing reality. With a moan, I swayed dizzily, lost in
a maze of insubstantiality.

Feliss scampered away, then returned. "It's not a race unless
you run too, Nadd."

"I—I'll run," I gasped. But when I put foot before foot, my
hand penetrated dimly perceived foliage and I staggered into
a darkly mossed trunk. Dark trees grew all around me, clutching
me in their musty arms, and somewhere, I knew with a swift
flash of panic, the huntress fitted arrow to string. Somewhere—
A rush of adrenalin made my feet pump. But they tangled in
the web-grass and I sprawled. Helpless, I heard Feliss' teasing
giggle as she ran away without me.

Bluewillows. They grew in dark clusters and small groves
all across the meadows. They were a slow-growing species.
No one knew how long a bluewillow required to reach maturity
because humans had not been on Destiny that long. But Trebb
had dreamed a grove of bluewillows to maturity in a single
summer. Bluewillows, and a solitary hunter stalking unseen
prey, a green-tufted arrow in her hand. Bluewillows . . .

I struggled to my feet, my breath coming in shallow sobs.
But the time was past for me to sob like a child. Corrie, Trebb,
Feliss, Ronna, Herrol—all the others were maturing. Secluded
at the cottage with Miss, I hadn't realized how rapidly the
process was proceeding, and how radically. Now I must mature
too. I could no longer afford to be a fearful child, helpless in
a context of wildly burgeoning powers. I squeezed my eyes

shut and forced myself to breathe deeply, regularly. When I opened my eyes, I reassured myself, there would be no phantom grove. When I opened my eyes, there would be only grass and sunlight and our new cottage.

I opened my eyes and no insubstantial forest impeded my vision. I stood in the swaying grass, sunlight sparkling through the tears I refused to shed. I saw clearly, I saw reality. Yet hadn't my vision been reality too? Reality of a profounder nature than the material world? I hesitated over the question. Often my visions revealed future reality, however veiled in symbolism. And today Corrie had betrayed her belief in my visions. Today Corrie, who had always insisted I saw nothing, had tried to force me to tell her what I saw.

Corrie, the huntress.

Yet at other times I saw futures that never materialized, futures that might well have been, yet (perhaps) were forestalled by the very fact that I foresaw them. Could I render any given future improbable merely by glimpsing it? Could I change the course of events merely by calling up a vision? If so, why was the effect so inconsistent?

Caught in a web of paradox, I staggered across the lawn and around the cottage. Refugees were clustered in the lane. I hardly saw them. They were present reality, a segment of now. The future had not touched them yet.

And yet they were of the future too, I realized reluctantly. For as I stared at their emaciated legs, the knobby knees larger in circumference than the wasted thighs or calves, I saw not human limbs but the trunks of a new species of tree. It was a species that proliferated so rapidly that we could walk into a sparse stand and, when we turned, find it grown into an impenetrable forest behind us. Dazed, I scrubbed a hand across my eyes, trying to wipe away the disturbing new vision of sallow tree trunks, knobbed, varicosed, bristling with hair.

Although Nira's voice seemed to come from deep within the new forest, her hand was on my shoulder. "Nadd, it's time to come put your things away."

"The trees," I gasped. "Nira, the trees." Why couldn't I communicate what I saw?

Her voice bent near, bringing warmth with it. "Nadd, are you having one of your bad spells again? Here, let me carry you. You're not too big, although you will be by your next birthday. Here, put your arms around my neck."

I gave myself eagerly to her enclosing warmth. But still the grotesque trees surrounded us, and I knew that this was the moment when I must cross some personal boundary. I drew one final breath of childhood and pulled resolutely from Nira's embrace. "I'm all right," I said. "If you'll just show me where the door is."

"It's right before you, Nadd. Reach. You'll find the knob."

"And my bed and my dresser."

"Nadd, if you don't feel well—"

"I'm just tired. It was a long walk. The sun—I'll put my clothes away later, after I rest."

"Of course, the sun," she said, gratified to find an explanation for my collapse. "You haven't been working in the fields all summer as most of the others have. You're not accustomed to the heat."

Or to the shade, the shade of those grotesque trees with their tattered black and white foliage. With Nira's help I groped down the hall to the bunkroom. Soon I stretched out on a firm new matress and the trees faded, leaving me in a merciful half-light. I forced myself to lie flat on my back with my eyes shut tight, breathing regularly. Soon I slept.

It was afternoon when Nira touched my forehead. "Just a touch of sun, Aldred. He'll be fine for the festival tonight. See, he feels cooler already."

Headfather Schuster's voice rumbled indistinctly and they both slipped away. A short while later I woke, aware of two circumstances: I was hungry and Ronna sat on the edge of my bed, silently caressing me. An aura of serenity surrounded us. "You'll be all right by tonight, Nadd," she murmured, her fingers slipping smoothly across my forehead. "You will be just fine by tonight, Nadd." Her eyes were deep wells of life. I had only to tap them for the very substance of health, of well-being.

But I knew I would never be fine, not so long as either forest grew in my mind, not so long as the huntress stalked the shadowy confines, bow ready. And even if I could successfully resolve the symbolism of this afternoon's vision, could render fully comprehensible the future it foreshadowed, I knew the cold dread that held me would scarcely loosen its talon-grip. Swallowing back the last tears of childhood, I closed my eyes and tried to sleep again.

CORRIE

FALL 0224

By daylight I could remain hidden in the trees, swirling a protective curtain of drizzle around me, but when dusk chilled the meadow, my shadow grew restless. And when the moons rose cold and distant against the starry sky, my shadow slipped from beneath the trees and drew me across the meadow. At once immaterial and compelling, it beckoned me through the tangled grasses, now extruding a phantom arm, now drawing it back, rippling with every breeze. It seemed to have a special affinity for the brightbushes that grew near the lane, their mirror-leaves shattering moonlight into brilliant splinters. My shadow merged eagerly with their bulkier umbrae without surrendering any of its compelling power over me.

On this particular night, Sunwaif Cottage stood deserted, its windows as vacant as my heart. I paused at the gate, staring up at its dark eaves. A tendril of cloud had followed me across the meadow. It swirled into the play yard and as it moved on the light breeze, nighmare shapes stirred across the cottage's dim glass panes. With a harsh breath, I squeezed my eyes shut. What had always given me greedy pleasure chilled me now, even as it compelled me. If I could just return to the grove, to the solitude of the trees, if I could isolate myself from the others entirely . . . But my shadow drew me on past the cottage and down the lane.

Reaching the village, I heard mingled sounds of chanting and hilarity from the northern edge of town. I paused, scanning the dark cottages that lined the lane. From within came only the occasional flicker of a house fire. I hesitated, wanting to return to the picnic grove, but my relentless shadow propelled me down the lane toward the refugees' meadow. As I drew nearer, the chanted undertone took an unexpected vibrance and became as joyous as the laughter that mingled with it. My features clenched in a deep frown. The drought seared the settlements beyond Drae's Crossroads; yet the heretics' crops spread omnivorously, devouring whole meadows at a bite, and their livestock dug its hooves callously into my Mother's hide.

And tonight the residents of Drae's Crossroads celebrated. As I drew nearer, scattered campfires sparkled against the chill night air. Skeletal figures, flapping grotesqueries who cast shadows three meters long, were outlined against the flames. The solid figures of the original heretics mingled freely with them.

I crouched in the shadows that lined the lane, detecting a disturbing note to the chant that rose from the center of the meadow. Drawn, I crept around the perimeter of the encampment, trying to distinguish the words of the litany. The breeze frustrated me, one moment whisking entire phrases to me, the next sweeping the chanting voices away. I peered warily into the tent settlement, then slipped through the deep grass to conceal myself in the shadow of a nearby tent. Moving silently, watchfully, I gradually picked my way from the outer perimeter of the meadow toward the communal campfire. Massed forms surrounded the bonfire, standing on their knees in the trampled web-grass, heads bowed. A discarded shawl lay nearby. I wrapped it around me, hiding everything but my eyes. Then I nudged my way forward until the heat of the bonfire stung my eyes and made my nostrils burn.

I gazed around surreptitiously until I isolated five forms in white clustered on a mat of freshly cut sheaves. Herrol glowered at me without recognition, his gleaming chest hair combed out over his collar in a defiant ruff. Ronna knelt beside him, her dun-colored face blank. As the chant rose around them, all five stared blindly into the fire, swaying as if moved by an unseen force.

"Clothe us in robes of web-grass and palm leaves, Secret Power," the litany went, *"and lead us through fields tall with grain. Bring the slugworms to our feet, deck our shoulders with sweet crybirds and brighten the air with the pastel grace of palemoths. Secret Power, guide our feet to the deepest and sweetest spring of this nourishing Destiny and let not our dipping hands be offensive to the waters. Teach us to adapt, teach us to worship, teach us to please the very soil upon which we stand. For we come not to inflict our will upon the existing biosphere but to live within the guiding rules. We come not to harm but to enhance. We come . . ."*

I shuddered, fighting enchantment. Normally a litany to the Secret Power moved with heavy stolidity, phrase upon sonorous phrase, masculine voices overriding feminine with uncompromising authority. But Headfather Schuster's disturbing new heresy echoed the sensuous ripple of the morning breeze, the graceful wheeling motion of the palemoths as they drifted through the summer heat, the cool murmur of the stream which gushed from my Mother's secret life-spring. Deliberately or not, Headfather Schuster had created a litany that seemed to rise not from human throats but from the grass of the meadows, from the rustling trees, from the soil itself.

Disturbed, I peered at the others. As they swayed mindlessly on the mat of sheaves, the bonfire etched their faces with an eerie radiance. A fist of tension clenched in my chest. I drew an unsteady breath, hardening myself to retreat from the circle, to escape the mesmeric spell. But the chant wound around me in silken ribbons, binding me to the grass where I knelt, binding me to the soil, binding me to Drae's Crossroads, binding me . . .

"We come not to exploit this welcoming world, with its graceful trees and glowing skies; we come not to plunder its rich soil; we come not to misuse, to abuse, to carelessly destroy in order that we alone may prosper. Instead we come to join ourselves to the very pattern of life here on this Destiny-world. We come to make more whole that which has already been created, to enhance the scene already so strikingly drawn, to fulfull. We come to offer our higher intelligence as a fitting culmination to this benign creation. We come . . ."

You come to suck my Mother's breast dry, I grated silently, fighting the silken spell. You come to tear her soil with metal blades, to rip back her cloaking grasses and destroy her whispering trees. You come to drive your cattle through grass never intended to be trampled, to build your homes of trees never meant to be felled, to wash yourselves in water never intended to be dirtied. You come—

But my private litany trailed away as a disturbing question wrenched me. Were these chanted words, these lying words, intended for the Secret Power at all? Or were they instead cleverly tailored to flatter my parents, to coax them into supporting the very intruders who plotted their destruction?

And did the words even lie? Stricken, I peered around the circle at rapt faces, intent faces, *shining faces*. Chill crept deep into my body, turning vital organs icy-brittle. If Headfather Schuster had directed his litany to the Destiny powers, however covertly, and if the heretics who chanted his words were sincere in their worship, if in the silent places of their souls they knew it was Destiny they worshipped and not the Secret Power, and if Destiny too knew . . .

My gaze flickered around the circle, cataloguing faces that had been gaunt with hunger and were now fleshing out ruddily, bodies that had been spindly and frail and were now hearty, elders who should have gone to the merging months ago, yet who chanted with their descendants. Was Destiny softening toward the settlers? Was Headfather Schuster deliberately—and successfully—undermining the aloofness of the native powers with his seductive chants and litanies?

Would Destiny ultimately adopt the intruders—and permit herself to be destroyed to feed them?

Alarmed, I tried to break free of the circle. I willed my knees to straighten, my legs to extend, but I remained kneeling in the grass, the chant winding gently around me, holding me captive. Gritting my teeth, I managed to bend far enough to put my palms flat on the ground but I could not push myself to my feet.

Caught, I crouched there with flame dancing against my eyelids. Around me heretic voices rose and fell in odylic chant, echoing the life breath of the soil, the rustle of the trees. Captive, I knelt there forever, knelt with my knees bruising the soil, my eyes blind with fire. Heretic voices murmured on, murmured like the breeze, murmured like the stream, murmured like the trees whispering secrets to Mother Destiny. And soon idyllic visions began to unfold around me. Angelic children swept across a sunlit meadow, flocks of crybirds billowing around them. Palemoths spiraled in their wake and slugworms appeared from the densely tufted grass, their elegantly patterned heads bobbing in unison. As the children rippled across the meadow, their voices rose sweetly on the morning air, an angel-chorus.

Behind them adults appeared in flowing pastel robes. Man and woman, woman and man, they ran through the grass, the broad sleeves of their robes belling out to create a mobile rainbow. Then came the elders, a paler rainbow, until the entire meadow was bright with celebrating people. They spread from horizon to horizon, child, adult, elder, their faces radiant. And although they did not throw back their heads, did not open their mouths, a thrilling paean united them, a chorus that rose from their silent throats like the mists rise from the meadow on a cool morning, wafting into the glowing lavender sky to form a lacy cloud.

I gazed up, and within the forming cloud floated five indistinct forms. Entranced, I peered at them and felt tears start down my cheeks. My sun-siblings floated freely within the lacy cloud, their faces indescribably beautiful, their heads crowned with vapor-diamonds. Feliss had discarded human garments for brilliant plumage. Hundreds of golden feathers lay sleekly against her flesh and her throat was soft with down. Her hair had turned to darker feathers which swept into a crest as the crown of her head. Near her drifted Herrol, his naked body clothed in glossy black hair, upon his head massive ivory horns which gleamed with mystic significance. His dark nails had become tiny separate hooves, five upon each hand, five upon each foot.

I drew a trembling breath, wondering tears wetting my face. My throat quivered as I tried to add my voice to the chorus of worship. Drawn, Trebb swam down through the misty veil and extended a green-fingered hand. His head was crowned with foliage and a cape of living vines swung from his shoulders. He mouthed my name, his living garment rustling, but I could not rise to join him.

Finally he drifted away to join the others, Ronna in her robes of light, Nadd in his ceremonial cowl, Feliss and Herrol. I called after him, an anguished summons. Because while they were united in the air, I was bound to the cold soil, an exile. Headfather Schuster's people worshipped beauty and light, health and plenty, completely disavowing the sensual beauty of darkness, the compelling necessity of death. And now they tried to deny my very existence. Angrily I fought to summon a cloud of my own, dark and turbulent. But instead of boiling above the enchanted meadow, my black cloud burgeoned within me, filling every chamber of my soul. Feliss danced daily among clouds of crybirds. Trebb called crops from the soil and made them dance on the breeze. Ronna and Herrol exercised their gifts at will. But I could create only drizzle, and that only when I crouched beneath the trees. Otherwise I was helpless.

Would I be equally helpless one day to abstain from exercising my matured power? If necessity grew so bleak that my Mother and my Father were forced to slay their god-children, the weapon would be placed in my hand. And that hand—must it slay, no matter how unwilling? No matter how I struggled to renege on my destiny, must I one day fulfill it?

It was already being fulfilled. Hadn't I just attempted to sweep away my sun-siblings' bright cloud and envelop them in my own darkness? And failed because the time was not now?

Or had I failed because Headfather Schuster's wind-blown litany paralyzed not only me, not only my sun-siblings, but my parents as well? A new shaft of alarm pierced me, driving splinters of apprehension deep into my heart. If Headfather Schuster lulled my parents into acquiescing in their own destruction—

Adrenalin spiked in my bloodstream and the dream-meadow darkened and was gone. I knelt again beside the crackling bonfire. With a strangled protest, I wrenched myself up and pushed through the kneeling heretics. Reaching the outer circle, I stared around the encampment. While the hypnotic invocation gripped the chanters, other heretics and refugees consorted casually before smaller campfires. They scarcely glanced at me as I fled the encampment.

I reached the edge of the meadow and plunged into the lane, barely aware of my shadow fluttering behind me. If the heretics flattered my parents into accepting them, into feeding them from their very life's soil—

As I ran the sound of the chant faded behind me and my pounding legs, my running feet soon exhausted the rush of adrenalin. I slowed and stumbled wearily up the path until I reached the new cottage. Moonlight reflected in clear sheets from its polished windows, beckoning me. But my feet did not carry me to the door. Instead they bore me through the deep grass to shelter of the massive trees that grew behind the cottage, trees I had scarcely noticed there before. Now I longed to hide myself in them.

But instead of being comforted by the musty dampness normal to mature bluewillows, I was repelled by an acrid odor. And the soil underfoot... Puzzled, I drew one foot across the ground. Instead of soft leaf mold and crumbled crybird shells, it met solidly packed soil. I squinted around, my eyes becoming accustomed to the darkness, then drew my foot back and peered up indignantly. The under-branches of the trees had been cut back to create a vast leaf-canopied cavern. And thousands of crybirds roosted on a series of lattice-work frames installed high in the trees.

I sucked a deep breath, trying to draw on the faintly spicy mustiness that should linger beneath the trees. Instead, I was overwhelmed by the offensive odor of crybirds nesting in unnatural numbers, sheeting the ground with their excrement. Revulsion rose in my throat.

My scream of indignation was silent, entirely silent, but the birds heard it anyway. Their alarmed voices rose in multitude, and the startled flap of their wings filled the air instantly, deafening me. They boiled from their roosting frames and swept out of the trees, a winged whirlwind. I whipped around, at first startled, then savagely elated by the furor. My second cry was audible, a shriek of elation. Screaming, I harried the panic-stricken birds against the night sky. They swirled into the air, darkening every moon, swooping around the cottage and grounds in noisy confusion. They they coalesced into a single massive flock and swept away toward the Crossroads.

Seeking Feliss. Quickly the birds disappeared, leaving only a few stragglers piping nervously around the chimney. My final cry died in my throat as my entire body deflated. Who would believe, when the rainbow swept across the meadow, that the birds had not come spontaneously to worship Feliss? Who would wonder if the storm were my creation? Who had even noticed that I had not attended the festival?

No one.

No one.

Absolutely no one. Bitterly I peered back into the empty trees, then set across the overgrown lawn to the cottage.

Hours later I heard voices in the hallway and Feliss winged into the bedroom, her eyes gleaming. Her nose wrinkled with distaste when she saw me. She retreated to the hall. "Nira, Corrie is lying on her clean bed in muddy clothes."

Ronna slipped through the door ahead of Nira, her face utterly pale by lantern light. She peered at me without seeing me, her breath rasping through her slack lips. Then Nira frowned at me from the doorway, her skirts gathered in white-knuckled fingers. "So you've decided to join us in our new home, Corrie. And how long have you been lying there muddying up your blankets?"

"For as long as it took to get them this dirty," I retorted, burrowing deeper into my nest of soiled bedding.

Her forehead compressed. "I don't suppose it's any use instructing you to change into clean nightclothes this late." She squelched a protest from Feliss with a weary gesture. "We're all tired, Feliss, and this isn't the time to argue. If the smell bothers you, bring your mattress into our bedroom and sleep there. Corrie will change into fresh clothes in the morning and we'll air the room."

"But this is our first night here. I don't want to sleep on the floor," Feliss protested, facile tears brightening her eyes. "Make Corrie take her mattress into your room instead."

Nira's gaze flicked briefly to me, then returned to Feliss, narrowing. "Feliss, you've argued with Miss all summer, but you will not argue with me. Bring your mattress along if—"

"But Corrie's the one who smells bad, and this is my bedroom too. Corrie—"

"*Feliss*. And don't cry. Unlike certain other members of the household, I can ignore your tears as well as your arguments."

Feliss' cheeks flushed. Her eyes sparkled at me accusingly through unshed tears. She tugged the mattress off her bed with a flounce and dragged it across the floor and through the door. "I'll sleep in Miss' room until Corrie leaves again," she announced.

Nira's lips compressed in irritation, and I hissed after Feliss, "I may stay until spring if I don't have to share my room with someone who smells like bird droppings."

"Corrie!" Nira snapped. "If you intend to stay here with the rest of us, you must—"

"Must what?" I demanded, coiling up out of my bedding. "You can't make me leave, Nira. This is my home too. And you're still responsible for me."

"Well, I don't much like the product of my guardianship,"

she snapped back. "Perhaps I was mistaken in leaving Miss in charge of the cottage this summer while I helped Aldred in the Crossroads. If so, it's an error I intend to rectify by insisting now upon acceptable behavior from you—as well as from the others."

"Well, you can start with Feliss!" I said vindictively. "Because I know why *her* clothes never get dirty when she spends the day tramping through the meadows. I know—"

Feliss reappeared from the hall with an indignant shriek, her hair flying. "You can't say things like that about me! You don't even know where I tramp. You're always out under the trees, wrapped up in a filthy grey cloud. You—"

"No, I'm not, Feliss," I said with barely repressed glee. "Sometimes I slip through the web-grass to the dell and hide behind the brightbushes watching you." I bared my teeth in Nira's direction. "She folds her clothes very carefully, Nira, so they don't even get wrinkled while she's dancing. And I'll tell you a secret. Some of the villagers think Feliss has feathers under her clothes, but she doesn't. All she has is skin, bare skin. She—"

"I *never* take my clothes off when I'm out tramping!" Feliss insisted, tears leaping to her eyes again. "You're just making it up so you won't be the only one in trouble."

"Then you don't mind if Nira asks Herrol whether you undress, do you?" I demanded. "He likes to watch you dance too."

"He—". Color drained from Feliss' face. "He—doesn't. He—"

"Yes, he does," I insisted, staring with fascination at Nira. Her expression combined anger, mortification and fatigue in equal proportions. Her fingers groped at her temple, pressing tenderly, as if to appease some tormenting inner demon. It gratified me to know that I could rouse her so easily. "Herrol likes the sun too, but at least he keeps his trousers on, Feliss."

Feliss spun around, pleading. "Nira, you won't talk to Herrol, will you? You won't ask him if he's watched me. You—"

The hand Nira took from her forehead trembled. "I don't know what I'll do, Feliss. We're all too tired to discuss this tonight. If you've been disrobing in the meadow, when I told Miss you could be trusted to tramp alone—"

"Just to dance. Just to dance with my birds, and then they cover me with their feathers. Just like they did tonight, when they came to the meadow and flocked around me. No one can see anything but feathers. No one—"

"No one but Herrol and me and anyone else who wants to watch," I said. "You never even look around before you undress. You just shuck off your things and—"

"Well, I never thought anyone would sneak up on me!" she squealed through her tears. "I don't sneak up on you when you—when you do whatever *you* do. I don't even want to see. I—"

"You're just a spoiled baby, Feliss," I said in disgust. "All you have to do is cry and everyone comes running to see what's wrong. Well, no one comes when I cry. No one—"

"*Children*!" Nira exlaimed, clasping Feliss by one arm.

Ronna's quiet voice cut through the rising fury of voices. "They're not children anymore, Nira."

I wheeled. Ronna's face was a death's head by lantern light. She gazed at us apathetically, her hair hanging in dusty streamers. Yet there was something in her voice . . .

"So they aren't," Nira agreed with a taut frown. "And I won't permit you to act like children. Feliss, we'll discuss this in the morning. I want you to find a place for your mattress now, lie down and think about what Corrie has told me. Corrie, you are to say nothing more tonight. I don't want to hear another word."

My face darkened angrily. "*See*, Nira. As soon as I say something bad about Feliss, we all have to go to bed. You don't want to hear because she's your little birdie girl. You worry whether it's safe to let Feliss go tramping alone in broad daylight but you hardly say a word when I come back after three days. You—"

"I don't want to talk about it now, Corrie. I'm sorry you feel neglected, but tomorrow is time enough to discuss all this, when we're fresh."

"But you know that tomorrow you'll be busy in the canning kitchen, and tomorrow night you'll be tired again, and the next day—"

"I'll make time for you to air all your grievances before I leave the cottage in the morning," she promised, releasing Feliss.

"Make her air her bedding too!" Feliss snapped and plunged from the room. A moment later she dragged her mattress down the hall toward Miss' room.

Nira frowned at me. "That too," she said firmly before retreating.

I whipped my hair around my shoulders, my indignation still running high. Ronna sat on the edge of her bed, her gaze dull. "You see how it is," I complained. "No one wants me here. They'd all be happy if I never came back. They—"

"If you want me to sit with you, Corrie—" Ronna offered half-heartedly.

"And do what? Make me well when I'm not sick!" I threw myself back on my bed and pulled up my covers in disgust. "Don't you even come near me."

She gazed at me with vacant brown eyes, then sighed and lay down. "Can you reach the lantern?"

"Aren't you going to change into your nightgown?" What was it I had heard in her voice a moment ago? What unexpected strength? And her gaze just now had taken a long measure of me, despite its weary vacancy.

"I'm tired now. I'm so tired . . ." Her voice trailed away.

Yes, she was tired. But everyone who had gathered around the bonfire had been revitalized, I realized bitterly, peering at her lax features as she fell asleep, one bony hand dangling. Everyone but me. I extinguished the lantern and flopped back into bed. For a while I nourished myself with angry thoughts. Eventually the regular flow of my breath anesthetized me and I slept.

I drifted back to wakefulness sometime later, aware of a warm presence. It seemed focused upon my temples and from there flowed through my entire body. Yet it enveloped me too, as if it existed not only within me but all around me, a cocoon of well-being. I lay for moments, my eyes shut, drawing deep, renewing breaths. A strange lightness—a rightness—tingled through my body. I felt as if I could incorporate the entire world into myself simply by drawing one lingering breath, then a second, a third. I felt as if I could possess life and beauty and death, as if—

Death . . .

My eyes flashed open and I peered up into Ronna's face. She sat beside me, moonlight falling across her face. But this was not the dull, exhausted Ronna I had known from earliest childhood. This was a Ronna I had never seen before, her eyes deep and shining, like sunken wells of light, the very planes of her face somehow altered. She looked down at me with a faint smile—a cherishing smile.

And the warmth, the enfolding warmth, the warmth that moved into all the secret places of my body, my soul... My lips pulled back from my teeth as I struggled against the usurping warmth. "I told you—not—to touch—me," I managed to protest, my very tongue resisting the words. "You—"

"It's all right. I'm rested now, Corrie," she responded, her voice a silver whisper. "I was so tired earlier, but then the moon reached through the window and made me strong again. And you're troubled. You've been troubled for so long and I've never had the strength to help you. I've been weak and afraid. But tonight, Corrie..."

She smiled again, and I wrenched at the bonds she had thrown around me, my teeth gritting. "I'm not sick!"

"But you are," she said, bending nearer. Her hair, silvered by moonlight, fell across her subtly altered cheek. "Your spirit is sick. It has been sick since you were conceived. You were troubled long before we were born. And I could never help you. Even now I can't heal you, but I can begin. I can begin making you whole, at peace within yourself."

For a moment my instinctive resistance weakened. Yes, I was torn. I suffered a desolation no one could know. It poisoned my days and turned my nights to terror: dreams of storm and death, followed by solitary tears. And the loneliness, the terrible loneliness—if she could make me strong and whole, make me the instrument I was intended to be—

The instrument of death!

"Trebb!" I cried, suddenly seeing him caught and torn by storm, *my storm*. "Trebb!"

"You've always loved Trebb best," Ronna said, her hair touching my cheek now, burning it. "When we were little, Daya and Miss always put you with Nadd to play. But Trebb was the one you loved."

Yes, Trebb with his dancing green eyes, his restless limbs, his infectious grin and irrepressible chatter. Trebb running through endless meadows, worshipped by every green thing. Trebb, rootless, boundless, growing in the sun. Trebb, who could make my shriveled heart a living organ.

If I let Ronna draw her web of healing warmth around me, if I let her expunge the conflict from me, the weakness, I would become the instrument my parents intended me to be—an instrument not of love but of death. And my deadly bolts would strike first at Trebb.

"No!" I cried, lashing out against her warmth, piercing it with my flailing arms. "No!"

Ronna sprang back from the terrible pain I projected, her eyes darkening in surprise. "Corrie—"

"Don't touch me again!" I shrieked, throwing myself off the bed, rolling away across the floor. Reaching the door, I took my feet again. "Don't ever touch me again! Never!"

The raw agony in my voice slashed through the spell moonlight cast upon her. Before my eyes she turned ugly again and tired, so tired she seemed scarcely able to stand. One hand groped uncertainly toward her bed. Her lips moved, but silently, dryly.

"Never," I repeated, and this time it was a whisper. I stood there for a moment watching her shrivel back into her bed, watching her eyelids drop, watching her bony hand fall lax upon the spread as utter exhaustion claimed her.

Then I ran through the cottage into the night and threw myself under a clump of brightbushes. There I trembled, sobbed and muttered to myself until finally my body surrendered consciousness. Then I slept the blackest sleep I had ever slept, slept it as if it were death.

CORRIE

FALL 0224

Sometime later I was wakened by a half-familiar rustling sound
from the far side of the cottage. I crept from beneath the brightbushes and sat, drawing a hand through my hair. Dense grey
shadow prefigured dawn. I listened intently for several minutes,
then stood and shadowed silently around the cottage. The pre-
dawn air was still and cool, the web-grass laced with dew. The
unaccountable rustling sound seemed to come from the meadow
east of the cottage. I slipped along the front wall.

Reaching the corner of the cottage, I peered around.
Through the dawning gloom I distinguished a fledgling stand
of fingerpalms silhouetted against the grey sky. Slowly, slowly,
as I watched, the slender trunks extended upward, becoming
perceptibly taller within the space of a dozen breaths. As the
trees grew, their stiff leaves extended, fluttering softly against
the still morning air.

I stood paralyzed at the corner of the cottage, my breath
shallow. After a span of minutes, I rubbed my eyes. The fledgling trees continued to creep upward, their trunks slowly ex-
panding in girth. The rustling sound grew more pronounced
as the leaves grew broader and stiffer.

I forced myself to draw a normal breath. I hissed from

between my teeth. *Trebb*. Palm saplings did not plunge up against the sky overnight. They required years to mature, a term only Trebb could abrogate.

And when had Trebb developed the ability to raise a grove in the space of a few hours? A chill touched my spine and tingled along my nervous system. The bluewillow grove behind the cottage had seemed unfamiliar earlier. How long had it been there? I frowned, sorting back through a series of mental images: the cottage two weeks before, windows unglazed, doors not yet hung, and towering behind it a dark crown of bluewillow; the cottage a month before that, no more than a framework, the heavy foliage of the bluewillows visible through its raw members; the cottage foundation at the beginning of summer, with web-grass unbroken in every direction except for an area directly behind the site, cleared for some crop not yet planted.

A crop of bluewillow. No wonder the ground under the trees was hard-packed. The trees had not had time to carpet the soil with fallen leaves. They had not been put into the ground until almost mid-summer.

And now they were a mature grove. I willed my limbs to thaw, to carry me down the gentle slope toward the rapidly growing fingerpalms. A long-legged form was curled in a tangle of blankets near the trees. Drawing nearer, I distinguished the expression on Trebb's sleeping face: blissful, intent. Whatever dream propelled the trees against the dawn, it was engaging.

My lips tightened. I slipped forward, my hand snaking out to snatch Trebb from sleep. But before I touched him, fingers bit into my shoulder. I whirled to meet Headfather Schuster's narrowed eyes.

He wore the same black suit he had worn earlier in the meadow. His lean body was taut, his hands knotted with dark veins, and his eyes held their usual poised alertness. "Let him sleep, Corrie."

"Let him sleep," I mimicked, trying to wrench free of his grasp. "You've filled the bluewillows with crybirds. I suppose these are husking trees for the palemoths."

He nodded, his fingers digging into my shoulder as he maneuvered me from the spot where Trebb slept. "They'll attract hundreds of thousands of palemoths when we have the husking frames in place," he said, gazing directly into my eyes, plying me with his mesmeric voice. "Hundreds of thousands of palemoths will husk here next spring, enough palemoths to paper the sky orange. When you step out of the cottage in the morning—"

"When I step out in the morning, I'll see Feliss dancing on the lawn with her moths and birds," I said abrasively. The unwelcome vision sprang to mind as vividly as if I had permitted him to complete his word-portrait. I regarded it sourly. "People will come from over the countryside to see Feliss and her moths, and if they accidentally catch sight of me, they'll make the sign of the broken cross and cover their noses. Not because I'm dirty but to keep the evil spirits from invading their lungs. Because you've persuaded them they can have all the bright things and none of the dark things. They can have Feliss dancing, they can have crops growing and cattle calving, but they can avoid night and death entirely. When their bodies are exhausted, they'll simply merge with the Secret Power and wear brilliant gowns of sunlight forever. They'll—"

"They'll die like any other flesh," he said flatly, abandoning the hypnotic lilt. My words had quenched the tight-focused alertness from his eyes too. His gaze became as flat and matter-of-fact as his voice. "I've never told them anything else."

"Oh, you haven't. You haven't told them. But you haven't weaned them from the pilgrim truths either. I've been listening. I've been listening to your new litanies, and I've compared them with the pilgrim litanies Nira taught us when we were children. You've led the people away from all the truths that were hard to live with, but the others—the doctrine of merging, of ongoing life—"

"But I believe in those doctrines, Corrie." He gazed intently into my face, then peered into the eastern sky, the first grey light of dawn shining upon the surfaces of his eyes. "I consider the doctrine of merging no more—and no less—than a symbolic expresssion of the return of the body to the soil. And what could be more ongoing than that? To feed new life with the physical remnant of your own?"

"The *return* of the body?" I demanded, giving his words a bitter twist. I shrugged free of his grasp. "Our bodies never came from this soil in the first place. They came from Earth. They don't belong here while they're living and they won't belong here when they're dead."

"Oh?" He lifted one brow, his reddish brown eyes meeting mine evenly. "How can you say your body doesn't belong here when every particle of it originated with the soil of Destiny? This is our land now. We've claimed it in the most fundamental sense—we've built ourselves of it, Corrie, literally created ourselves of it, atom by atom."

"We were never intended to!"

He shrugged, a casual lifting of lean shoulders. "Then why are we here?"

"We—because the First Pilgrims were foolish enough to set out in a ship they didn't even stock adequately. Because they were foolish enough to set out without so much as a clear destination in mind. They simply sealed themselves in and activated the lifters and—"

"And set course for their destiny, for whatever world the Secret Power might guide them to. They were trusting folk in those days. They gave their troubles to the Secret Power and kept their joy for themselves. And you're standing on the world the Secret Power chose for them. How can you consider it anything but destiny that both the fuel and food stocks brought us this far and no farther? If we weren't intended to be here, why did all the variables conspire to bring us here? And why have we survived? Consider our chances, consider—"

"Consider the way you've learned to exploit what you found here," I said, my voice dropping to an acrid whisper.

His gaze shifted briefly to the slowly growing trees. Their broad leaves rustled and flapped, rising in stark silhouette against the slowly brightening sky. A faint smile softened his lean profile. He seemed to enjoy our verbal sparrings. "Tell me this: what is life but the exploitation of resources?"

"But you're exploiting resources humans were never intended to exploit," I accused. "You came to our cottage starving and you recognized what we—what we were. And you deliberately set about annexing us. You were so eager to acquire us, to exploit us, you were even willing to court Nira. You—"

"And she was so eager to exploit me that she was willing to be courted."

That stopped me. I frowned, trying to grasp his point of view. "She—"

"Why do you think she let a ragged stranger, a heretic at that, return to the cottage repeatedly and cart away crocks of milk and sides of beef? Because she wanted human companionship for herself and for you. She wanted it badly enough that she was willing to let some very precious pilgrim truths slip through her fingers without much protest and contract herself in marriage to a heretic."

I expelled a reluctant breath. Why hadn't I seen the situation in that light, Nira as much exploiter as victim? She had always wanted to give us friends, schooling, all the elements of a normal life, long after she recognized that we were far from normal. "Nira—"

A taut smile tugged his facial muscles. "What is any human relationship but a process of mutual exploitation? At least in the beginning. The infant takes milk from the breast to fill its empty stomach, but the mother puts the infant to breast to relieve the pressure of fullness. Only later does the relationship—any relationship—deepen. And if you study the situation in Drae's Crossroads carefully, you'll see that the relationship of sunwaifs and villagers is deepening, is gradually becoming something more than mutual exploitation."

"Mutual?" I demanded, ready for him on that point. "What have you given us?"

A spark of pleasure lit his eye. My insistent questioning did not offend him. In fact he enjoyed the opportunity to match wits. Few in the Crossroads could challenge him as closely as I could. "We've given you personally something to rebel against, Corrie, a standard to reject, people to frighten and shun. Consider the frustration of a pariah who has none of these social advantages. We've given Feliss an admiring audience, a sense of her own uniqueness, a—"

"And she's a spoiled baby. She—"

"While you, of course, are a mature, well-balanced young woman."

I stiffened, suddenly aware of my caked coverall and smeared shirt, of my disheveled hair. "You think you can take all the good things and none of the bad," I spat back. "You think you can have all the life forces—from Trebb, from Herrol, from Ronna—without the death force. But you can't exclude me. You can't exclude me and still take what you want from the others. Because I'll be here waiting for you in the end."

"And you think I'm unaware of that fact?"

"Everyone is unaware of it! Wherever I go, people turn their heads and pretend not to see me. Tonight in the meadow—"

"Tonight you sat in our circle and we pretended you weren't there," he said. "And you feel that denies your power?"

"Nothing can deny my power!" I shot back.

"Exactly," he said, his voice soft now. "Everyone in the Crossroads recognizes the power of darkness and death. We've lived with them all our lives, Corrie. They stand beside us every day. By the very act of shunning you, the villagers admit your power. They admit you represent an inevitable force—one they have no hope of evading. They can only turn their heads when they meet you in the lane and hope you will pass and leave them unmolested.

"But tell me this, Corrie. Why consider yourself entirely a dark force? Who do you think brings the rain to the Crossroads?"

The rain? Startled, I glanced up. Even though there were no clouds, an aura of moistness veiled the dawn. From our first day in the Crossroads, I realized with a start, rain had blessed the settlement. "I—no. I don't bring that. I—" But my protest seemed empty.

"Then who does? Why do we have rain in Drae's Crossroads while the outer communities suffer a continuing drought?"

"You—" The suggestion threatened my entire self-concept. My body stiffened, but at the same time my face seemed damp with remembered tears, my own and my Mother's. In memory I crouched beneath a solitary bluewillow, drawing down moisture with which to veil my solitude. "No!" I said explosively.

"Oh, you don't bring it deliberately, at least not in the Crossroads. You have even less control over your power than Nadd has over his visions. But the rain is yours and the rain is what makes everything else possible. Without rain Trebb couldn't call the crops out of the ground. Without drinking water, Ronna couldn't keep the villagers in health. Without water for the stock—"

"The rain—the rain—" I groped, trying to find grounds to reject his thesis.

"The rain is a positive force? And you're our darkling, our death-child?" He had my attention fully now. He could afford to pace thoughtfully back toward the cottage. I had no choice but to follow. "There are two ways of looking at that argument, Corrie. After all, when the pilgrims arrived, it was rain and storm that delivered the First Warning. Before we harnessed the crybirds and the palemoths, it was rain that brought madness. Even a heavy morning dew meant no one could work in the fields until the day was almost gone. We came here a j/ people, believing that our god could guide us throug calamity untouched. We had only to listen for a voice in the night. But the rain, the spores, the madness—they turned even our god grim. And they transformed us from trusting children to bleak, repressive elders within a single generation. Certainly no one considered rain entirely a positive force until the drought."

"But then—"

"But then, fortunately—coincidentally?—your powers began extending. Two years ago Sunwaif Cottage was a tiny green island in a sea of brown. Now Drae's Crossroads is the island, and its boundaries extend well out into the surrounding countryside. We have moisture enough to grow crops for ourselves and for as many people more. And to provide meat and milk for an equal number. And the boundaries are pushing outward every week, Corrie. Slowly, so slowly I had to lay a line of stakes to convince myself they were moving. But they are, just as surely as my palm grove is growing."

I glanced distractedly at the trees, at the sleeping form beneath them. I had held Trebb responsible for the luxuriance of the web-grass around Sunwaif Cottage, later for the rich crops that grew in village fields. But where Trebb went I went too, I realized, and rain came. Not in torrents, not in floods, but in gentle mists and soft downpourings. And those mists contributed as much to the fields as Trebb did, as much to the cattle as Herrol did, as much to the health of the villagers as Ronna did. Even Feliss' birds and palemoths were dependent upon the rain for the mosses and spores upon which they fed.

The rain. I brought the rain.

But I didn't have to go on bringing the rain. Headfather Schuster leaned against the rough wall of the cottage, his face half-lost in shadow. Nevertheless I was aware of the probing alertness of his gaze. "You can't keep me here," I said, testing him. "You can't make me stay. I can go rain on some other settlement. Or I can live in the wild. I don't need you, not for anything."

"A pariah without a people?" he jibed. Slowly he shook his head. "No, Corrie, you'll stay here. Oh, not within the bounds of the village. You've hardly been in Drae's Crossroads all summer. But you'll stay near enough to keep the rain falling. And your province of power, your sphere of influence is enlarging. It's growing as your body is growing, maturing as your body is maturing. A year from now, even if the drought persists, we'll have twice as much land to work. And the others are maturing too. A year from now Trebb and Herrol won't even have to walk the fields. They can spend all their time in the Crossroads if they choose. Feliss is already calling crybirds from bluewillow groves for kilometers around, many kilometers."

"But none of that means I have to stay here," I insisted. "I'm not spoiled like Feliss. I don't have to have an audience. I don't even have to have meat and clean clothes. I can feed myself and I can weave a mantle of grass. There's nothing to hold me here."

He laughed softly and peered out into the rising trees. The first rosiness of dawn touched the horizon. The fingerpalms reached after it, clutching for it greedily. "Then why haven't you left before now? You've been trying to leave for months— and here you are, muddy, hungry, and sputtering with anger. You'll change your clothes, Nira will make you wash up and you'll eat like a starving calf for a few days. Then you'll run away again. But you'll run no farther than the picnic grove or Taddler's Hill. A few days later you'll be back."

"I—"

But he wouldn't let me interrupt him now. His face had hardened; his eyes had grown intent with some private vision. "You're bound to us, Corrie. While you thought we were shunning you, we were binding you. Any god, any power, however dark, craves worship. And once worshipped, the power must serve its subjects.

"Well, we have worshipped you in the most profound way, by publicly denying you, by struggling in a hundred ways that you are our eyes to you—by admitting in no look upon you. And now so threatening that we can't you are ours. us. Oh, even now she'd like nothing

"And Destiny she's learning the same lesson you must better than power, once recognized and worshipped, serves. changed worshipped Destiny and now she struggles like a crea- in a trap, knowing eventually she must capitulate."

"And serve," I whispered, stricken. Although I wanted to reject his claim, I felt the truth of it.

"And serve," he said.

"But I won't," I said with fresh passion. "I won't stay here. I—"

"Then run," he said. The intent lines of his face softened and he smiled, gazing out over his trees. "Run, Corrie. See where it gets you." Turning, he strolled back to where Trebb slept, leaving me alone with my seething denial.

I would not be bound here, a tool in his hand. I would not capitulate and serve.

My fists clenched. Turning my head sharply, I flayed the scene with my gaze: shadowy cottage, tangling gresses, growing trees. An unexpected spike of pain made me cry out. Then I flung myself away through the grass and down the lane, running like a storm-wind.

I ran through the meadow, through the village, through the fields beyond. I ran through harvest-ready grain, through withering melon vines, through expanses of staked plants, crawling plants, late-blooming plants. I ran away from the rising sun, toward the edge of night.

But I could not gain the darkness. My breath grew short, my side stung and the rising sun drove the last rim of night from the western horizon. And Headfather Schuster was right: the green ring was growing. Lush vegetation extended far beyond the boundaries of the previous year. Sheltering in my musty grove, I had not even noticed.

Finally, exhausted, I reached the perimeter of the green ring. The boundary of our influence was clearly marked. I stood in a field of luxuriant grass and looked out over a sere plain where ~~dead~~ web-roots wove a dry pattern across ground broken by deep crac~~ks~~. Even this early in the day, when the grass where I stood was ~~with~~ dew, the sun burned mercilessly upon the drought area.

I approached the boundary with ~~~~
boasted that I could feed and clothe my~~~~
My rains might follow me across the drought ~~~~idation. I had
me if Headfather Schuster were right. But coul~~d~~ ~~~~m what?
the land before I died of hunger and exposure? ~~~~

But to stay near the Crossroads, to serve Headfather Schu~~ster~~
and his chanting heretics . . .

A single brooding bluewillow stood a quarter mile distant,
~~sti~~ll within the green boundary. Turning, I ran toward it. The
~~ground b~~eneath its heavy branches was soft with leaf mold. I threw
~~myself~~ down against its mossed trunk, clutching my temples.

From somewhere a light breeze appeared and rustled the branches overhead. And soon I knew from the changing quality of the air beneath the tree that a dark cloud had come to swaddle the tree in mist.

I remained beneath the tree through the day, sometimes agonizing, sometimes falling into exhausted sleep. How could the settlers bind me when I had feet to carry me away? And how could they force my Mother and my Father to serve them with no more than chants and litanies?

The sun had already set when I was wrenched from sleep by a dream-glimpse of Trebb caught in a torrential rain, his mouth turned up helplessly in a drowned cry. I sprang up, trying to expunge the terrible image. Quickly I crawled from the leafy cavern. Mist surrounded the tree. It touched my face softly, trying to soothe me. But as I stood there, still reluctant to leave the green ring, I saw Trebb's drowned face again. And I knew I must go, even if I died on the drought plain. My calves tensed and I launched myself through the tangled grass, running toward the drought-burned land where I could evade both Headfather Schuster and the terrible necessity my parents seemed to urge upon me.

I tripped twice in the deep grass and each time scrambled up, wind tossing my hair into my eyes and stinging my bare legs. Only when I reached the boundary and attempted to burst free of the green ring did I realize that I struggled forward against a rising storm. Mist had turned to cloud so dense I could no longer see the meadow. And I ran not beneath my familiar cloud but deep within it, choking with every breath.

I halted, peering up wildly. A sudden gust smashed against my chest, driving me back from the boundary, making me stagger and fall. I fell to the grass on my back. For a moment I was too dazed to move. Then I struggled to regain my breath and my feet.

But I quickly discovered that more than storm held me flat. As I lay stunned, tendrils of web-grass had curled around my arms and legs and woven themselves into my hair. They were wiry, stubborn. I arched my back, I drove my elbows against the soil, but I was caught tight. I couldn't even raise my head. My pulse pounding, I lay back against the ground. But despite my physical helplessness, I refused to surrender. I projected rage against the coiling grasses, against the buffeting wind, flailing out at them fiercely.

As if in retribution, the lightning came, its serpents' tongues flickering down through the cloud, teasing me with terror. They tasted soil all around me, making dew sizzle and grass wither. They were delicate, they were blinding, they were deadly.

And they were not mine! I shrieked at them, I reached for them with my consciousness, I fought to turn them back. But they continued to hiss and sizzle around me, beyond my control. With a tremendous effort of will, I tried to dissipate the cloud they sprang from, to melt it into impotent wisps. Instead it darkened, grew denser and grumbled with thunder.

Let me go! Afterward I never knew if I cried these initial words aloud. *Let me leave, let me run, let me go!*

You will stay, lightning answered and thunder underscored the command.

No! No!

You will stay, daughter. The voice was no softer with the second command.

And serve the humans? I demanded bitterly. I fought the binding grasses hopelessly.

You will stay and serve your Father and your Mother came the thundered reply.

But it was useless. The boundary was scant meters from where I lay, but the elements would not let me cross. Only when I gave up the struggle and lay spent did the grasses release me. I sobbed as lightning-tongues withdrew and thunder grumbled back into silence. Slowly the storm cloud dissipated until no more than a familiar mist hung over me. Weakly, tear-blinded, I took my feet. *Please*, I begged one last time.

Stay. The voice was faint but final.

Yet Destiny was no more pleased with her imperative than I. As I trudged back through the meadow toward the Crossroads, the ground wriggled beneath my feet, the throes of a trapped animal. I could almost imagine its pain, could almost hear its squealed protest.

Yet my Mother and my Father had ordered me back to the Crossroads to serve Their will and I had to go.

DESTINY

NADD

SPRING 0226

"Nadd, Nadd!" Trebb urged, shaking me awake. "Nadd, there's another brush fire south of the Crossroads. Aldred says we can watch it if we don't leave the green ring."

"Mmmm?" I struggled to full consciousness. Trebb had set his lantern on the floor beside my bed. It underlit his thin features, casting flickering shadows into the hollows of his eyes. Yet his pupils, as he bent over me, remained dark and fixed, midnight-green orifices from which some other entity entirely seemed to study me. I wiped a sleepy hand across my own eyes. "A—brush fire?"

"Yes, it's burning up from the direction of Wursterville and Cannebury. Hurry and get your clothes on. Aldred will change his mind if it gets much closer to the green ring before we leave."

"I—" I sat and tried to react clearheadedly to his urgency. His thin hands moved without volition, describing impatient arcs in the air, but the uncannily blank pupils regarded me fixedly. "We? Is everyone else going?"

Puppet-stringed by his growing impatience, he bobbed up and dodged across the room to toss my clothes to me. "No, Herrol has to stay in the calving barn. He's expecting his breeders to let down forty or fifty calves tonight. And Nira hasn't let Ronna out of bed all week. And you remember what happened last time Feliss watched a brush fire and some of her crybirds caught sparks on their wings."

I shuddered, remembering the birds' burning shrieks and Feliss' hysteria. "I—I don't want to go either, Trebb. The smoke makes me cough. And tomorrow is the final day of school. If we don't pass the orals and Maid Tetner refuses to graduate us—"

He laughed sharply. "You know she doesn't want us around another year. You and Feliss are the only ones who could even fit into the desks."

He peered around the room, one arm flexing rhythmically, the fingers snapping. "Where did you put your boots?"

"I—"

But he had already located them at the foot of the bed. He plunged his hands into them, extracted my socks and tossed them at me. "Hurry up, Nadd. Aldred won't let me go alone."

With a hopeless sigh, I pulled on my shirt and coveralls. Trebb jittered across the room to peer out the window. We had celebrated first our thirteenth birthday in the new cottage and last winter our fourteenth, and Trebb had fleshed out a little with maturity. But the energy that drove his long limbs was as relentless as ever. He turned from the window, his mobile features reflecting a quick succession of inner states: excitement, anticipation, impatience, and something else I couldn't identify, something that lived deep behind his distended pupils. As I pulled on my socks and boots, he snatched up the lantern and launched himself into the hall. The cadence of his boots was urgent on the smooth-scrubbed floor.

Neither Nira nor Headfather Schuster emerged as we passed the master bedroom. The girls' bedroom was dark and silent. Outside the chill spring air carried the scent of smoke and the southernmost moon wore a lacy grey veil. It peered out plaintively, its silver face unsmiling. The fire rimmed a narrow arc of the southern horizon. I paused at the edge of the lawn, night touching my cheek with cool fingers. Despite distance, the fire flickered with angry scarlet clarity. Trebb had already plunged down the lane and grass whipped around my boot tops, urging me after him. Even the stiff foliage of the palemoth grove rustled with nervous anticipation.

"Nadd, hurry!"

I cast a reluctant glance back at the cottage, then plunged down the lane. Brightbushes chattered in agitation, tossing splinters of light after me.

In the year and a half since we had moved into the new cottage, Drae's Crossroads had added three distinct growth rings, sod-roofed cottages built of materials scavenged from Wursterville, Cannebury and other abandoned settlements. As we ran through the sleeping settlement, the cottages were brightly swaddled in moonlight, silent testimony to the compelling power of hunger and thirst over pilgrim faith. Polished windows mirrored distorted images of the three risen moons, and an occasional house fire launched a thin streamer of smoke against the sky. By the time we reached Herrol's breeding compound at the southern edge of the Crossroads I was gulping for breath. Trebb straddled the fence that bounded the empty day-pen, gazing down at me with frank lack of compassion. "You need more exercise, Nadd."

From the big barn, a bovine bellow underscored his verdict. "I—my legs aren't as long as yours," I pleaded, throwing myself against the fence. The odor of the cattle yard discouraged me from gulping for breath. "Why don't you run ahead, Trebb. I'll catch up later."

Trebb glanced impatiently to the south, where smoke veiled the horizon. His hands twitched in staccato rhythm. His gaze returned to me, the pupils green and distended, assessing me unwinkingly. "You're not that tired. Come on. I'll run circles so you can keep up."

"Trebb—" But he had already jumped down and was plunging through the breeding pen. He ran in broad arcs, covering twice as much ground as necessary. As he hurdled the far fence and swung into the meadow, a ferocity of energy seized him, lashing his limbs in spastic furor. He flung his arms up, yelping, and swaths of web-grass were ripped from the soil and whipped through the air. They floated back to the ground as he passed, their wiry roots writhing blindly for purchase. A wriggling tendril of web-grass caught my trouser leg and clung, its writhing roots bunching the fabric. Shuddering, I slapped it away and stumbled after Trebb.

We plunged alternately through the meadows and cultivated fields until we swung across the final green headland. The fire was still kilometers away, but the smell of smoke was distinct and over the harsh intake of my breath, I imagined I heard the fire's angry crackle. "Trebb, we can't go any nearer," I pleaded.

He swung around, completing a wide, running arc at my side. His limbs continued to flex, inciting the web-grass to riot. "The fire line isn't as near as it looks. We can run another twenty minutes and still be this side of it."

I stared at him in dismay. "But you told Headfather Schuster we'd stay inside the green ring. You—"

He laughed, a sound at variance with the flat vacancy of his fixed pupils. "Aldred's asleep. Come on!" He plunged ahead again, limbs thrashing.

The grass swept at my boots, urging me after him. "Trebb, if we get too near the fire and the wind picks up—"

He turned back in disgust, his pupils narrowing in a gaze that probed me to the core. "You don't see anything like that happening, Nadd," he concluded. "And it's no use saying you do. I can tell you don't."

"I—"

"You *don't* see us getting caught by the fire, do you?" he pressed, his gaze concentrated.

"I don't see anything now," I admitted. "But I don't always see everything. Sometimes I—and if you promised Headfather Schuster—"

"I've promised Aldred lots of things," Trebb reminded me airily, his pupils distending again. "Come on. We won't even get singed. And we might see pilgrim flashes. Remember last time? Remember—"

A knot of nausea closed on my stomach. "Trebb, that's just a story, something the refugees tell to—to—"

His sandy brows drew together, rendering his expression briefly intense. "No, it isn't, Nadd. I've heard about the flashers from people who had just stumbled across the green line. They were too weak to make up stories, and they wouldn't lie to Aldred. There's a whole sect of flashers in the outer settlements. When something sets off a meadow fire, they soak their gowns in lantern oil and run out into the flames. They believe—"

"I know what they believe," I whispered, choking back nausea. "I—but it's not true. Even if they exist, those weren't pilgrim flashes we saw. They were just patches of dried brush flaring up. They—"

"Then why do you look sick?" he parried. "Come on, Nadd.

You know what Aldred will say if you let me leave the green ring alone." With a summoning toss of his head, he darted away through the grass, his lanky limbs silhouetted against the moonlit sky.

I peered back toward the settlement, agonized, then squeezed my eyes shut in a concentrated effort. My vision was unreliable, sometimes permitting me to tap it at will, other times refusing me even an accidental glimpse of the shape of events. Tonight I could dredge up no snatch of disaster. But that meant nothing. Hugging myself, I peered toward the advancing line of fire. Late the summer before, Headfather Schuster had plowed a safety strip deep in the scorched web-grass that surrounded our green island. Over the intervening months, our boundaries had expanded until the safety strip lay barely half a kilometer beyond the green ring. If I followed Trebb no farther than that—

Trebb called impatiently. With a sigh, I stumbled after him. We crossed the drought boundary and my boots crackled through dead grass and brush. Trebb didn't stop until he reached the safety strip, where he threw himself down on the plowed soil. I tossed myself down beside him, breathing hard. "Trebb—"

His head turned slowly. Uncannily, when he met my startled gaze he still held flame upon the surfaces of his eyes. It flared intensely red, limned in orange and green. He peered at me through the brilliant blaze, unblinkling, as if the flames held him entranced. "You know what she's trying to do, don't you, Nadd?" His voice was husky.

I gazed into his blazing pupils, totally disconcerted. "She—"

Deliberately, without lowering his unwinking gaze, he hefted a clod of soil and held it out to me. When I stared at it uncomprehendingly, he tossed it away. "She: this planet. She's alive, you know. She's aware. She has feelings and thoughts and dreams, just like any living being. She sleeps and she wakes, she uses energy and secretes waste. She—"

I tongued dry lips. "I—I don't understand, Trebb. I—"

"Corrie calls her Mother Destiny," he informed me in the same husky, dispassionate voice. "But she doesn't want to be our mother. She's never wanted to be our mother. She's been trying to shake us off her back ever since we came here. First she tried to drown us, then she tried to kill us with lightning. Later she tried to drive us all mad. She poisoned our cattle with web-grass and she gave us pnurrhea and skinspot. And none of it worked. We're still here, still clinging to her back. So now she's using the drought against us." A bare smile touched his lips, but it failed to soften his oddly vacant features or neutralize the scarlet holocaust that possessed his eyes. "The drought and the grass fires."

I shivered, unable to draw my gaze from his burning eyes. "Corrie—told you that?"

"No, I figured it out myself, from the way my roots feel, from the way her soil fights to keep them out. Didn't you notice what happened when we ran through the fields? I uprooted web-grass and the tendrils reached right back down into the soil, and it accepted them. But when I pulled up wheat and rye, their roots couldn't penetrate the soil again. They hardly even tried. She doesn't want the wheat and rye and they know it. They know it as well as I know it."

"I—I didn't notice, not about the wheat and rye," I admitted weakly, remembering the wiry strand of web-grass that had clutched my pants leg.

"Well, my roots are the same. She doesn't want to accept them. It's always been like that, from the time I was a child, but I didn't understand it then. I didn't understand why I had to keep running—running all the time. It's because she closes the soil against me. All my life I've been like a vine trying to survive on a brick wall. I can squeeze a few capillaries through the cracks between the bricks, but there's never enough soil to keep me alive. Not unless I keep reaching, not unless I keep sending out streamers and roots. I can't survive in one spot because she won't let me. She won't let me put my roots deep enough."

"You—" I wanted to argue, to rebut his analysis, but his claim had the impact of truth. From early childhood he had raced in every direction, limbs waving, like a creeper desperately seeking a place to anchor. Shivering, I hugged my drawn up knees. "But you—you've put down roots," I argued. "All the fields, all the meadows—"

He laughed, a derisive sound. "A few square kilometers."

"Enough to support everyone in Drae's Crossroads. Enough—"

"I don't care how many people the fields support if I can't sink my own roots."

"The trees then. You—"

"They're *her* trees, Nadd. That's the only reason I'm able to drive their roots down. But my roots, *my* roots—" A flurry of agitation gripped his thin features, quenching the flames that threatened to consume his eyes. Abruptly his pupils narrowed to dark points and he jumped up, his limbs moving restlessly. "She knows what we did to Earth, Nadd. She realized as soon as she felt us crawling around on her back that we had come to destroy her. And so she fights us. But she's harming herself too. If the drought goes on, she's going to kill all her own vegetation, and our crops and meadows will be the only things left. She—"

"She—dirt doesn't feel," I pleaded feebly. "You're anthropomorphizing. You know what happened to Earth and you're afraid you'll help it happen here by stimulating enough crops to support everyone who comes to Drae's Crossroads. But there are just a few thousand people on Destiny now. What happened on Earth took centuries—and billions of people, careless people, people who hardly realized what could happen. We—"

He caught his head, his arms dancing loosely, like streamers of vine caught in a gale. He swung his gaze toward the advancing grass fire. The surfaces of his eyes remained dark, refusing to record the crackling flames. Only when he turned to me again did a phantom blaze briefly appear, flickering palely before it was quenched by some inner darkness. "I can contain the fire if I want to."

I took my feet, alarmed. "Trebb, we'd better go back. If we ruin our clothes—"

"They're only field clothes." His legs joined the loose-jointed dance. He peered at me intently, trying to impress me with his own emotion. "Nadd, whether she likes it or not, she's our mother. And we're her sons, her true sons. If I let her burn off her own meadows when I can stop the fire, if I let her destroy herself—" His voice trailed away, but he continued to stare at me. Finally his voice dropped a key. "Nadd, didn't you ever want to meet your mother, to do things for her, to make her proud, to make her comfortable?"

The probing force of his gaze touched off a sympathetic pain in my chest, a wordless longing that had lain semi-dormant from earliest childhood. How many times had I tried to imagine my mother's face, her hair gleaming by lantern light? How many times had I struggled to touch her still features with a smile? If I could believe that this soil was my mother, that it had cradled and fed me, that it knew me, knew my dreams and my nightmares . . . My lips were stiff as I rejected the notion. "We have Nira."

"Nira isn't our mother."

"Then our biological mothers. They didn't give us up voluntarily. The Council of Elders ruled that none of the families could keep their children that year. Otherwise we—we would both have had mother."

"Human mothers," he corrected. "But we're not just human. We're—we're a part of Destiny too. We—" He thrashed his loose-jointed fingers against the air, struggling to formulate his argument. "She was pleased when the Elders took us from our families. She hoped the Elders would lock us up and we could never learn—learn to do the things we do. She hoped we would die. Because she knew we would harm her if we lived to grow up. But if we can show her that we don't want to harm her, if we can make her understand that we don't want to kill her like we killed Earth, that we just need a little space to live, some fresh water and clean air—"

"Trebb—" I protested uselessly.

He was too restless to continue his argument. "You stay here," he instructed. He cast a darting glance back toward the crossroads, then launched himself across the safety strip. Before I could protest again, he was plunging through the drought-scorched meadow.

Tension brought me to the balls of my feet. As he ran toward the scarlet horizon, the plowed soil seemed to heave an impatient sigh, eager to shrug me off. An involuntary cry escaped me. Choking back a second cry, I hurried after Trebb. *Our mother, our mother was burning*, a thin voice in my brain screamed, and the harsh rasp of my breath couldn't drown the irrational cry.

I ran, choking on the smoke-laced air, until the distant crackle of flame became a dull roar. Ahead of me, Trebb ran effortlessly, still describing broad arcs through the dry grass, arms and legs flailing. Swaths of tinder-dry vegetation answered the motion of his limbs, waving brittle seed stalks after him.

We bounded across the meadow endlessly, until my legs were numb and my throat raw. Finally Trebb halted and I staggered against him, gulping for breath. The fire line was a quarter kilometer distant, but a quickening breeze fanned it forward relentlessly. Occasionally a stand of brightbushes or a lone tree ignited, creating a brief flare of brilliance. I rubbed my eyes, refusing to see outflung arms and agonized faces in the flames.

"Don't go any nearer, Nadd," Trebb instructed. The encroaching flames deepened the hollows of his eyes and darkened his pale eyebrows, transforming him from lanky adolescent to elemental force. "You can run along beside me, but don't get between me and the fire."

A brisk breeze blanketed us in smoke, then whisked it away again. I choked, tears coming to my eyes. "You—what are you going to do?"

He didn't answer. Briefly his face seemed to flicker, flame-like, as if he stood at the brink of another dimension. Then he was running again, legging across the dry meadow parallel to the advancing wall of flame. As he ran, he threw his head back and pumped his arms violently. Incredibly the dead vegetation through which he ran responded. Reluctantly at first, then with brittle eagerness, dry tendrils of web-grass tore loose from the soil and arced through the air. Soon entire swaths of grass were ripped from the ground and curled into huge, golden balls which rolled away toward the fire.

With a hoarse shout I pounded after him. Massive puffs of uprooted web-grass bobbed and bounced away from the barren strip he was creating, bounding upwind toward the wall of flame. I peered back along the lengthening strip incredulously. If he could create a second safety strip kilometers short of the strip Headfather Schuster had plowed, *if he could halt the fire and save our burning mother* . . .

My foot caught and I stumbled, tearing my cheek on the brittle reflector leaves of a drought-parched brightbush. *Our mother?* A hysterical titter forced passage up my throat and ended in a rasping laugh as I struggled to a sitting position. My mother was no hostile ball of soil, no grass-cloaked geological entity. My mother was flesh and blood and human tears. My mother was a warm body, longing arms, and gleaming hair. My mother—

The soil stirred beneath me resentfully. I leaped up with a gasping sob, briefly mobilized by the displeasure she communicated. *How could I denounce the only mother whose arms were always open to me, who had fed and cherished me from infancy? How could I deny her when she had created every atom of my body from her own life substance?*

I jammed a clenched fist against my teeth. *Madness*. With a sobbing breath, I peered after Trebb. He ran with undiminished energy, his arms pumping rhythmically, violently, tearing the dead grass from the soil. A dark band of bare ground broadened behind him, bisecting the golden-brown meadow. I fought back a momentary urge to retreat to the green ring. My muscles protesting, my breath coming with increasing difficulty, I hurled myself after Trebb.

He ran until he reached the eastern extremity of the fire line, then arced around the fire line, creating a quarter circle of bared ground which prevented the flames from moving either eastward or northward toward the Crossroads. Then he wheeled and ran back toward me, widening the bare strip as he came. His thin face was silhouetted against the wall of flame, caught in a strange exaltation. When he passed me, I turned and loped unsteadily after him toward the western extremity of the fire line.

But if he were right, if in our Mother's earthen heart she wanted us dead, and if I let Trebb quench the grass fire, let him subvert our Mother's efforts to destroy the intruders, if I let him compromise her attempt to save herself from the parasitic human colonists . . .

As if I had summoned it to us, a tongue of flame raced to the edge of the newly created safety strip and leapt at it with a snarling crackle. I stopped in my tracks and watched, unbelieving, as the fiery tongue sent a gout of flame blazing across Trebb's safety strip and into the dried grass barely twenty meters from where I stood. "Trebb!" I cried, as a second blazing tongue snarled at the barrier and conquered it. Flame scurried through the grass helter-skelter, as if seeking prey.

As if seeking us!

"Trebb!" But my voice was lost in a sudden wind. It seemed to spring from nowhere, soil-born. As I turned to run after Trebb, it buffeted me rudely to the ground.

At the same time the wind reached for Trebb, lacing invisible fingers around his pumping arms, binding them to his sides. Roughly it spun him to face me, then whipped him back toward where I lay. His face was ashen, distorted with shock.

As I watched his helpless approach, a third tongue of fire leapt the safety strip. Not five meters from my feet a parched brightbush flared alight. Its brittle leaves chattered as flame took them. For a few moments the uppermost leaves scattered tiny shards of light across the dry ground. Then flame engulfed the entire bush.

Trebb's face was twisted with the same terrible fear that brought an inchoate cry to my lips. He struggled futilely against the invisible turbulence that propelled him through the dry grass. As he fought, as I cried out, the three strands of flame that had jumped the barrier seemed to sense our location. Abandoning their random course, they raced in our direction. Even the turbulence that swirled around us did not divert them as they blazed toward us.

My mouth worked dryly. I struggled, trying to regain my feet, and shouted to Trebb, gibberish. His answering cry was lost in the wind.

Run, I tried to say, but he could no more run that I could stand. I could almost feel his straining effort as he fought the wind. His teeth were bared in a soot-streaked face; his pupils blazed with fear. With mammoth effort, I managed to pull myself a scant quarter meter toward him, clutching at clumps of dry grass, dragging myself forward a centimeter at a time. Even the grass had changed, becoming wiry; my grasping fingers neither broke its dry stalks nor pulled its clutching roots from the baked soil.

Seeing my progress, Trebb deliberately let his body fall limp against the wind. His eyes shut, his head bobbing forward, he managed to sink first to his knees, then to his stomach, until he lay sprawled a few meters from me. Immediately he imitated my agonizing crawl through the dead grass, pulling himself forward hand over hand. He bunched his shoulders and pushed himself forward with his toes.

But three angry tongues of flame pursued us, and when I peered across the safety strip, I saw billows of burning material sweeping toward us through the dense smoke. I wiped at my eyes, clearing them a little, and saw that the great golden balls of uprooted web-grass which Trebb had swept toward the fire line were tumbling back toward us now, burning. I shouted warning, the words garbled.

Trebb raised his head and peered blankly at the fresh on-slaught. Weakly he rolled to his stomach and tried to pump his arms in the motion that had torn web-grass from the soil only minutes before. If he could create a barren area around us, a haven against fire...

But the grass resisted his effort. It clung stubbornly to the hard soil. And the grassy billows swept forward, somehow unconsumed by the very flames that fed upon them. Choking, I could almost feel the agony of fire upon me, searing me.

With a sobbing cry, I burrowed down against the soil, instinctively trying to hide in the arms of an unseen mother. This time my outcry was silent, focused upon the soil. *No, no, no, nonononono!* And then there were not even words, just the inarticulate babble of a mind lost in the culminating agony of death-fear. My fists clutched, my feet pounded, I tore my cheek on the rough soil as I tried to burrow back into the earthen womb that had given me birth. If I could crawl back to that dark place, if I could render myself unborn, unconceived, if I could retreat into nothingness, unbeingness—

When I first heard the terrible, wrenching moan of pain I thought it was my own. Then I realized that it came not from my raw throat but from the very soil beneath me. And suddenly the dry grass I clutched became silken, turning to hair in my hand. And the rough soil, the parched ground—flesh. I lay upon my Mother's breast, her long hair clutched in my fists, shrieking while she moaned with my pain.

It was her own pain as well. For if she was my Mother, I was her child, her own. I was flesh of her flesh, blood of her blood, and the fire that snapped at my feet now, that crackled at my trousers legs burned her as well. Her entire body heaved, almost throwing me off. But I clung, babbling with my pain, *her* pain.

And at last she relented. As suddenly as tongues of fire had leapt the safety strip, they drew back. Flaming balls of uprooted web-grass halted bare meters from where Trebb and I lay and collapsed into ash. Turbulence died. Freed, Trebb jumped up and threw himself across my blazing legs. He extinguished the flames with his own body.

Then we lay side by side, exhausted, while the brushfire died, growling at us angrily from behind the barricade of cleared soil. I let my torn cheek fall against the soil, hardly feeling the pain of my burned ankles and legs. The soil was silent now, still.

But it had granted us the right to live another day, whatev

the cost. My eyes fluttered shut gratefully. My nostrils stinging with smoke, my face seared, I lapsed into a profound sleep, the sleep of an infant at its mother's breast.

NADD

SPRING 0226

It was near dawn when we tramped silently back toward the Crossroads, our faces smeared with soot, our clothes torn and stained. Just before we reached the green headland, Trebb turned and stared back at the blackened horizon. A wispy finger of smoke curled across the face of the lowermost moon. Trebb sighed. "Maybe she understands now," he muttered.

Understood that we did not want to destroy her, that we could not idly permit her to destroy herself? Then why had I pleaded for my life? Why had I wrested it from her reluctant breast? I gazed into the east, where impending sunrise made a cathedral of the sky. For a moment I felt an intense longing to be enfolded again in earthen arms, to be protected and comforted, a beloved child. I experienced a concomitant need to protect the great warm soil-entity who had borne and nourished me, who tonight had spared me. Tears pricked my eyes and threatened to escape down my smeared cheeks.

But my cheeks were flesh, as were my hands, my arms, my feet and legs. My entire body was flesh, blood, sinew and bone. How could the soil be more than inert matter, a globe of rock winding mindlessly around an orb of fire. *This soil my mother?* Could it be true? Or had I been too shaken by hysteria tonight to distinguish reality? Had we simply been victims of a vagrant wind, which had shifted at the critical moment? I peered back, trying to isolate the madness that possessed Trebb and stalked me. But we were alone in the drought-scarred meadow, alone with the sunrise.

When we reached the breeding pen, urine-scented steam rose from the trampled soil. We slipped silently into the tank room of the barn. Bending over the wooden tub, I rolled up my charred trousers legs and splashed my blistered calves to a rising accompaniment of bovine trumpetings. I had just bent to slip off my boots when Herrol thumped into the tank room, bare to the waist, his glossy pelt damp. He glowered, his shallow forehead compressed with displeasure. If I was still a child, if Trebb was a weedy adolescent, Herrol was a young-father, his muscles hard with maturity, his face heavy-jowled and set. And judging from his lowering expression, we were not welcome in the breeding barn this morning.

Trebb's hands swung in nervous arcs, sending drops of water flying. "How many calves did you deliver last night, Herrol?" he asked, an attempt to distract Herrol from his obvious displeasure.

"Forty-two," Herrol muttered, his dark nails drawing up into hairy fists. "I just provisioned the stock," he went on in an accusing voice. "They should be quiet now. Instead they're restless. They don't want you here."

"They—I guess they don't," I agreed lamely. Since we had stepped into the tank room, the volume of protest had risen steadily until the timbers of the barn throbbed with it. But we couldn't go back to the cottage in our ruined clothes. I raised my voice to a nervous treble, drying my face on a coarse brown towel I had found on a hook. "Are you going to the cottage for breakfast?"

Herrol glowered at the misappropriated towel. "I have to eat, don't I?" It was more bullish mutter than human response.

"You—of course you do. And Trebb and I have to go to school for graduation exams, but we've ruined our clothes. If you'll bring us fresh ones from the cottage without telling Nira, we can—we can leave the barn."

"You can leave the barn without clean clothes."

"But we'll be in trouble if we go back to the cottage like this," I pleaded over the cattles' bellowing protest. I gestured to my ruined trousers and blistered ankles and calves. "Headfather Schuster told Trebb not to go beyond the green ring, but we did. We almost got caught in a brush fire. Nira will cancel the picnic tomorrow if she finds out. But it we can bury these clothes before we go to school, she'll probably never guess."

He lowered his head and thrust it forward between his powerful shoulders, a bullish stance. "Feliss is supposed to dance at the picnic," he rumbled. "If Nira cancels the picnic—"

Trebb and I exchanged a guarded glance. "Nira—Nira said Feliss could dance if we made sure no one from the village followed us," I agreed. "And if we don't mention it to anyone, not even Angelicus."

"She's supposed to dance wearing feathers," he pressed, fixing me with a belligerent gaze. "If she's going to wear coveralls, I don't care if Nira cancels the picnic."

"If she was going to wear coveralls, the whole village could follow us," I pointed out.

The dark hair that peaked between his eyebrows rippled as his shallow brow furrowed. Without change of expression he snatched the damp towel from me and scrubbed it across his arms, shoulders and chest. He first ruffled his matted belt, then smoothed it with uncharacteristic delicacy. To my surprise, he ran a caressing hand over his hair, then slicked down the dark bristles that grew down the backs of his hands to his fingertips. A final touch, he smoothed the hair on his arms into a series of gleaming whorls. "You wait in the harness shed and I'll bring your clothes," he instructed.

Trebb shot me a knowing grin as Herrol stamped away, but I gazed after him in puzzlement.

"He knows he'll see Feliss at breakfast," Trebb explained. "Haven't you noticed how he preens for her? And he's not the only one."

I shuddered. Half the men in the Crossroads brightened when Feliss swept past. She had grown from rebellious child to irresistible nymph in the past year, her eyes alternately sparkling and teasing, her birds always fluttering somewhere near, ready to cloud the air with color. "I've seen how she teases him," I said. Sometimes it drove Herrol to near-fury. Then he muttered and bellowed like one of his bulls, shoulders bunched, eyes glittering. "But it doesn't mean anything—not to her." Nothing that I was ready to deal with today.

"Doesn't it?" Trebb demanded, grinning again, aggravating my sense of unease.

It was aggravated further the next morning when Nira called me into the sitting room while the others finished packing our picnic lunch. She motioned me to a stiff wooden chair, selecting a second for herself. Sitting, she laced her hands in her lap, a gesture that suggested more serenity than her face expressed. "Nadd, as you've guessed, I'm concerned about the picnic."

"I know you didn't want us to go without Miss," I conceded, "even though when we were young you let us run the meadows alone." Fortunately my burns had healed before she had had a chance to notice my awkward gait.

"But then you were young," she pointed out. "You were mischievous and irresponsible, but young. Certain concerns were absent." Her voice trailed and away she sighed lightly. "But within the year now you'll be fifteen, the age of final majority, and you'll take your places in the adult community. You—yourself, Trebb and Herrol—will be designated young-fathers, and the girls will be eligible for maternity." Her fingers slid apart and one hand rested on her abdomen reminiscently. "Fortunately they'll have some choice in the matter. Aldred did well to abolish the maiding hut and all the coercion that accompanied maternity among the pilgrims. But the fact remains that certain mature interests have begun to develop. I'm sure you've noted both physical changes and alterations of attitude in the others over the past years."

Reluctantly I realized why she and Headfather Schuster had argued about the picnic behind closed doors. My cheeks burned. "Nira, I'm—"

"Oh, I realize you're not interested in these things yet, Nadd. It's Herrol and Feliss I'm concerned about. Herrol lives much too close to the mating process. We've all seen how he reacts when Feliss teases him and we've all seen how Feliss delights in doing just that. Physically you're still very much a child, but I rely upon your judgement. I want you to watch them both today. Don't let them go off alone. And if Feliss becomes too provocative, you must speak to her. Warn her—"

"But you've already promised she can dance with feathers. Herrol—"

"I promised," she agreed with a sigh. "Aldred feels there is a pattern which you must elaborate among yourselves and that we must not prevent your doing so. But I can't help being concerned. Although Feliss is obviously not ready for maternity, she seems determined to flutter the senses of every male in the Crossroads. It's up to the rest of us to protect her until she reaches the age of reason, whenever that may be."

"If Miss could follow us at a distance—" I suggested, reluctant to accept responsibility for Feliss.

She shook her head. "Feliss delights in disturbing Miss. If Feliss caught sight of her, she would be twice as unmanageable as otherwise."

"Then Headfather Schuster, if he isn't too busy with the field crews. Or—"

Nira sighed, her fingers clasping again, whitening at the knuckles. "No, Aldred is right. We can't supervise you like children forever. The time has come when we must permit you to begin finding your way as young adults. But even so I will speak to him. I'll see if he can't find time to look in on your picnic at some point."

I was hardly reassured. Burdened, I slumped in my chair. If Herrol and Feliss ran away from the group, what could I do? They would never mind me. And if—I peered up owlishly as Nira laughed.

"Not so solemn, Nadd. I'm not laying the entire responsibility upon you. I've spoken to Feliss and Aldred has talked with Herrol. And I've asked Ronna to be alert too, although she is still terribly frail. I must ask you to see that she doesn't tire herself again today. It's been almost a month since she was well enough to leave the cottage."

I nodded dully, my unwelcome burden doubled instead of halved. The boundaries of the Crossroads had pushed well out into the countryside over the past two years and the population had doubled several times. Trebb's abilities and Herrol's had kept pace with the growing population. Even Feliss' flocks had grown in proportion to the increasing need. But the presence of hundreds of new refugees had strained Ronna's powers to the breaking ooint. New arrivals were pitifully susceptible to disease and had little strength to bring to the healing process. At the end of our first winter in the new cottage, Ronna had been frail. At the end of this, our second winter, she had appeared near death. A month's isolation had restored some flesh to her spindly limbs, but her eyes remained dull and her hair had fallen out in patches. "If she asks to walk—"

"She may walk a few steps. No more. Herrol and Trebb are perfectly capable of shouldering her carry-chair all day. She weighs hardly anything. And she mustn't know yet about the three refugees who died last week. She would only blame herself."

I sighed and hunched in my chair, glumly expecting to be burdened further. Instead Nira stood, smoothing down her skirts, and smiled at me. "None of this must spoil your day, Nadd. Do have a good time and don't eat too much cake."

Dismissed, I retreated from the sitting room. As I sidled down the hall, I heard Feliss and Trebb arguing in the kitchen. I hesitated at our bedroom door. Herrol stood at the mirror painstakingly grooming his glossy pelt. He shot me a forbidding glance. Demoralized, I turned and slipped down the hall and out the front door. At the end of the lane, I threw myself down in the shade of a cluster of bushes and peered anxiously back toward the cottage.

Several minutes later Angelicus skipped out the front door. She paused on the lawn, peering directly up into a shaft of sunlight. The golden halo of her hair lent her a special innocence, a particular vulnerability. A remorseless hand closed around my heart as she raced away to meet a playmate.

A playmate much like herself, a playmate with still-vestigial features and slight body, with gifts no more profound than a special facility for numbers or perhaps a sweet singing voice. Not for Angelicus and her friends the exercise of unaccountable powers, the command of the elements themselves. Normal human children came into the world wielding no weapons beyond the direct power of their muscles and the limited scope of their minds. Injury and disease held them prey, and if they survived most would grow into a limited adult awareness. Even Headfather Schuster, whose special qualities were recognized by everyone in the Crossroads, could not heal a sick infant or glimpse the shape of the future.

But we, the six of us, could bring down wind and rain, could tug crops from an unwilling soil, could feed growing herds on grass which should have been poisonous, could swirl crybirds and palemoths through the spore-ridden morning air, and if we chose could tease the veil from the face of the future. And how did our powers serve us? Corrie was a voluntary exile, Ronna a living skeleton. Feliss teased and flirted almost desperately, as if male homage were her life's blood. Herrol stamped from breeding barn to cottage scowling belligerently. Trebb struggled with delusions of an earthen mother who rejected us. And I---?

I hunched in the shade, trembling because today we would be alone together. Heavily I got up and crossed the lawn to the eastern corner of the cottage. The straight, dark trunks of the fingerpalm grove striped the lavender sky. Hatchling palemoth skimmed the air, their papery wings spread to the morning sun. If I could sit in the dewy grass facing the morning sun and draw anything short of disaster from my seeing mind—

Drawing a steadying breath, I placed myself against the eastern wall of the cottage. Briefly I gazed into an unfocused cloud of color, flecks of pale green, yellow and orange surging against a backdrop of delicate violet. Then my eyelids slipped shut and I monitored the random surges of my own nervous system.

But instead of images and impressions I slowly became aware of the physical sensation that I sat not in the grass but in the palm of a giant hand, a hand which cradled me in fingers of rock and soil. Its pulse throbbed through me, slow, heavy, jarringly powerful. Fragrant breath flowed past me as it was drawn into mammoth lungs. A long sigh escaped me. I relaxed and gradually attuned myself to the steady rhythm of the pulse, my troubled thoughts throbbing alive with each beat, then fading into blissful dormancy between beats. Soon, listening closely, I heard the distant snore of the rock-entity's massive inhalations.

She loved us. Our earth-bound mother cherished us as bits of herself briefly set free to run and dance, cry and sing. We had been forged from her elemental resources by the surging energy of the sun and cast into human form—but not confined by it. We were created of sunstorm and hurricane, moonlight and frost. And thus had we lived, alternately wreaking havoc and glazing our environment with enchantment.

Thus had we lived, and in the context of our years did she love us, deeply, warmly, totally. But surely now she found our continued existence prohibitive. Our every laugh, our every pirouette consumed massive resources. If the humans had disturbed the balance that had existed through long Destiny-ages, we could destroy it entirely. How could the sun continue to channel us the energy we dissipated so prodigally? How could the soil spare us the vitality we drained from her? Hadn't the time come to gracefully accede our lives, to die and permit this ancient earthen entity to continue her slow way without us, stolid, mute, enduring?

Gracefully accede . . . I felt the compelling necessity of my own death as I crouched there, the morning sun on my face. But I also felt perspiration on my face, each cold bead a separate stinging reminder that I was human as well as other, that I wanted to live. I struggled against the stony grip, against the controlling rhythm of the jarring pulse, desperate to present my argument for life. But paralysis held me. My mother's earthen hand would not release me.

Then, as if in answer to my unvoiced plea, a vision appeared. I was gliding through a dense forest of bleak pilgrim trees, tugged forward by an invisible force. The trees' foliage was black and their trunks were barked with decaying human flesh. Intermingled were the even gaunter trunks of the refugee trees, their lower extremities disfigured with pulsing varicosities. The trees crowded together densely, denying each other sunlight. Nauseated, I skimmed through the grim forest. As I neared the heart of the forest I caught at the trees' lower branches, trying to hold myself back. But the flesh-bark sloughed off in my hands and I was drawn on.

The heart of the forest . . . I dreaded it without knowing why. Soon the trees were larger and more widely spaced, their leaves glossy, their trunks sturdy. When I caught at their lower limbs, the flesh-bark scraped my plams instead of peeling way. And soon the forest giants began to take on human form and features. Maid Tetner peered at me disapprovingly as I swept past. Youngfather Breeze bared yellow-barked teeth. Headfather Dressler furrowed his leafy brow at me. Fleetingly Larissa— sweetly mischievous Larissa, swept away in the first storm of our power—smiled at me and was gone. Behind her, peering around her trunk—

But suddenly the forest was behind me. Before me stretched a clearing saturated with sunlight. Web-grass grew in a luxuriant tangle and palemoths colored the air. Upon six separate knolls stood six totally disparate human trees. Trebb's bare roots splayed across the grass, writhing for purchase in the unreceptive soil. Feliss bowed to the breeze, crybirds in her leafy hair. Herrol glowered, trying to force a bellow from a deeply carved mouth. Ronna, Corrie—and then I approached a final tree, smaller than the others. Its bark was pale and smooth, featureless, and its foliage rustled nervously in the breeze.

As I approached the virgin tree, its bark assumed individual features, my own nose, beneath it my mouth, trembling slightly, above it my eyes, distended. At an appropriate distance beneath the forming face, a faint pulsation began. Within the pale trunk my own heart had begun to beat, pounding in time with the pulse that animated the earthen hand which still gripped me.

My heartbeat, swelling the slender trunk, drew me across the final meter that separated us. Then, just as I became embodied in the tree, just as my blood turned to sap and my hair to foliage, I became aware of the arrow. It glided across the clearing stealthily, tipped in silver. Trapped in the woody trunk, I stared at it, trying to bring my stiff upper limbs down to ward it off. But the arrow moved swiftly, moved surely, and my limbs moved not at all. Silently the arrow pierced my newly assumed bark, tore through my pulp and penetrated my heart.

My death cry echoed across the clearing. The lavender sky, the golden sun, my brothers and sisters slowly faded. In the moment before my eyes slid shut I saw them all turn toward me, saw the entire universe turn toward me with eyes of fire, sucking greedily at the spectacle of my death.

Dead, I stood there hunched around the silver-tipped arrow for hours, for days, for centuries, my bark drying and cracking, my limbs withering. Then I woke with a start, suddenly flesh again. The world I stared at with panic-blown eyes was the world I had always known: pastel sky, emerald grass, rustling trees no more sentient than I was dead.

Dead? I savored a trembling breath and treasured the stiffness of my legs as I stood. Then I leaned against the cottage wall and closed my eyes, listening for the pulse of the earthen hand which had cupped me. But there was no rock and soil hand, no sunlit clearing, no woody faces, no arrow. With a sobbing breath, I opened my eyes in time to see my sun-siblings disappear down the lane. Herrol and Trebb carried Ronna's invalid chair between them, and Feliss' moths and crybirds spiraled joyfully after the group. With a half-hysterical laugh I recognized the sounds I had mistaken for my own dying cry. It was the call of Feliss' birds.

"Wait!" My voice was hoarse and my legs stiff, but I ran after them, alive as they were alive, alive on a world that was not a stone and soil entity, not a violated mother, but an inert orb, unfeeling, unresisting, possessing neither whim nor will.

I was alive, but as I ran, as crybirds swooped back to mock

me, I experienced a single disturbing flashback. Unwillingly I relived the moment when the arrow penetrated my heart. The sensation that had accompanied the trauma was not pain, not shock, not outrage—but ecstasy. The silver tip had blundered through my vital tissues wreaking not destruction but exaltation, even a soaring sense of fulfillment.

In death? "Wait!" I called again and stumbled down the lane, too disturbed to walk alone.

CORRIE

SPRING 0226

I had squatted behind the brightbushes at the fork of the road for over an hour when Angelicus and her friend raced past and darted up the hill toward the burying ground. Stiffly I stood and emerged from my hiding place. My mood today was strained, tinged with foreboding, almost as if I were having a taste of Nadd's uncomfortable gift. Yet the early morning sky was lacy with golden cirrus, and dew turned the meadow to a garden of jewels. Stooping, I caught a sheaf of web-grass between my palms and drew my cupped hands up, harvesting a small ration of dew. I licked it off my palms thirstily, weary of waiting for the others, weary of trying to ignore the ominous tingling at the very perimeter of my consciousness. If Feliss had insisted on picnicking in the dell beyond the east meadow instead of in the abandoned play yard at Sunwaif Cottage, if they had left the road and cut through the wheat fields, they would not even pass this way.

I caught a flicker of motion through the line of fingerpalms that bounded the burying ground. Frowning, I crept up the hill in time to see Angelicus and her friend bound away through the brush at the far side of the burying ground. *Only children playing.*

We had once been children too. Playing.

I peered around bleakly. The burying ground was long overgrown with vines and tangled web-grass. Only three fresh mounds near the trees were distinguishable as graves. Until recently it had been months since there had been a fresh grave in the Crossroads. Another time I might have gloated. Today I shuddered and retreated into the bushes.

A few moments later I heard the first distant call of Feliss' crybirds. It rapidly became a shrill din as the flock swept down the road. Feliss was barely visible through the flurry of bright wings. I glimpsed her face, laughing, provocative. She wore a bodice that hugged her budding breasts too snugly and trousers that boldly delineated her developing form. Palemoths floated at the perimeter of her rainbow flock, their weightless serenity contrasting with the noisy sweep of the birds. Nadd trotted after the flock lugging a picnic hamper, his face pinched with anxiety. Herrol and Trebb followed, supporting Ronna's invalid chair between them. Ronna lay lax against its fabric panels, her heavy-lidded eyes dull, her skeletal features lifeless. Even sunlight seemed to lie heavily upon her, stressing her parchment-fragile flesh to the tearing point.

I didn't emerge from the brightbushes until they had passed. Then I trudged down the path after them, keeping my distance. I lay every night with my face pressed to the soil, listening to my Mother groan in her sleep, torn by the dark conflict of her dreams. I woke regularly with tears on my face and the phantom sensation of a bow in my hand, of the cutting pressure of the bowstring and the clenching pain of cramping muscles as I prepared to loose the arrow. Did Ronna's deathlike weakness mean that my Mother was preparing even now to turn me against the others? If she were, would I be as helpless to resist her imperative as Ronna had been to heal the three settlers who lay buried on the hill? Did I have any will in the matter? Frowning, at once reluctant to join the others and powerless to resist, I set off down the road.

Time had diminished Sunwaifs cottage, rendering it little more than a long bleak shed with dusty windows, its chimney fallen, its roof molting weathered shingles. The play yard was choked with web-grass and brush, but the climbing frame was intact. By the time I reached the cottage, Feliss perched upon the top rung of the climbing frame, hidden in a spiraling cone of crybirds. Occasionally a single bird peeled from formation and darted at Nadd, who crouched at the base of the frame. When I approached the gate, Feliss' face appeared, her black eyes sparkling maliciously at me. "I don't care who told you I was going to dance with feathers, Herrol. I'm not. Why don't you ask Corrie to dance instead?"

Herrol stood bare-chested in the overgrown play yard path, his pelt ruffed angrily, his feet planted wide. His dark eyes were belligerent. "Corrie doesn't dance. And if you won't dance like you promised—"

"I didn't promise anything," Feliss jeered, her birds taking up the chorus.

"You did! You told me—"

"She's teasing you, Herrol," Trebb interjected uneasily. Ronna sat on the bunkroom steps, leaning weakly against the door, and Trebb stood guard over her, his hands jiggling nervously at his sides. They all seemed on edge, as if this day represented a pivotal point in our lives and each of us sensed it. "As long as she can make you bellow, she'll never dance. You know how she is. She's a tease."

Herrol's narrow forehead compressed so fiercely his eyebrows disappeared into his hair. "I know," he rumbled. "And if she doesn't dance—"

"I never said I would," Feliss jeered again. At her signal, the spiraling cone of crybirds swept back to form a surging curtain behind her. As sunlight struck her bare arms, it seemed to plume them with color. I frowned uneasily, remembering the golden bird I had seen twice this spring soaring far in the distance, larger than any crybird. Disturbed, I rejected the image that tried to introject itself into my consciousness. Feliss wore close-fitting blue trousers edged with scarlet ruffles. Her yellow bodice molded her small bosom provocatively. Her fine black hair was feathered to frame her gamin face. "I asked Aldred and Nira if I could dance with feathers and they said yes. But I never promised anyone I would, Herrol."

Herrol's voice rumbled from deep in his chest. "You told me—"

"You can't prove it!" Tossing her head, Feliss arched backward, swinging full circle around the smooth rung. She had every eye; she knew it and relished it. As she flipped back into position, she raised a hand and a rank of crybirds peeled away and dove at Herrol.

He swiped at the birds with a bellow of fury. They responded by darting directly at his face, sweeping aside at the last moment. His muscular jowls set with rage. Reaching out, he snatched a pair of birds from the air. "If you won't dance—" He raged over the alarmed scream of the captured birds.

Quickly the entire flock took up the cry, darting back to Feliss with an indignant clamor. A cry as piercing as the birds' sprang from her throat and she handed herself down the frame and threw herself at Herrol. "Let my birds go!"

"Not until you dance!" Now there was as much challenge as fury in his bellow. He thrust out his muscualr chest, dark ruff of hair gleaming.

Feliss flung herself at him, screeching with rage. They disappeared in a cloud of feathers, Feliss' indignant voice, Herrol's enraged one drowned by the fury of the birds. Alarmed, Nadd scrambled up from the grass and threw himself into the melee. As he pawed his way into the feathered cloud, crybirds launched themselves at him, driving their shallow bills into his bare arms and unprotected face. He fell back, shielding his eyes with one forearm, blood oozing from a dozen punctures.

Instinctively Ronna started up from the steps. Tree pushed her back. "I'll take care of him." Quickly he dampened a napkin from the water skin and ran across the yard to where Nadd huddled by the fence.

But Nadd resisted Trebb's ministrations. "Don't let them— don't—"

"They won't hurt each other," Trebb declared, but his face was strained and he glanced back at the surging cloud anxiously. "They're just playing. They—"

"They're not playing, Trebb," Nadd insisted, his narrow face contorted. "Listen to them! It's not—"

"Nadd—"

"Listen!" Nadd cried, pushing aside the damp napkin.

Frustrated, Trebb crumpled the napkin, a frown tightening his mobile lips. I crept into the play yard and the three of us peered into the feathered cloud. As if forced aside by our combined wills, the protective screen of crybirds parted to reveal Feliss and Herrol wrestling in the grass. He had half-torn away her yellow bodice, revealing one small pink breast, and he tugged at her trousers, his nostrils dilated, his eyes glittering. Feliss fought him with shrill laughter, resisting just enough to inflame him.

Nadd clutched Trebb's arm apprehensively. "Trebb, Nira told me—"

But Trebb had already interpreted the situation. He shook

loose from Nadd and launched himself at Herrol, limbs thrashing. "Herrol, if Aldred hears that you—"

Herrol hardly seemed to notice Trebb's attempt at intervention. With a bellow he lashed backward, toppling Trebb. Before Trebb could regain his feet, Herrol seized Feliss' bodice and ripped it completely away. Delighted, Feliss jumped up from the grass with a shrieking laugh. She lunged and fought him for her ruined garment. Snorting, Herrol caught the waistband of her trousers and wrenched.

"Feliss, your birds!" Nadd shrilled. "Your birds can make him stop!"

Feliss laughed, a mocking trill. Then, breaking free from Herrol, she covered her breasts with one hand and with the other signaled to her birds. Her eyes sparkled with malicious delight. For instead of diving at Herrol, the birds spiraled outward and darted at Nadd. He retreated with a frightened cry. "Feliss!"

She laughed as the birds drove him to a corner of the play yard and barricaded him against the weathered fence. When Trebb immediately jumped to his feet and tried to grapple with Herrol again, Feliss swept her hand through the air and a second phalanx of crybirds formed, cutting Trebb off from Herrol. Trebb threw a protective hand over his face and it was immediately pocked with scarlet. Jeering, the birds drove him across the yard and against the fence.

I rose to the balls of my feet, an angry cry in my throat. But when I ran across the yard to Trebb, the birds surged between us, mocking me in a hundred voices. *"Feliss!"* My voice was raw. When had she grown from vexing flirt to willful minx, intent upon inflaming Herrol despite the cost to us all?

As if she had read my question, Feliss crowed with delight. "No one wants to watch you dance, Corrie. You could tear off all your clothes right now and no one would even look. You could run through Drae's Crossroads naked and everyone would turn his head the other way. But they look at me! Everyone looks at me, even when I'm wrapped in my birds. And everyone loves me, no matter what I do. I get everything I want! All I have to do is take it! *Everything!*"

"Then you'd better be careful what you want!" I shrieked in warning.

But she didn't hear me. "So you want me to dance with feathers, Herrol?" she demanded. "But I don't dance the way

I used to, when you spied on me. I've learned a new way to dance with feathers." Slowly, provocatively, she unbuttoned her trousers and let them slide down. With a teasing smile, she stepped free of them, kicked off her shoes, and threw her head back, catching sunlight on her face. Still partially concealed by a lacy curtain of wings, she rose to her toes and began to spin. Faster, faster she spun, first tucking her arms against her body, then letting them rise, borne up by the force of her motion. Within minutes her naked pink body had become a blur. As she spun, the birds that guarded Trebb, Nadd and Herrol gradually withdrew to join the rainbow tapestry that rippled above her.

Trebb smeared blood across one cheek absently, transfixed as Feliss' naked pink body slowly took the color of plumage: scarlet, emerald, violet, gold. Her limbs shimmered, at first luminous with color, as if she had become a light source, then gradually taking first down, then plumage, until she was entirely covered with brilliant golden feathers. "Everything!" she shrieked, with the voice of a crybird. "Everyone looks at me and I get everything I want, Corrie!"

As I watched, every joint frozen, her spread arms became wings, and her breasts swelled into pectorals. She settled to her feet, spinning slowly now, peering at us with the tiny round eyes of a crybird. "*Everything!*" she screeched again, and her lips pursed up into a shallow yellow beak. She waggled her head and her hair became golden plumage which crested at the crown of her head. With a surge of her pectorals, she swept her wings against the morning air. Her hands had disappeared entirely, and her feet had become claws.

The soaring bird I had seen twice in the distance—Feliss!

A trumpeting bellow sounded from across the yard. As we watched Feliss' transformation, Herrol had sunk to all fours. Now, his bull's torso swollen with muscle, he pawed the grass with incongruously delicate hooves. He tossed his head, a second belligerent declaration emerging from his muzzle. As I stared at him, dabbing my cracking lips with a leathery tongue, spiraling horns grew from his skull. They were of purest ivory, gleaming in the morning sun, gleaming as white as his pelted hide gleamed black. He kicked at the grass and wagged his massive head, sweeping his horns against the air. With a final lusty snort, he pounded across the yard toward Feliss.

Woodenly I retreated, expecting Feliss' flying guard to

launch itself at Herrol. But as he charged, I realized that the canopy of crybirds had disappeared, as if Feliss had feathered herself with them. Numbly I looked to Nadd and Trebb. Nadd huddled against the fence, blood streaming from his wounds, his entire body shrunken with fear. And Trebb stood rooted, his feet lost in the soil, his ankles grown with bark. His arms extended stiffly parallel to the ground, the blood that oozed from his wounds clear and sticky now, sap.

Had either of them given any more credence than I had to the village tales of a magnificent bull with spiral horns, seen mingling with the herd only by moonlight?

Certainly this was no creature of myth before us now. It was solid flesh. As Herrol moved with heavy grace toward Feliss, head lowered, massive hindquarters surging, she screamed inarticulately, a sound at once frightened and mocking. With a swift flurry of wings, she rose into the air. She tested her wings briefly against the air, then drew her fragile yellow claws up against her breast and swept from the yard, screaming with exultation.

Herrol's indignant bellow seemed to jar the very earth as he thundered from the yard, following Feliss' teasing flight across the meadow.

"No!" Nadd croaked, half-rising, staring after them with horror-struck eyes. "I promised Nira—"

"You promised you wouldn't let anyone turn into a bird today?" I cawed, my voice ragged with hysteria.

"I promised Nira—" But his words turned to gabble high-pitched nonsense flavored with the white foam that appeared on his lips.

Slowly, woodenly, Trebb lowered his arms and disengaged his feet from the soil. He peered at us with blank green pupils. His voice, when it came, was little more than a rustle. "We can't let them—"

"We can't stop them," I cackled, the bird in his tree.

While we gaped at the scene in the meadow, massive bull and brilliant crybird charging and darting, Ronna stood. Her gaze was white-eyed, fainting, but her deliberate pace, foot before foot, took her as far as the gate before she sagged to the ground. She lay limp for moments, moaning almost inaudibly. Then she placed both palms flat against the ground. Limp-wristed, she pressed her palms against the soil, trying to raise herself. "I know I can draw the strength," she whispered. "I feel it. It's tickling my palms. I know..."

I stared at her, frozen. Her voice was a harsh whisper, little more. Yet I sensed something in it I had heard there before, some bare promise of strength.

Trebb went to her stiffly, the blankness of his eyes terrible. "Don't try to walk, Ronna," he creaked. He slipped one arm around her and raised her slack-jointed from the ground. The effort seared the glaze from his eyes, substituting pain. "Corrie, help me get her back to the steps."

Why did I hesitate, staring at them as they leaned against each other, Trebb wooden-limbed, Ronna so slack she seemed to have no bones? Trebb's pain touched me in the place where I still cherished images of a long-limbed infant, of a running boy, an earnest adolescent. But my muscles were locked. And somehow there was strength in Ronna's voice, even in her fainting eyes, as if she were on the verge of tapping a hitherto undiscovered well of energy.

"I know I can find it," she whispered again and I shuddered. If this were the moment when my Mother intended me to play my destructive strength against the others' weakness, before Ronna found her strength—

At first I didn't recognize the sound that froze the others, turning Nadd to a cowering child, making Trebb bare clenched teeth, driving the last blood from Ronna's ashen cheeks. It ululated across the overgrown play yard, an almost-tangible mourning wail, a thing apart.

Yet it came from my own throat. Recognizing its source, I pressed my hands to my throat, extinguishing the sound. Then, without speaking, I slipped one arm around Ronna and helped Trebb carry her back to the steps. Trebb wet another napkin from the hamper and stroked her face until she opened her eyes and peered emptily at us. After a moment her vacant gaze slipped beyond us to the meadow. Deep beneath the dull surfaces of her eyes, apprehension stirred. Her dry lips moved, forming a single incomprehensible word of warning.

I turned. In the meadow Herrol stamped and snorted, his ivory hooves a dainty contrast to the massive bulk of his bull's body. Feliss darted teasingly at him, sunlight dancing on her gaudy plumage. When he charged, she swooped at him, then darted aside at the last moment, barely avoiding his ivory horns. She winged up against the clear sky, swimming the air currents, her wings spread. Staring up, I could hear her teasing laughter as she swept high overhead, freed from the gravity that bound the rest of us.

But Herrol's bellowed protest quickly drew her back down. With a shrill cry, she dived at him again. He lowered his horns, bunching his massive shoulders, and galloped heavily through the grass, stung by her mocking assault. Screaming with delight, she returned again and again, rasing his dark pelt with the rushing wind of her golden wings, slipping past his horns by bare centimeters.

Apprehension gripped me. I threw myself against the ground, spread-eagled. Herrol's pounding hooves tore at my Mother's hide, sending a series of silent screams through her surface layers. And each time Feliss drew at her pectorals, lashing her wings against the air, my Father's rays weakened perceptibly as they fell across my back.

"No!" When the protest rang through the air, I thought I had uttered it. But it was Nadd who jumped up and staggered down the overgrown path, his face twisted . "No!"

No sooner had his second cry lanced the air than Feliss made her final dive. Overconfident, she swept at the ivory horns and failed to pull away before the surging power of her own wings drove her into them. Instead of gliding up and swiftly away, she impaled herself upon the horns, driving them deep into her feathered abdomen. With a shrill cry, she threw her crested head back and spread her wings in agony.

Herrol halted mid-charge, his eyes rolling up. Before I could move, Trebb raced past me, restored to full mobility. He dashed through the meadow in a welter of agitated web-grass. "Herroll, pull in your horns!"

Wheeling, Herrol shot him an agonized glance. He bellowed, a vain attempt at speech. Blood had begun to run down his ivory horns in scarlet rivulets.

"Take back your shape!" Nadd screamed, hurtling after Trebb. "Your human shape!"

Instinctively Herrol tossed his head, trying to throw Feliss free of his horns. When that failed, he lowered his head and pawed the ground, as if to scrape her free. His eyes were wild. His bellow seemed to shake the very ground.

Trebb reached him and somehow found the strength to wrestle his head erect again. As he struggled, shouting in Herrol's ear, Feliss' spread wings closed in a sudden spasm. Her bright-feathered body shuddered and her plumage began to molt, each separate feather first dropping, floating lightly for a moment, then taking life of its own and fluttering away. Within moments a cloud of crybirds surrounded them, screaming with fright. Reaching the three of them, Nadd beat at the confused birds, driving them back. His voice was as shrill as Feliss', his commands as meaningless.

But the frightened birds yielded to him, drawing back like a curtain to reveal Feliss lying naked in the grass, two gaping wounds in her abdomen. Herrol stood over her, hooves and horns gone, his face human again, transformed by brute fear. Feliss stared at him with the blankness of shock, one grey hand pressed to each bleeding wound.

"Was that everything, Feliss?" I ground out when I reached her. "Was that everything you wanted?"

Her eyes rolled toward me, suddenly lost in weak tears. She tried to turn back my accusation, but shock had numbed her lips. All she could do was whimper, staring at me accusingly. Then she gazed past me, and her eyes widened.

I turned and stared back toward the cottage. Ronna stood erect at the center of the overgrown path, her head thrown back sharply, her arms raised straight overhead. She had cupped her palms, turning them toward the sun like receptors. She tossed her head, making her feathery hair billow on the breeze. She stood poised for minutes, staring straight overhead, her emaciated body swaying.

Then she brought her head slowly erect until she peered directly into the sun. Incredibly her normally dull eyes seemed to cradle their sun itself in the depths, growing, deepening, overflowing with light. When she had peered for minutes directly into the sun, she began widening and narrowing her eyes rhythmically, rocking her head back in a drawing motion each time they widened, then letting her head slip forward sinuously as she narrowed her eyes.

Feliss whimpered, but Ronna continued to rock her head forward and back, forward and back, widening and narrowing her light-struck eyes, until a concentrated beam of energy became visible, linking her to the sun itself. Slowly she let her head drop back, raising her light-flooded gaze until she stared up at her cupped hands. The connecting beam rose, as if directed, and focused upon the palms of her hands. She lidded her eyes and stood for minutes, light-energy making first her hands, then her wrists and arms glow. Finally she moved her hands apart, each describing a half-arc, spreading light with it. When they hung at her sides, still cupped, she stood in a brilliant ring of light.

When she opened her eyes again, the ring became an orb, a blinding manifestation that radiated from Ronna's emaciated body to a radius of meters. Within the orb of light, web-grass crackled and died, and a lone brightbush burst into fierce green flame. The climbing frame charred visibly and cottage windows melted.

And Ronna's emaciated body, I realized, was no longer skeletal, no longer fainting. Fed by the sun, her bony limbs had become full and smooth. The curves of her newly fleshed body pressed tautly against her coverall. The contours of her face rounded as I watched, the proportions of nose, jaw and forehead altering until she was almost unrecognizable. Half-lost within the nourishing cloud of solar energy, Ronna tossed hair that for the first time was thick and glossy. *"I can draw the strength,"* she had said, and now she drew it.

Feliss squirmed, color returning faintly to her ashen face. "Ronna?" she said uncertainly.

With a strange smile, a smile full of knowingness, of mastery, of poise, of all the things Ronna had never possessed, Ronna raised her arms again, sweeping the enveloping orb into a compact ball of fire which she tossed back toward the sun. When it disappeared into the sun's surface, a halo of light lingered round her, faint, blue-white. She dropped her arms and inhaled deeply, drawing in the ghost-light, retaining it.

Then she floated down the path, her eyes still glowing, her face radiant with an impossible beauty. The smile that touched her generous lips promised bounty, well-being, strength and health. She swept her glossy chestnut hair across her shoulders with obvious pleasure.

It took her forever to cross the short distance with her strange, gliding stride. When she reached us, the sun still glowing in her eyes, I realized that she had grown taller by almost half a meter. The hem of her scorched coverall barely reached her calves and the sleeves of her bodice had split. She kicked away her shoes, the seams burst, and stood before us a goddess, smiling an unreadable smile, the sun-glow of her eyes enveloping us in a cloud of warmth. "Feliss, do you know how much energy it takes to heal the mortal wound of a sunwaif?" Her voice was a purring contralto.

Feliss squeezed her eyes shut, sending tears down her grey cheeks. "I didn't mean to hurt myself."

The golden eyes studied her unwinkingly. "Do you ever mean to hurt the people you hurt?"

"I don't hurt people," Feliss protested pettishly. "People want things from me—they always want things from me—and I give them what they want."

"But only after you've made them beg," Ronna reminded her without condemnation. "That's your way, isn't it? To tease, to flirt—"

"Well, people must like to be teased then! They always come back!"

"People like to be healed too, but I never make them beg," Ronna said gently. "I never ask them to surrender their dignity before I heal them."

Feliss' voice had grown noticeably stronger. Color stung her cheeks. "Well, you're doing it now, aren't you? To me!"

"And do you enjoy it? Do you like being teased?"

Feliss' features puckered indignantly. "You know I can't do what Herrol really wants. If I did, you'd tell Nira and Aldred and they'd never let me out of the cottage again!" Her voice had risen to an injured squeal. "What does everyone expect me to do? Corrie keeps saying I'm a spoiled baby, but people don't follow her around and beg her to make the birds dance. Old men don't paw her every time she walks through the Crossroads. Children don't beg her to talk like a crybird. She doesn't even have to come home at night or change clothes or wash up before she eats. She doesn't have people watching everything she does, petting her and—"

"And you love it!" I grated. "If people didn't notice you, you'd turn somersaults at devotions just to get their attention. Just like you came to the picnic in clothes you knew Herrol would want to rip off you. If you didn't want him to bother you, why didn't you wear your old coverall and your work bodice?"

"Then he wouldn't have come at all," Feliss charged. She squirmed up from the grass, forgetting to cradle her wounds. "Do you think he'd come just to share lunch with you and Ronna? You don't even comb your hair and Ronna's so ugly she—" Abruptly she bit her lip and turned fearful eyes to Ronna.

Ronna was so ugly . . . I drew an unbelieving breath, staring at the gaunt girl who swayed weakly against Trebb, her glowing eyes extinguished, her scorched clothes hanging emptily on her emaciated frame. Her eyes rolled up and she gestured to the grass with one skeletal hand. "Trebb . . ."

Feliss gasped, running her hands down her bare abdomen. All that remained of her wounds were two puckers. Her face was a study in conflicting emotions: relief, elation, mortification, pique. She stared wordlessly as Trebb lowered Ronna to the grass, turning her to face the sun, her cupped hands at her sides.

Ronna's breath rattled in her windpipe. It was minutes before her eyes fluttered open. She smiled weakly. "I knew I could draw the energy. I've been so weak, so tired all month. But I've felt the tingling in my palms every day. And today, when the need came, I knew what to do. I knew how to draw the energy directly from the sun."

Trebb knelt beside her, smoothing a feather of dust-colored hair from her forehead. "Can you do it again? Can you make yourself like that again? Whenever you please?"

Briefly she closed her eyes. "I can do it," she said distantly. "I can do it but it's too soon now to do it again. The change—"

"Does it hurt?" Feliss demanded, summoning something like concern.

Ronna smiled faintly. "It—burns. It burns me. Inside where no one can see."

"And I'm the only person you've every done it for?" Feliss demanded with selfish wonder.

"You're the first. Later I'll do it again. Later. But not now. Not again now. And not . . . not . . ."

"You shouldn't talk," Nadd decided, glancing around officiously. "Bring the chair from the play yard, Herrol, so we can carry her back."

Herrol had forgotten his fear of minutes before, had forgotten any debt he might owe Ronna. His shallow forehead creased rebelliously. He had never tolerated Nadd's officiousness. "I have calves to tend," he announced. Turning, he stamped away across the meadow, his pelt disarrayed.

Nadd called after him, but Trebb shook his head. "Corrie, you fetch the chair. You can help me carry her back to the Crossroads."

I edged away from his earnest gaze with a sensation close

to panic. I only wanted to lose myself in the sheltering mustiness of my bluewillow tree, to forget everything I had seen this morning. "I'm not going back to the Crossroads," I declared, trying to make my voice as hard as Herrol's.

But Trebb could bend me when no one else could. "You have to, Corrie. Nadd's too short to hold up the other end of the pole. And I can't carry her by myself. It's too far."

Trapped, I peered from one to the other. Ronna lay like a bundle of sticks in the grass, dry, grey, angular. Feliss had covered herself with crybirds. They perched upon her arms and shoulders and clung to her abdomen and back, mewling softly. Nadd's eyes still bulged with apprehension, and Trebb knelt at Ronna's side, the grass worshipping at his ankles.

Trebb. . . . A torturing fist clutched my heart. My parents had had opportunity to destroy Feliss and they had faltered. And so Trebb had been spared too, I had been spared, Nadd and Herrol had been spared. Even Ronna had been spared.

Had I misunderstood my parents' urgency? Had I even misunderstood their ultimate intention?

I tried to fashion hope from the morning's events. But as I walked back to the play yard, I could feel my Mother quivering underfoot. The entire yard was scorched, the grass charred. I peered around bleakly, distinguishing the burned remnants of the picnic hamper and, beside the step, the few remaining fragments of Ronna's invalid chair. The climbing frame had been almost entirely consumed, as had Feliss' clothes, and the wall of the cottage was scorched, all the window panes melted.

Trebb peered at me questioningly as I returned to the meadow empty-handed. "There's nothing left. The chair was burned," I reported.

"We'll have to make a litter then," he concluded "We can use some pieces from the play yard fence for supports. Then if we can find some canvas—"

"We left storm curtains behind when we moved to the Crossroads," Nadd interjected.

Trebb nodded. "See if you can find them, Nadd. Some of them have probably rotted but there should be a couple of sound ones." Turning back to me, he flashed me a rare smile of reassurance.

But as we carried Ronna back to the Crossroads between us in the makeshift litter later, Nadd and Feliss trailing behind,

I knew that Trebb was as keenly alert as I to the mood of the soil underfoot. And I knew he shared my unease about our future as daughters and sons of this troubled Destiny.

NADD

SPRING 0226

We had not gone far before Feliss skipped past Ronna's litter and raced ahead, her crybirds darting after her. Glimpsing her bare back as she pirouetted down the lane, I shuddered, unable to throw off the apocalyptic visions that had gripped me just before she had impaled herself. Had the images that rushed through my mind at that moment taken reality, none of us would be walking home now. We would lie drowned in the meadow, victims of a storm more violent than any ever known.

But my vision had not been fulfilled. Feliss chattered happily with her birds and Corrie walked meekly under her shared burden. And the sun shone down on us all.

The sun shone down with a special intensity, its rays increasingly oppressive. Twice I turned and glanced back. Once I seemed to peer into a glowing face, its brilliant eyes hypnotic. With a shudder, I turned away. When I glanced back moments later, the sun was an impassive orb, distant, featureless.

Still I felt as if it had chosen this day to focus upon us with particular intensity, as if it worked some profound alteration both upon us and upon the fabric of time, stretching it, creating an eternity of our brief walk back to the Crossroads. I shivered, trying to escape the sense that we had just reached a point in our personal evolution from which we could never turn back. From here, from now, we could only move forward.

But into what future? Toward what consummation?

We climbed a grassy hill and at its crest Trebb and Corrie eased Ronna's litter down to rest. They immediately stepped back, Trebb's features wooden, Corrie startled. Catching up with them, I stared down at Ronna. She had not become the goddess of the meadow again, but in the brief interval since we had left Sunwaif Cottage her thin cheeks had taken flesh and her hair had grown smooth and dark. When she stood, her ragged coveralls fell far short of her ankles again.

I peered up, feeling the pressure of the solar gaze again. Sunlight: it touched us with probing fingers, fingers that reached deep into our tissues and touched alive potentials long dormant. They yawned awake, stretched, and now—

Ronna hardly seemed to notice Trebb's shock, Corrie's surprise. "You won't have to carry me any farther." She smiled at us abstractedly, as if she were in a dreaming state, only marginally aware of us. "I feel much stronger now."

"Ronna—" Corrie's voice was strung tight, her lips a pale gash.

Briefly Ronna's gaze focused on Corrie and her smile took depths that went beyond the human. Languidly she extended one hand, as if to grasp Corrie's clenched fist. Corrie drew back as if stung, her face darkening. "No!"

Ronna admitted no rebuff. Her smile was dreaming. "I won't touch you if you aren't ready, Corrie."

Feliss had swept back to join us, her bare pink breasts shimmering, her birds fluttering in excitement. "There are people in the Crossroads you can touch if you're strong again, Ronna," she said ingenuously. She seemed not to notice Corrie's ashen face, her stricken eyes. "A lot of people got sick this spring. Three of them—"

"Feliss!" Trebb hissed.

"It's all right. I know about the three who merged," Ronna said with the same unwordly smile. "I've been so weak this spring and there have been so many who needed me. But it was a preparatory weakness, my final test. Now I'm growing strong—so very strong. Soon I will be able to help everyone, even the people in the far settlements, the people who have not accepted the new way. They will accept it soon now." Turning, she directed her gaze at me. "Will they not, Nadd?"

"I—" My throat constricted. Her gaze was like sunlight ᵤcused to a searing coherence. I could feel its energy probing ₑe, dazzling hidden potentials awake, stimulating them to life. ₗdrew a gasping breath and images flooded into my conscious‐ ₑss, so many tumbling images I could not sort them, images ₜat flashed through my awareness too rapidly to be evaluated. ₗwas overcome by rapid visions of a hundred contradictory ₗtures, all of them equally vivid. And I knew these crowding ₗtures were not new to me. My mind had always seethed with ₗsions and images of hundreds of futures. I had repressed ₗwareness of all but the most vivid for the sake of my own ₗnity. But now, under Ronna's dazzling gaze— With a chok‐ ₗg cry, I pressed the heels of my hands to my temples. For ₗ moment the flow became less rapid, less erratic.

Trees. Trees sprang up all around us, pressing in upon us. ₗrees barked in tattered black cloth, trees with scabrous flesh ₗnd bony knees. "There's no room!" I yelped in panic, feeling ₗe pressure of jostling bodies. "We don't have room for the ₗlgrims. We don't have water, we don't have food. We—"

"But we will have all those things soon," Ronna said quietly. ₗThat's why we were born, to bring the people to the land, to ₗake them truly of the soil, to create the link they could not ₗreate for themselves. I was born to give them health, Feliss ₗ give them sanity, Trebb and Herrol to give them meat and ₗain."

"And I was born to give them death!" Corrie hissed, stepping ₗack from Ronna's prophetic presence, her shoulders hunched. ₗer hair fell across her shoulders like living snakes. In her ₗyes was storm and death, wrought as vividly as if they marched ₗcross the morning sky. Yet her features were marked not with ₗalevolence but with fear, fear as intense as my own.

"And rain," Ronna said gently. "You bring rain to the Cross‐ ₗoads. Soon you will bring it to all the settlements."

"I will bring storm!" Corrie cried, her voice terrible—and ₗtill wrenching fear lived in her face, sobbing fear. "I will bring ₗvinds that will tear the walls from houses and dismember ₗumans and stock alike. I will bring lightning to destroy every‐ ₗhing that flees my winds, rain to drown what remains behind. ₗ will bring thunder so terrible that anyone who survives will ₗe deafened for life. I—"

"That is one facet of your potential," Ronna said, undis‐ ₗurbed. "When I look to the future, I see life because I am born

of light. You see death because you come from darkness. Eac
of us sees a different vision of the future."

"And I see them all!" I cried in despair. Because sudden
they all rushed in upon me: Ronna's visions of life; Corrie
visions of death; Herrol's visions of thundering herds; Felis
visions of crybird flocks so dense they darkened the sky. I
my mind I walked across the meadow and felt Trebb's belea
guered earthen Mother writhe underfoot. Even Headfathe
Schuster's vision of a human contingent grown into a might
host unfolded in my mind. Armies of settlers trampled me
their booted feet grinding me into the soil. They spread acros
the plain into the distant mountains, crushing everything i
their path.

The sun shone down, the sun touched me where I had neve
been touched before, the sun peered at me from Ronna's eye
and I saw every future that any human or sunwaif had eve
seen—or would see—in dream or in nightmare. Every possibl
and every probable future dashed itself against the shores o
my awareness, crashing, thundering, foaming. The rushin
images drowned me, destroyed me. Yet still I stood on th
grassy hillock in the morning sunlight.

"Yes, you see them all," Ronna said. Her gaze seemed t
shed a special beneficence upon me, separate from the poter
tializing warmth of concentrated sunlight. "Yet a year fro
now only one of the todays you see will be valid. The other
will have become ephemeral. Your function—"

"But they're all there!" I protested. "Every one is as rea
as the others. What you see is as real as what Corrie sees
Trebb's Mother is as real as Herrol's herds. The storms, th
trees, the earth tremors—the pilgrims—"

Ronna shook her head, her voice gentle. "They all appea
equally real now, Nadd, but how can they be? Only one of th
todays you see can come to pass. Only one. Move deeper
Nadd; think. From every point in time stretch hundreds o
divergent futures, each as possible as any other. But we ca
walk only one path, and when we choose that path, all other
fall into nonexistence."

"But I'll never know which future is the true future,"
moaned. Was it my destiny to go through life battered b
images that held no validity?

"Because there is no true future. There is only the one futur
we validate over all the others by choosing to live it. It is you

function to see all probable futures, to evaluate them, to point out to us the consequences of our choices and actions at every point along the way."

"I—"

"It is your function to stand outside of time and direct us."

But I hardly heard her. I shook my head, mutely protesting. "No. NO. It's jumbled. Everything is piled on top of everything else. Nothing makes sense. I can't sort it." Even as we spoke, chaos continued to tumble through my mind. Fragmentary visions, fleeting images, pressing foresights, all contradictory, pressed in upon me. "I can't—"

"But you can," she said with smiling certainty. "Perhaps not now, not this moment. But soon. We are all maturing. I have felt the ability to draw energy directly from the sun tingling in my palms for weeks and today the ability matured. Today I learned to draw and to channel and to discharge. And tomorrow, if I am ready to draw the full strength I need from the sun again, and if you are ready to receive it, I will give you the ability to sort the images you see and choose a path for us all. Tomorrow, if we both are ready, I will make you a seer."

I stared at her, at the gleaming hair that fell to her waist, at the strength of her lightly downed arms. "You—"I choked.

"I am the actualizer," she said simply. "Just as Corrie is the destroyer."

Corrie: we all turned and stared at her. She crouched as if in mortal fear, one fist pressed against her teeth.

"I am the actualizer," Ronna repeated. "When the time comes, I will bring even Corrie to her full function. I must. Look, Nadd, and you will see that on every path to the future: Corrie fulfilled."

Feliss' birds had settled into silence. Now they began to cry again as Feliss demanded excitedly, "And me? Are you going to fulfill me?"

Before Ronna could respond, Corrie unleashed a wail of despair. Then she pounded away down the lane and cut into the field, her hair lashing around her shoulders. Ronna gazed after her undisturbed, then turned her sun-struck gaze back to me.

And I fell to my knees, suddenly gripped by swirling visions of Corrie fulfilled, of storm and death, of destruction unparalleled in vision or imagination. I was distantly aware of my shrill scream, of the froth on my lips, of the thrashing of my limbs as the others tried to quiet me. Then my body arched under the stroke of imagined lightning. Almost gratefully I fell into an unconsciousness that seemed to have its place outside time. I lay there forever, collecting myself for the long journey back to consciousness, back to the torture of bombarding images and visions.

When I woke I swayed in the litter, carried between Ronna and Trebb. I peered for a moment at the bright morning sky. Then I slipped away again.

I was only marginally aware of the events of the next hour. The sun continued to burn down upon us, charging the morning with energy, making it a day like no other. As we neared the Crossroads, grasses, brush and trees yearned toward Trebb, rustling and sighing, as if they would uproot themselves for him. Massive clouds of crybirds from dozens of kilometers distant swept into view and joined the flock that already swirled around Feliss, creating a vortex of bright plumage that towered hundreds of meters over her head. Herds of cattle lined the sides of the lane.

The people of the Crossroads sensed our approach long before we reached the village. They came silently to watch us pass. Swimming back to consciousness, I closed my eyes, trying to blot out the awe I saw in every face. But I knew, just as they knew, that our lives were changing, radically, permanently. Though I struggled, I could not gain shelter of unconsciousness again.

We reached the cottage and Trebb and Ronna lowered the litter. I stood, shakily, and peered around at the people who pressed near on every side. One hand flew to my throat, trying to claw away an invisible obstruction.

Nira and Headfather Schuster pushed quickly through the gathered people. Nira halted when she caught sight of Ronna. Color drained from her face and one hand flew to her mouth. When Headfather Schuster took her other hand, pressing it, she turned and stared at him. "You expected this, Aldred," she gasped, an accusation. Her gaze flew back to Ronna. "Aldred, you—"

"I expected—something," He said. As he assessed Ronna, his lips tightened to a hard line. "But not today. Not so soon." Quickly he glanced around the yard. Every blade of web-grass that was not trampled underfoot bent toward Trebb, quivering.

Both groves, fingerpalm and bluewillow, rustled and moaned toward him. The chatter of brightbushes was audible over the whispers of the crowd. "Not so soon," he repeated, and in that space of time he accepted what he saw and prepared to deal with it. "Feliss, I believe you need to dress yourself again," he said, addressing the slight form almost invisible within the tumult of crybirds.

Laughing, Feliss swept aside her curtain of crybirds. "In feathers or in clothes, Aldred?" Somewhere along the road she had shed her ruffled trousers. Sunlight shimmered provocatively on her naked body. She laughed up at Headfather Schuster, prepared to relish his discomfiture.

But Headfather Schuster's smile was at once unaroused and unoffended. "How would you like to dress, Feliss?"

She tossed her fine black hair, her smile wanton. "I've already worn clothes today and I've already worn feathers. I think I will just wear nothing now. The breeze feels good on my skin."

The breeze of a thousand beating wings. Nira's forehead compressed in a taut frown. "Young miss—"

"I'm not a young miss anymore, Nira," Feliss pointed out with a trill of laughter. "I'm a golden bird and I fly in the sky."

"You are a young miss until you reach your second majority this winter," Nira snapped. "And you will go inside and cover your body."

"I'm a golden bird and I will go where I please," Feliss shot back. With a rebellious cry, she arched to her toes and began to spin, her pink flesh shimmering in the sunlight. Crybirds swept around her in brilliant spirals, calling in shrill voices as she spun faster and faster. Within moments her body was entirely plumed and she peered at us with the impudent black eyes of a crybird. She tossed a mocking cry at Nira, then spread her wings and joined her flock in the air.

I was the only one who heard Nira's fainting moan. Everyone else peered up as the gleaming host of crybirds swept across the sky, following the golden bird whose plumage blazed in the sun. Screaming ecstatically, the entire flock swept away, leaving not a single straggler.

Nira had crumpled to the grass. I pushed my way to her, kneeling, cradling her head in my lap. Her cheeks were pale; her eyelids barely fluttered. Headfather Schuster knelt beside her for a moment, then quickly slipped his arms under Nira's still body and lifted her. "Stand aside," he instructed the settlers who crowded around us. "Let me pass."

They yielded reluctantly. Inside the cottage, Headfather Schuster placed Nira on the master bed. "Get a comforter to cover her," he directed. As I did so, he bent over her, touching her face, her neck. "She'll be all right, Nadd," he said finally. "I want you to stay with her. She has only fainted. She shouldn't be alone and I can't leave the others alone with the crowd."

Alone with the trees, the black-molting trees. "Head father—"

Briskly he took me by the arm, a shake of his head refusing to pamper my weakness. "There are times when each of us must be strong. This is your time, Nadd."

And I knew he was right, with Nira unconscious under the hand-pieced comforter, her breathing shallow, her face blanched of life. "I—will. I will be strong," I assured him, swallowing back my own hysteria.

"Good." And he was gone.

Later, that day became legend. Later, I heard about the mass healing Ronna performed there on the lawn before our cottage. I heard about the cattle that gathered in thundering herds in the fields, about the screaming flock that darted everywhere, about the living grasses that reached out into the burned drought area so rapidly that the green ring could be seen to expand visibly. I heard about trees that grew by meters when Trebb was borne through the village on the shoulders of the people. I heard about the living tapestry Feliss created in the sky when the people gathered to chant, about the sunlight that continued to shine long after the disk of the sun was seen to set. I heard about the new litany that was created spontaneously and how the earth shifted underfoot when first it was chanted.

I heard about all these things later but I did not see them. Instead I sat with Nira while she groped for the sanity that had never before threatened to elude her. We talked for hours about homely details: how many jars of beans were left from the previous year's canning, whether Angelicus needed a new bodice to wear to our graduation ceremony, if Maid Tetner could successfully nurse the baby she had impulsively conceived in the last fertile season of her life, a hundred small matters. By the end of the day, when we heard chanting from the unplanted field far to the south of the cottage, she had reestablished her hold on sanity. She smiled at me, touching my cheek. "Thank you, Nadd. I thought for a while—I thought that reality and I could no longer coexist. Now I believe we will go on together for a while. If you would like to go to the services, please run along."

Run to the forest? Let the trees crowd around me, suffocating me? Mutely I shook my head and retreated to my own room. There I fell into an exhausted sleep. I didn't even wake when the others returned to the cottage near midnight.

When I did wake, sleeping silence lay upon the cottage. Sitting, I peered across the dim room, trying to locate the source of the sound that had wakened me. It came again and I saw Trebb standing outside the window, tapping the pane with his fingertips. His face was stiff and wooden and his hair twined down his neck like streamers of ivy. "Nadd!" he hissed when he saw I was awake.

Herrol snored heavily in his bed. I swallowed down reluctance and fear and crept to the window. Trebb stood waist-high in web-grass that still grew, reaching loving green tendrils for him. "What—"

"Nadd, come with me to the streamside," he said, speaking with terrible effort. Why was his voice hollow? Why were his eyes blank? "Come with me."

"No. Please," I said instinctively, peering beyond him at the tangled grass. If I went outside, it would strangle me, trying to reach him. Trees would spring up in our footsteps and snatch at us both. If I went with him, I would be caught in a maze of living tendrils. "No, Trebb."

"Come," he insisted. "My roots—I feel the soil opening for them. I feel—" He waved his hands, groping for words. "This may be my last night to run. Tomorrow I may be bound forever. Tomorrow I may be rooted." His hands moved awkwardly, as if the arms that wielded them had grown fibrous. Tears gathered in his staring eyes. "Come with me, Nadd."

"But you couldn't—you—" I started to argue, then stopped myself. Trebb could never be rooted, trapped forever in one spot? But things just as incredible had happened today. And change was still in the air. I saw it in the moonlight that turned the growing web-grass silver. "I'll come," I said, torn by the fear in his eyes.

It was the wildest of all our runs together. Once he uprooted himself from the spot outside our window, Trebb's limbs grew supple again. Arms waving, legs flexing, he dashed away through the worshipping grass, calling back to me.

We ran through the village, we ran through the fields. We ran through meadows that rustled and cried after us. We ran along the perimeter of the green headland, and that same perimeter reached rapidly out into the drought area. Trebb whooped as he ran, hectic cries of celebration and fear so mingled I sometimes could not distinguish between them. Occasionally a bush or sapling uprooted itself and stumbled clumsily after us for a few steps, roots writhing. Once I glanced back and saw an entire glade of young bluewillows struggling after us. But soon their roots tangled in the thrashing web-grass and they toppled.

We ran until I could no longer catch my breath and my legs were numb. "Trebb!" I pleaded, collapsing into the grass.

If he heard, he did not heed. Instead he ran on. I tried to gain my feet again, but I was too weak. With a ragged sigh, I threw myself down and lay staring up at the starlit sky until I felt strength returning to my legs.

He had asked me to come to the streamside with him. Indeed the grasses and trees all yearned in the direction of the old cottage and the stream. My chest still heaving with exhaustion, I wanted only to return to the cottage, to my bed. But if this were Trebb's last night of mobility, I couldn't desert him. Half-stumbling, I took the direction of the rippling grasses.

Reaching the abandoned cottage, I paused for a moment, peering at the charred steps and melted windows. Then I gazed out over the meadow. By moonlight the grass rippled like a field of silver, each blade standing out in shimmering detail. In the distance I detected the shadowy blur of a human shape. "Trebb!" I shouted, running again.

As I ran a night breeze swept through the grass with a rustling sigh, scattering reflected light around my ankles in metallic spikes. I shielded my eyes, disoriented by the shifting pattern of light-shards, haunted by the sibilant voice of the grass as it stirred with increasing agitation, yearning toward the streamside.

But this time it was not Trebb who drew the grass. Ronna stood at the center of the meadow, an increasingly luminous cloud of silver forming around her. As I approached, I saw that she had flung her head back and raised her cupped palms overhead, as she had earlier in the play yard. But this time she moved in a slow, stylized dance, presenting her cupped hands, her glowing eyes, first to one moon, then to the second, finally to the third, each in its separate quadrant of the heavens. I stopped short, afraid to approach, afraid I would be drawn into the invisible web of energy she spun around herself. As she moved, her body swaying, her hair shifting across her bare shoulders, her limbs fleshed out magically, growing both longer and fuller. Her naked breasts, already full, blossomed voluptuously. Her hair became molten metal, a solid mass, but when she began to spin more rapidly, presenting her receptive palms to each moon in rapid succession, it swung loosely around her, a cape of silver.

I was helpless to retreat as her spinning dance enveloped more and more of the meadow in a cloudy luminescence. The force of the breeze increased, making the web-grass bow before her, and the brightbushes chattered in brittle agitation. A gale, the wind ruffled my hair and tugged at my coverall, propelling me into the glowing energy web. I caught an apprehensive breath, remembering the scorched grass and charred picnic hamper.

But within the silver cloud I met not heat but bitter cold. It fell upon me like some snow-pelted beast and bled away my body heat. My fingers numbed and my feet slipped into hibernation. "Ronna—" I pleaded, my breath a cold fog emerging from lips frosted with rime.

She lowered her cupped palms and abandoned her sinuous dance with a flourish. Approaching me, she towered over me, cradling a globe of blinding brilliance in her outstretched hands. Her naked flesh seemed to fit her like a sheath of silver, a precious metal casement from which her eyes gazed like drops of liquid mercury. Her voice was again a purring contralto, compelling in its husky timbre. "Nadd, did you know that you are imperfect?"

I tongued my icy lips. "Ronna, I thought you—"

"You thought I could not draw the energy again so soon?" She laughed softly, a chorus of bells. "I thought the same thing this morning, after I healed Feliss. I thought I could not bear the burning again so soon. But I was worshipped today by all the people whom I healed and tonight I woke with moonlight tickling my palms. I came to the meadow and it followed me, ready to be mine again. And so I drew it directly into my core, I assimilated it into myself, and now I am at last as I was intended to be. I have fulfilled my genetic endowment.

But you are still imperfect, Nadd."

My voice was a frozen croak. "I'm not. I'm—"

"But you are, Nadd. I can read human physiology as easily as other people read the printed page. I can find deep hurts simply by laying on my hands and I heal them the same way. I can identify and destroy invading micro-organisms without even touching their host. And now I have reached the time in my life when I can read the genetic code and see what each of us was intended to be, if we hadn't been stunted." She bared her silver teeth in a silent laugh. "Don't you want to know what you were intended to be, Nadd?"

I tried to retreat from her, from the terrible freezing brilliance she held in her cupped hands. But my feet would not move. And yes, I did want to know. I wanted to know. "Was I—was I meant to be tall?" I faltered, peering up at her.

"Oh yes. Yes. You were meant to have the body of a god, with legs like pillars and arms and shoulders as strong as a bull's. As strong as Herrol's. You were meant to have eyes that could see for kilometers and hands strong enough to crush a bull's skull, yet delicate enough to play a harp." Smiling, she moved toward me, her cupped palms held out before her, an offering. "I've drawn the strength to make you whole, Nadd. If you will hold out your hands, if you will take sunlight from me, sunlight reflected from below the horizon, if you will permit all the starved cells of your body to drink with me, drink what I offer, *sunlight, moonlight, starlight, lifelight...*"

Her voice fell into a coaxing chant. Instinctively I reached out, touched by a thirst I had never known before, deep, ravaging, urgent.

The brilliance she offered was blinding, her voice hypnotic. "Feed from my strength and you will know, Nadd, *sunlight, moonlight, starlight, lifelight*; feed and the opaque will become clear and the clear transparent, *sunlight,* moonlight, starlight, lifelight; the hidden will become apparent and the apparent understood. When you touch my hands and draw my strength, Nadd, you will step outside of time. The future will become now and now will become forever. *Sunlight, moonlight, starlight, lifelight...*"

Numbed, I let myself be drawn into the spell she wove. Images of power blazed through my mind. When I touched her hands and drew upon the icy energy they cradled, when my body blossomed with sinew and muscle, when my vision intensified, reaching out effortlessly both across the physical world and across the future itself—

With a sharp quiver, my hands flinched back from hers, a subliminal burst of vision had flashed through my awareness, terrible devastating, promising things no human could ever want to see, in the present or in the future. If I drew from the energy she offered and saw all the disaster and death that lay within the realm of probability, saw it as clearly as I saw the meadowgrass, as clearly as I saw the stars, if I could never again put it out of mind, if the future became now, always now, pushing in upon me night and day, crowding my dreams with every horror...

She had touched me with the light of her eyes that morning and the spate of images and visions had been crippling, overwhelming. How much more overmastering would they be if I took the light from her hands?

"No!" I cried, a shriek that broke the spell of her chant long enough for me to throw myself beyond her net of moonlight. "No!" I would not be an exile at the border of time, a solitary figure cursed with all the terrible probabilities that stretched out from every event, every action. Sooner I would be a frightened gnome for the rest of my days, hiding behind Nira's skirts.

"The light, Nadd!" she called after me, but my feet were already pumping again, carrying me across the meadow, through the lashing grasses, away from the terrible light she held in her hands.

NADD

SPRING 0226

When I glanced back from a safe distance, she had returned to her sinuous dance, offering her cupped palms to each moon in turn, her hair swinging around her shoulders like a cape of silver. And surely I only imagined that the wind which swept toward her from every direction cried as it trailed reluctant fingers through the web-grass. Surely I only imagined that the moons dimmed as she wove more and more of their reflected light into her energy-web. Surely I only imagined that the entire meadow shuddered underfoot as I fled.

I ran blindly, the entire future pursuing me. I ran until Ronna had become a distant form at the center of a silver cloud. Then I threw myself down in the grass, fighting for breath.

It was several minutes before I sat and peered around. I was several dozen meters from the streambank. The water muttered angrily as it flowed between the husky young saplings which stood sentinel on its banks. I rose slowly, frowning. It took my numbed mind moments to pinpoint the discrepancy. Instead of frail saplings, these were well-established young trees. And they were growing. Their trunks, silhouetted against the sil-very-grey sky, expanded visibly as I watched, and their branches arched outward. Tiny tongues of moss appeared, licking mischievously at the air.

I tongued dry lips. Trebb must be near. Downstream the saplings were still frail, but upstream they were several growth stages ahead of the ones in my immediate vicinity. I touched my temples, gingerly, and a vision of massive trees blinded me. With a crushing sense of unreality, I shook the vision away and crashed through the streamside brush, running upstream with a growing sense of urgency.

Twice I stumbled over protruding roots. Both times I picked myself up, muddy and frightened, and ran on. The trees became increasingly larger and more heavily bearded as I ran upstream. Soon the moons could insinuate only slim fingers of light through their dense foliage. As the trees grew more imposing and moss slapped at my face and clung to my coverall, I became aware of a cloying odor, at once spicy and musty. I covered my nose but the insidious odor penetrated my fingers, choking me with every breath.

Finally, with a floating sense of unreality, I reached a spot where the restored trees stood in ancient dignity, their limbs arched high overhead to create a natural cathedral. I halted, my fingers and toes tingling, my head bobbing loosely above my shoulders. I let my hands drop and inhaled deeply, remotely surprised to find my fright displaced by an uncanny serenity. There was peace here, as if these trees were eternal, not only the guardians of some sacred power but an integral part of it. And the power, *the power* . . .

Slowly, swimmingly, drawn, I entered the cathedral of trees. Despite dense foliage, its interior was bathed in ghostly grey light. A vagrant breeze stirred through the upper branches and high overhead patriarchal beards of moss swayed, raining down grey dust in silent blessing.

I inhaled deeply, no longer choking. As the dust's magic reached my nervous system, I felt ten meters tall, a giant, my arms like girders, my legs like pillars. Slowly I turned my massive head and peered around. The stream flowed in rhythmic surges, as if it were pumped by a powerful heart embedded deep in the earth.

The spicy mustiness of vision dust thick in my nostrils, I strode upstream. As I progressed, I became aware of the deep, thudding contractions of the buried heart that pumped the silver stream. Twice I stopped and placed my hands and forehead against a tree trunk. Abandoning my own consciousness, I experienced the surge of sap through woody limbs as it was forced to the extremities of the tiniest capillaries by the same heart that sent water surging through the stream.

As I walked, the contractions intensified, until finally I reached a spot where they seemed to emanate from directly underfoot. The ground itself vibrated to every beat, and the driven water foamed and swirled. Even here, in the very heart of the cathedral, the trees continued to grow, their trunks gnarling, their limbs becoming more and more massive. I peered across the rippling water and watched dark foliage unfurl, crinkling rapidly from the tips of every growing branch.

Then my gaze swung back. A few meters from the stream's edge the unearthly grey light that illuminated the cathedral of trees came to shimmering focus. Contained within its silver-white cone were two figures, one crouching, her tangled hair tumbled across her shoulders, the other lying curled on his side, his knees drawn up, his head hunched between his shoulders.

"Trebb?" As I approached, my legs seemed to contract, my head to sink, until I was no longer a giant or a god. "Trebb?" My voice hung uncertainly in the mote-laden air, a wispy emanation.

He rolled his head to peer up at me. His voice was slack and his eyes were silvered surfaces, blankly reflective. "The trees are returning," he said, his voice little more than a breeze.

"They—yes. They're growing." With a twinge of dread, I realized that his arms and legs were no longer lanky but emaciated, as if he had grown the trees from his own flesh. And why did the soil heave underfoot as if in distant agitation? "Trebb—"

Corrie rose to her knees, tossing her tangled hair back from her face. Despite the silver-paleness of her face, her eyes were dark pits. I seemed to teeter on their brink. "How far downstream have they grown, Nadd?"

"I—I don't know," I hedged, struggling for balance. Again the earth shifted uneasily. "I'm not sure how long I've been walking."

"Ten minutes? Fifteen? Did you walk that long, Nadd?"

That long and longer. Forever. "I don't know," I repeated, wrenching my gaze back to Trebb. He peered at me emptily, no shadow moving on his silvered irises. Was this what he had meant when he said the soil was opening to him? That he was to invest his substance in the streamside trees? "Trebb, are you—why are you—"

Briefly he lidded his silvered eyes. Then he uncurled and rose to a sitting position. He rubbed absently at the bark-like scales that covered his forearm. "It's the only way. It's the only way we can save her."

I tasted my lips uneasily. "Our...Mother?" How could I deny her reality, her presence, when the soles of my feet conducted her throbbing heartbeat through my entire body?

He nodded. "I've worried about what it cost her to green our fields and meadows and I've worried about how it hurt her to sear and burn the fields and meadows beyond the green ring. I've worried about the energy we use every day, just to live, and to foster the settlers's survival. But until today I never realized how we wounded her when the pilgrims burned the trees from her stream. I never knew how she must have cried when sunlight fell on her waters for the first time in forever. Her voice was the mew of a crybird, the rustle of the grass, and I was deaf to it. I ignored it.

"But today, when the settlers created their spontaneous litany, I heard her voice at the very center of the chant. She begged for her trees, the trees I'm growing for her now. I'm restoring them all, Nadd, every one. And the brush—I'm growing the brush for her and the lichen and the moss. Everything that was destroyed that day we first came to our power. Then she will be whole again. Her waters will be protected. She will be able to rain again. She will be able to rain and put out the brush fires and feed the grasses. She—"

"She's waiting," Corrie hissed. "She's waiting for us to restore everything we destroyed, Nadd. And then she can destroy us."

Suddenly a flotilla of arrows seemed to hang in the air, their silver heads poised bare centimeters from my chest. "Destroy?" A dry whisper.

"She has no choice," Corrie said. "Name me one other Mother who would feed her children from her very heart for so long? For fourteen years, Nadd, without complaining. Name me one."

"Nira would," I stammered. Must the arrows find their target? Was there no way to evade them without destroying the very soil underfoot?

Corrie laughed sharply. "From her heart? We've been feeding Nira, Nadd. Trebb grows the wheat she grinds into flour. Herrol breeds the cattle that produce milk for her custards. Fruits and vegetables, meat and suet—everything. Haven't you ever noticed that the older we get, the more we come into our power, the fatter Nira gets?"

"She—everyone gets fatter when they grow older," I pleaded.

"If they have someone to feed them they do. If they have *us*. But we can't go on fattening all the refugees who come to us while our Mother suffers. They'll have to go back to the old way now. They'll have to fight for every bite, and sometimes there will be nothing to chew. Sometimes they'll eat and sometimes they'll go hungry."

"You—you'll let the settlers starve?"

Trebb's voice was a dispassionate rustling of branches. "They didn't starve before, Nadd. Before the drought."

But I remembered gaunt pilgrim faces and shadowed eyes. And I remembered the joyless dogmatism of their faith, the heavy chants and somber litanies. Headfather Schuster had said the pilgrims came to Destiny a joyous sect, glad to escape the hardships and chaos of a dying Earth-Then, pleased to find a place where they could hear the whispering voice of their own Secret Power, the power no other people on Earth recognized. "But the death rate then—" I faltered.

"The death rate was normal under the circumstances," Corrie rasped. "What could they expect when they came out here beyond the reach of technology? For centuries the unfit bred with the fit on Earth-Then. People who were genetically defective were snatched from death by medical science to become the parents of more genetic misfits. Massive benefit programs let the incompetent breed in numbers and mingle in turn with the unfit. And now is the winnowing. Now, on Destiny, the people who are too weak to live must die. Trebb and Herrol can't feed them any longer and Ronna can't heal them. Because the energy they are drawing to foster these people is not *theirs*. The energy is being drawn from our parents and they can't spare it any longer."

"They can't," Trebb echoed. "We have to set the balance right and let ourselves be destroyed. Otherwise everything will be destroyed."

Everything. Shuddering, I tried to will away a sudden vision of a rocky world floating dead in space, her rivers and lakes dry, her veil of greenery stripped away, not even a spot of lichen left to protect her naked crust. But I could not. The vision persisted, becoming more real with every moment. Nor could I ignore the stirring of the ground beneath my feet. And it moved not in dying spasm but in silent rebellion.

A moan escaped my lips and a yawning emptiness drew at my soul, emptying me of visions. Blinking, I saw for a moment only what actually lay before me, unshadowed by past or future. And that was a spewing stream, an ominously growing forest and my two sun-siblings, Corrie, agent of destruction, and Trebb, agent of restoration. Two opposing forces, allied.

As I watched, the silvery brilliance of Trebb's eyes darkened and he turned his head, peering beyond me. Corrie followed his gaze, half-rising. Puzzled, I turned, briefly ignoring the subterranean muttering underfoot.

Ronna moved silently through the trees, her cloud of energy concentrated to an intense silver cocoon. She strode at its center, her molten hair pouring down her naked shoulders, her liquid mercury eyes glowing. She was almost lost in the brilliance of the energy web she had spun around herself, but when she stopped short of us I could distinguish the smile that transformed her luminescent face. "I have drawn the energy, Trebb. Are you ready?" she purred, her hands floating up from her sides. Upon each open palm she held an orb of light so intense, so concentrated, I could hardly look at it. "Are you ready to become what you were intended to be, Trebb?"

Mesmerized, Trebb stood. He stared into the blinding light she held, bark slowly creeping up his neck. "I am already— so," he said in a wooden voice. With one stiff hand, he indicated the restored trees. "And I have done this."

Ronna shook her head. "No, this is not your ultimate fulfillment. This is only an expression of your limitation. But you need be limited no longer, Trebb. Aren't you ready to feel your roots penetrate deep into the mother-soil, reaching for the sweet water that that lies there? Aren't you ready to lace the sky with your limbs, ready to feel morning sunlight on your foliage, ready to be as you were intended to be, Trebb?"

His lips gaped stiffly, but before he could answer, Corrie demanded roughly. "And what about me?"

Ronna swung her molten hair across her shoulders. Her smile remained dispassionate. "This afternoon you would not permit me to take your hand. Are you ready now to accept my light?"

Corrie appeared caught in ambivalence. Peering at the silver orb in Ronna's left hand, she took a single step forward, her own hands extended. But at the same time her eyes seemed to deepen with some image she did not want to see. She touched her temple, as if stroking away pain. "I—how was I meant to be?" The demand was plaintive. Did she, this late, hope to hear that she was not our destroyer? That, fulfilled, her function was something other than she had already declared it?

Ronna tossed her molten hair, her smile deepening. "You don't need me to tell you the force of your power or the directions in which it can carry you, Corrie. You know all that, if you will only recognize it. The truth is there if you choose to see it."

"But you know too," Corrie probed, resentment coloring the demand. "You know I come from darkness. You said it yourself."

"I said it," Ronna acknowledged simply.

"You—" Corrie wet her lips, her eyes swirling with turbulence. When she spoke again, her voice was the wind, bitter with cold. "You know my origin, you know my intent, yet you will fulfill me if I ask?"

"I will," Ronna said.

Paralyzed, I stared at the tableaux they presented: Ronna majestic within the swirling brilliance of her energy-cloud; Trebb peering with blank silver eyes at the brilliance she offered; Corrie reaching out one clawed hand, yet reluctantly, cringing from the very thing she sought. The scene was etched in sharp contrasts, silver upon black, black upon silver. I saw only the now of it, the very moment in which the gift was offered, and nothing beyond. But fear closed my throat. Choking, I tried to swallow back its sour taste. "Trebb, if you take the light—"

"I will use it to put things right," he creaked. "You see how weak I am now. And you know how many more trees were burned." His voice fell to a murmur. "I will return every tree that was burned, every beard of moss, every clump of lichen. I will set the guardians beside the waters again, and our Mother's heart will beat without fear. I will return the fields to grass, the meadows to brightbushes, the groves to trees. All the timber that has been cut and made into homes will leaf and bloom. The village will become a forest of green-growing cottages. Every fence post will put down roots, and cart wheels and wagon wheels will refuse to roll. Plank walls—"

"Trebb—" I pleaded.

But he was blinded by his forested vision, blinded by images of a world restored, a Mother appeased. His voice ran on, murmuring, sighing, conjuring, until he had turned the entire face of Destiny green again. Then his voice became a woody sigh emanating from deep within his trunk. I looked down and saw that his toes were spreading across the soil, knotted roots groping for purchase. His face was lost in bark, his hair a mass of foliage. Only his arms remained recognizably human, despite the rough bark that fleshed them. Stiffly they reached for the orb of light Ronna cradled upon her right palm. "My roots," he sighed with timeless longing. "I want to put down my roots, Ronna."

As Ronna glided forward, her hands extended, Corrie's face contorted with sudden pain. She stood frozen as Ronna proferred the orb of light to Trebb, her silver cocoon swirling. At the last moment, as Trebb's twigged hands accepted the light, Corrie lunged, a grieving cry jarred from the depths of her throat. "No!"

No! No, no, *no, no,* NO! My own cry was silent but no less pain-spurred. As Trebb cradled the ball of light in his shriveling palms, a holocaust of visions burst into my awareness, visions too terrible for any human to endure. But I could not retreat from them. They flared violently through my mind, whining, droning, shrieking, cast in inferno, limned in flame, too terrible to behold, too real to deny. I tried to utter a protest, but when I opened my mouth nothing spewed forth but a long, wailing cry, hardly human.

It was too late. The orb of light had already burst, releasing its energy in a blinding silver flare. I flung my hand up to shield my eyes. Energy arced from the burst orb and billowed around Trebb, swirling and crackling, now half-concealing him with its glare, now sweeping aside to reveal his captive body. His foliage rimed with frost, and his thrashing limbs froze in stiff attitudes, glistening with ice. His roots curled into agonized knots, surrendering their blind efforts to penetrate the soil.

Then, as I watched, my voice frozen in my throat, his roots became feet again, his limbs arms, his foliage hair. What had been trunk became torso. His face emerged from the encroaching bark, flesh once more, but caught in an expression I could not read. Agony? Or ecstasy?

Whichever, it did not last long. As I struggled to break free of paralysis, Trebb matured before my eyes. One moment he was an adolescent, the next a youth, then a youngfather. His thin face filled out, his features became sharply defined. But early maturity passed quickly into later maturity and middle age. Almost too rapidly for my eyes to process the tumbling images, he was an old man, his features shriveling, his hands withering.

Terrified, I tried to halt the dizzying process with a cry. But Trebb had already sunk to his knees, a bearded ancient, and was lost behind brightly surging curtains of energy.

When they swirled aside again, Trebb had disappeared. All that remained was a single slender green stalk dappled lightly with brown. Quickly a second stalk sprang up, and a third. The pliable young stalks pushed through the soil eagerly, multiplying rapidly throughout the cathedral of trees, vibrating with joy. Soon the cathedral was filled with their thrumming chord, their quivering, throbbing celebration of life. The chord grew, trembling through the trees, making the foliage shimmer, the long beards of moss quiver and convulse.

A chill passed up my spine. *Mother Destiny had accepted Trebb's roots* and he was springing up everywhere. Peering downstream, I saw his dappled green stalks leap to life beneath every tree, multiplying with dizzy rapidity. The vibrating chord of celebration became a chorus, a chorale, and every tree, every bush joined in. Brightbushes chattered with brittle joy and ancient trees boomed in woody voices, their dark trunks throbbing. I felt the individual organs of my body quiver in frustrated muteness and recognized the bony chatter of my vertebrae against one another.

Caught in the throbbing enthrallment of the moment, I hardly realized that Corrie had stepped forward, her hand clawing toward the second orb of light. She was limned in brilliance, eagerness and dread struggling for possession of her features. She snatched at the second orb of light and a second blinding silver flare lit the cathedral of trees, throwing barked trunks into sharp relief. Corrie stood at the center of a roiling cloud of luminescence, her dark pupils yawning pits, her black hair snarling across her shoulders, a living mass.

Stricken, I backed toward the stream. As curtains of energy swirled around Corrie, briefly concealing her, then whipping back to reveal her again, the ground groaned underfoot. With a sharp crack from somewhere far below, the soil rumbled and boomed and the stream no longer flowed in rhythmic surges but gushed forth in a frenzied cataract.

And Corrie became storm. She threw back her head and her hair became snarling black clouds. She flung up her arms and lightning snapped from each fingertip. When she opened her mouth, thunder boomed forth, a deep-cracking voice that made the trees thrash in dread. The earth vibrated underfoot, as if Mother Destiny's heart were bursting, and the stream gushed once with such force that it overflowed its banks, then subsided to an anemic ribbon of water which lay slack and pale in its bed.

If I screamed, my voice was lost in the tumult. Corrie had risen to her toes, silver luminescence still swirling around her. Throwing her head back, she spun on her toes and the silver light became the funnel of a tornado. A glowing presence, it towered high into the trees, crackling with thunder, lightning leaping from its apex.

"The trees—" I cried. Deadly fingers of lightning crackled at them, igniting their wind-withered foliage.

Corrie lashed me with her winds, drying my nasal passages, cracking my lips. "The trees must die, Nadd, and I am the instrument."

"No, Corrie!"

"I am the instrument!" Briefly she danced around me, tugging at my hair with her tornado gales, drying my skin until it itched intensely.

"But Trebb—"

Her hair swirled around her shoulders, concealing her face. When it whipped away again, her features twisted in agony. "I have to do it, Nadd. If we live, we will destroy the sacred cycle and dance in the ruins of everything beautiful, everything bright. If we live, one day the crust of the earth will crack open and the sun will plunge down the sky like a blinded god." She tossed her hair again, and suddenly, superimposed between us, I saw the arrow, its silver point gliding toward me.

But it was not an arrow, I realized. It had never been an arrow. It was a finger of lightning, pristine, deadly. And it was not directed at me. It was directed at the sheafs of dry moss that clung to the trees, at the foliage from which Corrie's tornado winds had sucked all moisture. And it was directed at Trebb, at the quivering, thrumming stalks he had become, springing eagerly from the soil everywhere.

"No!" I shrieked, throwing myself at her.

But who can catch the wind? She spun away, giving me one final glimpse of her anguish. "I didn't want to do it!" she cried. "I didn't want to be the one!" Then, rising on her own tornado winds, she whisked through the upper reaches of the cathedral, her lightning fingers sparkling and crackling.

Mossy beards were already igniting when Headfather Schuster stepped from the shadows. With a start, I realized he had been there for several minutes, silent, immobile, only his eyes alive. "You don't have to be the one, Corrie," he said, his voice carrying through the tumult of her winds. "None of this has to happen."

Startled by his emergence, by his words, she drew her winds into a silent knot and peered down at him. "Why are you here?"

"Because I knew you would come here tonight. This is where it began, when you caught the pilgrims at worship and later when the pilgrims returned to burn the trees." He looked up at her unafraid. "And now I'm telling you: this second burning is unnecessary. It need never take place."

"Then why is my Mother rumbling?" Corrie demanded, still suspended in mid-air. "Why are the waters roiling?"

"For the same reason you have sensed disturbance all around you these past few years. Your Mother and your Father are offering their final resistance to the Secret Power."

"Your false god!"

"Our true god, the god of all humans," he retorted. "He has existed in many forms for many races. He has been worshipped in many tongues under many names. Our forefathers made the mistake of thinking that only they knew the truth of god and so they worshipped only one of his facets. They worshipped the whispering voice that comes in the night.

"Even so, they could not limit the god of all humanity by calling Him Secret. He came here with them and He has brought them alive through these two troubled centuries. And at the same time He has been preparing to merge with the Destiny powers, so the god of place and the god of people may be one. But the Destiny powers have fought our Secret Power—and us—with the strength of desperation. It has taken this long, two and a quarter centuries, to bring them to their knees. Even now they have not fully accepted the merging that is about to occur."

"It will never occur! I won't let you destroy them!" Corrie hissed, sinking to earth. "I'll kill you with the others. I'll burn the Crossroads. I—"

"No, Corrie, there will be no destruction. Our god is slowly accommodating itself to Destiny and her powers just as Destiny is slowly—unwillingly—accommodating herself to us. You— the sunwaifs—have accelerated a process that was inevitable from the moment we landed. We have only to survive this final resistance and we will enter the golden age, the age of gods merged, gods working hand in hand for human benefit." He turned, finding me where I crouched behind a mossy trunk. "Tell her, Nadd. Tell her what the future holds."

I stared at him, quivering with disbelief. Plumb the future and suffer the pain of death not only in reality but in vision as well? Overhead trees ignited with a loud crackle. The mossy beards that clung to them burst into flame, wagging with blazing excitement, passing the fire eagerly from tree to tree. Suffer the fire twice in such rapid succession that each death, the vicarious and the actual, would be superimposed upon the other? "No," I begged him. "*No*. Don't make me look!"

"See? He knows what he will see," Corrie cried, her face twisting with pain. "He knows he will burn twice if he looks at the future now."

"No, he will burn if he refuses to look at the future." He clutched my arm, pulling me fully erect. His gaze was impelling. "Look, Nadd, and tell us what you see."

Squirming, I tried to resist his authority. "No! Even if I do look, even if I tell you what I see—it won't be true. I see—I see too much! It—everything opens up in every direction. I see every future that could be and I can't tell which is right and which is wrong. I—"

"You can distinguish if you take my light," Ronna said. Her silver cocoon spent, she stood almost forgotten in the shadows. Now she stepped forward and extended her hand. A globe of energy blazed alive in her palm, as if translated from another dimension. "If you accept my lifelight, you will see the roads to the future marked clearly before you. You will see where each fork leads. You will see what will pass if Corrie burns the trees and you will see what will pass if she does not. You will see what will pass if Trebb burns, if you burn, if Headfather Schuster burns and you will see what will pass if no one burns. You will see all you need to see to guide us."

"No!" I protested. The responsibility was too heavy, my shoulders too narrow. I could never bear the burden and live. I cringed from her extended hand. But Headfather Schuster did not release me. And where could I run? Into the burning trees? In the confusion of the moment I grasped one fact clearly. If the trees continued to burn, I could never escape them, no matter where I ran.

"Look, Nadd," Headfather Schuster said, supporting me. "Look."

Fire leapt at the dry foliage overhead. My fear was so overwhelming I hardly realized I had lunged for the light until it burst around me. Freezing silver brilliance rained upon me. I was caught with my mouth gaping, my eyes frozen wide. The terrible cold moved deep into my body, freezing me into immobility. With terrible effort, I moved one arm a bare centimeter, and ice crystals crackled in my joints.

I stood at the center of cold for seasons, for years—for moments. Then came the glowing warmth and my body began to grow. My legs surged upward, bursting the seams of my trousers. My arms rippled with forming muscle and my chest expanded, splitting my shirt. Briefly I was choked by a ring of new muscle that cordoned my neck. Then my skin stretched to accommodate it and I breathed again.

There were other changes, changes I didn't discover until later. Although my hands grew, I didn't know then that their touch simultaneously became precise to the point of delicacy. I didn't know that I had developed the power to extend my gaze far into the distance, picking out detail no one else could see.

That night I extended my gaze into the future instead, fearfully, expecting the worst.

Instead I saw the Destiny powers and the Secret Power, gods of place and people, reconciling and merging, becoming Three-That-Are-One. None of the three surrendered its unique identity; yet between them they created a unity that permitted them to reconcile the needs of the people to the needs of the land so that neither need suffer at the agency of the other again.

Thereafter I saw Corrie directed by the Three-That-Are-One

o bring an end to the drought. I saw rain come to the land
again, greening stricken meadows, quenching brushfires. I saw
Trebb springing up everywhere; I saw Feliss leading flights of
birds and moths wherever they were needed; I saw Herrol's
herds fanning across the broad plains, their hooves causing the
soil no pain; and I saw myself walking down village lanes, my
inner sight focused years ahead, preparing settlers and sunwaifs
to choose the path to peace and prosperity.

Corrie seized my arm. "There is no Three," she said through
clenched teeth. "Destiny is two, Mother and Father."

"And the Secret Power is another," Headfather Schuster
said gently.

I had spoken without realizing. But now I proclaimed my
vision. "And the Three are One," I intoned. Then the entire
vision rolled off my tongue, the beauty, the wealth, the peace.
Men, women and children spread across the land, offering
culmination to a creation that until now had been without higher
sentience. Their songs and chants rose in a continuing paean,
until the Destiny powers forgot there had been a day when their
creation had been mindless and mute. "We have come to speak
for the Destiny powers," I said. "We have come to give them
voice and intelligence."

Corrie's gaze shot upward, at the flames that consumed the
roof of the cathedral. "You lie," she grated. "You lie, Nadd."

But I was no longer the gnome she remembered, frightened
of my shadow. She had to reach up to clutch my arm and I
peered down at her, my voice thundering. "Then try this vision
instead, Corrie. Imagine a ball of soil and stone spinning lifeless
around the sun. Imagine barren fields, dying trees, rivers and
streams dried to nothing. Imagine Destiny stripped of everything living, everything green."

She drew back, her fingers still biting into my forearm.
"Who—how?"

"Who will strip her—and how? You, with your fire If you
destroy us, the Destiny powers and the Secret Power will con-
front each other over our burned bodies. And there will be no
reconciliation. They will plunder this globe of every scrap of
life—the one in grief, the other in anger. They will strip away
everything, down to the smallest patch of lichen. They will
wipe life off Destiny's face and send her on her way barren
forever."

"They—no! No!"

"Yes," I said, and my voice carried utter conviction. "You must rain now. You must extinguish your fires or all is destroyed."

Her eyes whipped around the clearing, beseeching each of us. "But I'm the dark force. I'm the destroyer! I'm—"

"You are duality, Corrie," Ronna said quietly, her molten eyes glowing. "Look into yourself—you have the power to do so. You have always had the power. Look and you will see your other face. You are the agent of fire and water."

"And they bring death!"

"But they bring life too. Used correctly, both of them are indispensable to humankind. And it is your function not to unleash them upon us but to strike a balance between them, to see that both are used wisely, for our benefit."

"I—" Hope fought in Corrie's face, peeling back layers of anger and fear. I watched in fascination as years fell from her. Had she always been so old, as old as the soil itself?

Now she was becoming young. "You control the two forms of death-force we dread most," Ronna said. "They are also the two forms of life-force we depend upon most heavily."

"You wear two faces, Corrie," Headfather Schuster said. "You have shown us the face of death and you have frightened yourself as much as you have frightened everyone else. Now you must show us the face of life."

"Now you *will* show us the face of life," I declared, letting my new voice boom.

Corrie's hair writhed of its own accord, teeming back across her shoulders. She resisted my imperative, the imperative of her own dual nature, for a moment longer. Then she sighed, "Yes," and the last layers of bitterness and rage fell from her. She wore the face of a child, radiant, vulnerable. She laughed, a wondering sound. "Yes. I am two. And I will rain."

And in a moment her rejoicing tears fell all around us. She laughed and they fell, laughed and they extinguished the flames that licked at the cathedral of trees. For the first time there was neither malevolence nor pain in her laugh. For the first time it was a laugh of pure joy—of life. "I will rain!" she cried, rising upward on the force of her winds, her head thrown back in ecstasy. "I will rain!"

And we knew, all of us, knew, from the rumbling of the earth, from the roiling of the stream, from the sighing of the trees, that at that moment Three became One and that They were pleased.

EPILOGUE

Sometimes now Corrie smiles as she walks through the Crossroads and children run after her, laughing. At other times she storms and frightened settlers slam their windows and bar their doors. Occasionally, on a spring morning, Feliss takes flesh and dances on the village green. More often she appears as a winged shape in the distance, flirting among the clouds. Herrol loses himself in his herd for weeks at a time, then reappears in human form, grooming his shining pelt to go courting some village miss. And Trebb...

When I began this manuscript, I was concerned about the solar storms I saw in our future, afraid of the births that would follow. Now I have learned that another kind of genesis is already imminent.

In a small cottage north of Wursterville a young woman awaits virgin birth. She insists she has known no man. Late one night, she says, she woke to find her cottage besieged by dappled green stalks. As they sprang from the soil, they thrummed and sang to her, wordless songs that held her spellbound. As the light of first one moon and then another fell across the celebrating stalks, the stalks flowered and released a golden pollen that fell upon her, touching her in all the hidden places of her body. And now she is large with child, Trebb's child.

How many others carry the same seed, I have no way of knowing. Perhaps many, perhaps few. Time will tell.

Time will tell much: whether settlers who were once devout pilgrims can accept the birth of dozens of children as strange as the six of us or stranger; whether any of us can tolerate the presence and proliferation of gifts that at first appear bizarre or destructive; whether the original sunwaifs can adapt to a new generation without jealousy and conflict.

And time will tell more. Although Aldred claims no personal gift beyond well-developed intelligence and intuition, he saw the future as clearly as I did that night in the cathedral of trees. He has said many times that there is almost as much left unfulfilled in the average settler as there was in the sunwaifs at the beginning of that last day. Ronna can bring physical health to him and to the others, but she cannot fulfill their latent gifts as she did ours.

But perhaps one day a child will be born who has that fulfilling touch. Perhaps one day every settler on Destiny will be as he or she was intended to be.

Perhaps one day we will all be gods, at home on a world that is our greater god.

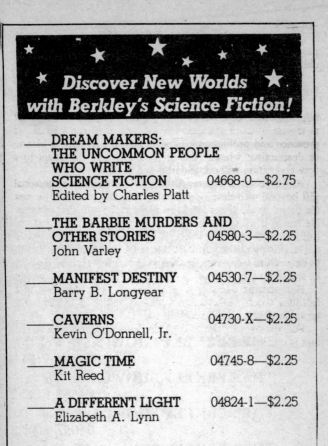